refuge

refuge

Stephanie M. E. Gallentine

Refuge

by Stephanie M. E. Gallentine

© 2009, Word Aflame Press
Hazelwood, MO 63042-2299

Cover Design by Laura Jurek

All Scripture quotations in this book are from the King James Version of the Bible unless otherwise identified.

All rights reserved. No portion of this publication may be reproduced, stored in an electronic system, or transmitted in any form or by any means, electronic, mechanical, photocopy, recording, or otherwise, without the prior permission of Word Aflame Press. Brief quotations may be used in literary reviews.

Printed in United States of America

Printed by

WORD AFLAME PRESS
8855 Dunn Road, Hazelwood, MO 63042
www.pentecostalpublishing.com

Library of Congress Cataloging-in-Publication Data

Gallentine, Stephanie M. E., 1969-
   Refuge : a novel / by Stephanie M.E. Gallentine.
      p. cm.
Summary: Fifteen-year-old computer hacker Kevin Ramsey is forced to plant a computer virus and then must find a way to stop the real criminal without exposing family secrets--but first he must find a way off a research facility in the Pacific Ocean where he is challenged to find new faith in adults and in God.
   ISBN 978-1-56722-736-9 (alk. paper)
   [1. Computer crimes--Fiction. 2. Computer hackers--Fiction. 3. Fathers and sons--Fiction. 4. Child abuse--Fiction. 5. Christian life--Fiction. 6. Manned undersea research stations--Fiction. 7. Science fiction.] I. Title.
PZ7.G13638Ref 2009
[Fic]--dc22

                                          2009015963

Contents

ACKNOWLEDGEMENTS	7
CHAPTER 1	9
CHAPTER 2	19
CHAPTER 3	31
CHAPTER 4	45
CHAPTER 5	55
CHAPTER 6	67
CHAPTER 7	79
CHAPTER 8	91
CHAPTER 9	101
CHAPTER 10	111
CHAPTER 11	123
CHAPTER 12	133
CHAPTER 13	141
CHAPTER 14	155

CHAPTER 15	163
CHAPTER 16	175
CHAPTER 17	187
CHAPTER 18	201
CHAPTER 19	211
CHAPTER 20	221
CHAPTER 21	231
CHAPTER 22	241
CHAPTER 23	251
CHAPTER 24	263
CHAPTER 25	271
CHAPTER 26	283
CHAPTER 27	289
CHAPTER 28	299
CHAPTER 29	307
CHAPTER 30	315

Acknowledgements

As with any lengthy writing endeavor, one does not accomplish it alone, and this novel would not be complete without taking a moment to thank those who helped me.

First off, I want to thank God, who not only gave me the desire to write, but also listened to me and helped me through every step of the way. No words can express my appreciation of His hand in my life.

My family, Robert, Heather, and Andy—thank you for your patience during all those writing marathons. You are the greatest and I love you!

My co-workers, Bettie, Debbie, and Lillie—thank you for listening to me go on about this project for the last three years and for rejoicing with me along the way. I appreciate all of you.

My first critique group partners, Mandy, Renee, Annie, and Lisa—you saw my writing at its very worst and yet you encouraged me to keep trying again, no matter how many times you ended up reading chapter one rewrites.

Suzanne, Susette, and Therese—each of you brought a different strength to the critique table. Thank you for the chats, the crits, and the friendship. God truly blessed me when he blessed me with you.

My Christian Young Adult Readers and Writers Group—all I can say is what an awesome group of people whose greatest passion is writing for today's teens. Thank you for all your honest critiques and your wonderful encouragements. Diana,

Jill, Vernona, Deb, Lynn, Mary, and Gretchen—you are all truly a blessing.

My local ACFW group, Debra, Sue, and Shirley—you have all been a wonderful blessing and have given me something I thought I never have: real life writer friends whom I can visit and plot with face to face. I appreciate each of you so much.

Bethany Calloway—you were the first young person who asked to read my book. What an honor it was to have you read and share your thoughts. You are awesome.

Lastly, I would love to hear from my readers. My email for this book is *stephgallentine@aol.com*.

chapter 1

One hour and fifty-nine minutes.

Sixteen-year-old Kevin Ramsey shoved his hands into the fleece-lined pocket of his hoodie. His fingers, stiffened by the cold, clasped the folded bus ticket. In less than two hours he would be free, and for the first time, in control of his life.

He quickened his pace against the chilling January wind. White flecks of snow swirled about him, dotting his jacket and melting within seconds. He shivered and pulled the straps of his backpack tighter. A sudden gust of wind blew his hood back, and dark strands of baby-fine hair whipped in his face, catching in his glasses.

Frowning, he tugged his hood back up and double-checked the zippered interior pocket for papers that showed his new identity. Sean Childers. He repeated the name under his breath. Puffs of frozen air escaped his lips and disappeared—like he would, once he got out of McKeltic, Texas. Finding him would be like finding Cosmic Warrior's secret identity. No one would know whom to look for. His own life proved that. In the twelve years since his original identity had been changed, no one had ever guessed he had a secret past. Why would this time be any different?

His cell phone chimed. Kevin slid it open and read the text message from his best friend, Aiden Rollings.

GJ NOW.

Kevin nodded and then texted a reply. Galactic Jitters, a popular sci-fi coffee shop, was only a few blocks out of his way. He could meet Aiden and still make his bus. He shivered and folded his arms tightly across his chest. At least at Galactic Jitters, he wouldn't freeze into a human iceberg.

As he turned onto Marsh Avenue, a truck with oversized wheels sped by, spraying the sidewalk with the gray slushy remains of last night's snowfall. Kevin jumped back, but slush seeped into the fabric of his jeans and forced the chill deeper into his bones. He glared at the offending truck and wished for a snowball-encrusted rock. A glimpse at the ground told him he'd have to forego revenge—nothing underfoot but rock salt and barely visible snow flurries.

Two blocks later, Kevin hurried to the entrance of the familiar hangout. Inside the rich aromas of coffee and vanilla wafted through the air, while overhead hundreds of artificial stars glimmered from the black ceiling. Teens clustered at tables around laptops and video games, surrounded by a wall-to-ceiling space mural.

Chapter 1

"Hey, Kevin." Joe, the owner, waved to him from behind the counter and wiped his hands on his apron. "The usual? Quadruple shot mocha latte?"

Kevin nodded and then inched back his sleeve to uncover his watch.

One hour and forty-five minutes. Freedom was so close.

He paid for his drink and headed to the back corner booth where Aiden sat. Sliding into the bench seat, Kevin wrapped his cold hands around the steaming cup and breathed in the vapors. He tipped back his head and let the hot coffee slide down the back of his throat. "What's up? I thought your mom had you on lockdown."

Aiden brushed at charcoal bangs that shaded his half-opened hazel eyes. A mischievous grin pinched his fever-tinged cheeks. "She did but her boss called her in for a couple of hours. I figure by the time she gets home, I'll be back in bed."

"You shouldn't have come."

"I had to." Aiden cupped his hands in front of his face, muffling his sneeze. "I wanted to see if you'd changed your mind."

Kevin stared down in his coffee and shook his head. "No, but the bus doesn't leave till five. We can hang out here till then." His cell phone vibrated in his pocket. He pulled it out and grimaced when he saw the caller. "It's my dad."

"You think he found out?"

"Nah, I doubt it." Too bad Kevin's nerves didn't agree. Beneath his hoodie, his heart raced at the speed of light. "He couldn't have. Right?"

"I just hope they don't send you back to juvie."

Stephanie M. E. Gallentine / refuge

One quick push of the ignore button and the vibrating ceased. Kevin pressed his lips together and narrowed his eyes. "They won't."

In the past year, he had spent more than his share of time in juvenile detention. He wasn't going back. Especially since it wasn't his fault—this time. But who would believe him? He was a juvenile delinquent, and like a character in one of his comic books, Kevin bore a label. The world labeled them—some heroes, some villains. But every character had one thing in common: they longed for a place their reputation didn't follow them, a place they didn't have to fight, a place they could just be normal. But did a place like that even exist in the real world?

"You need to tell someone about the file you found that night," Aiden said.

"It wouldn't matter. That file doesn't exist anymore."

"Then why are you running?"

Kevin clenched his fist and leaned forward. "You know why."

"Just let me tell my dad like we should have done in the first place. Let me tell him about everything." Aiden voice held a touch of pleading. "I'll make him believe you."

Everything.

Kevin groaned. Aiden couldn't possibly understand what he asked.

"I can't." He crushed the empty cup. "I don't need his pity."

"But you need his help."

Kevin crossed his arms while his gaze shifted to make sure no one was close enough to hear. "I wouldn't be so sure about that."

Chapter 1

Aiden set his cup on the table. His hazel eyes grew as round as the twin planets painted on the wall mural behind them. "Oh, man, what did you do?"

"I went back."

"To The World's Gateway?"

Kevin nodded. The small, travel business, co-owned by Peter Damon and William Tyke, had been his and Aiden's latest assignment as part-time penetration testers for Rollings Securities. Their job had been to help with the attempt to infiltrate the company's computers and detail any potential security threats. They reported everything except for one file, never knowing how much trouble a single encrypted file could cause.

"Are you nuts?" Aiden lowered his voice another notch as a teen passed by. "You're already in so deep, you'll be lucky if they don't lock you up in juvie till graduation."

"I wanted to find proof one way or the other." Kevin paused. Now it was his turn to plead with Aiden. "I had to know."

"Know? What more did you need to know? Didn't finding the first file get you into enough trouble?" Aiden shook his head. "Why is it so hard for you to break down and ask for help?"

"I told you, I don't need anyone's help."

"Oh yeah? Keep telling yourself that. Let me know when that starts working for you." Aiden sighed, massaging his temples with the tips of his fingers.

Kevin stared at his friend. The pink-tinge in Aiden's cheeks intensified to a deep scarlet in the dim lighting. "You okay?"

"No."

"Want me to drive you home?"

Stephanie M. E. Gallentine / refuge

Aiden's head popped up. "No thanks. The only way I'll ever hand over the keys to my car is from my cold, dead fingers. You'd either kill me with your driving, or my dad would when I got home."

Kevin rolled his eyes. "Thanks for your vote of confidence."

"Who said anything about confidence? I'm not gonna let you wreck my car the way you wrecked your dad's."

"But that was an accident." Six weeks ago he had "borrowed" Dad's car, only to ram it into the back of a parked car three blocks later. "I just need more practice."

"Well, you're not gonna get it in my car." Aiden twisted in the booth and leaned back against the wall. "So what happened when you went back to The World's Gateway?"

Kevin scooted further into the booth so Aiden could hear his low tones. Galactic Jitters probably wasn't the best place to have this conversation, but it would have to do. "I waited until one o'clock when I knew everyone but the receptionist would be at lunch. It only took a few minutes to pick the locks on the back door and then Mr. Tyke's office."

Aiden gaped. "Man, the things I miss when I'm stuck at home."

Kevin scowled at him. "At first, I was just going to check his file cabinet, see if I could find some sort of documentation on his investments. Then I spotted a laptop tucked in a crevice between the desk and the file cabinet."

Aiden's brow creased with interest. "Did you find anything on it?"

"Not at first. Then in one of the subfolders I found a zipped file called PThomas. When I tried to open it, I dis-

Chapter 1

covered the file was password-encrypted." Kevin reached into the outer pocket of his backpack and pulled out a small flash drive. "I didn't have time to figure out the password, so I copied it onto this." He held up the device.

"Why? What's so special about that file?"

"I'm not exactly sure, but Mr. Tyke acted as if he didn't know something as simple as emptying the recycle bin could free up space on his hard drive. Why would he know about encryption?"

Aiden shrugged. "What did you do?"

"I got nervous when I heard voices in the lobby, so I did something really stupid. I locked up his laptop with a virus I had stored on the flash drive."

"You didn't."

"I did."

Aiden shook his head. "So it wasn't enough to plant a virus in their company's computers? You had to put one on Mr. Tyke's personal laptop? Kevin, you are going to be so dead."

"Not unless they catch me, and in another hour, I'll be outta here."

"Then what did you hope to accomplish?"

"Let's just say I bought us some time to prove who the real criminal is."

"Yeah, time in juvie." Something in Aiden's expression changed. His mouth moved silently as he tried to form words. A single phrase became audible. "Uh-oh."

"What?"

"Adult alert."

Kevin turned. Like some silent alarm had gone off, the incessant chatter around them died down to whispers. Laptops snapped shut as Dad strode through the room.

Kevin groaned. Dad wasn't supposed to get off work until after the bus left. Through the dim lighting, his gaze traveled to an iridescent, moon-shaped clock. One hour and twenty minutes.

Kevin grasped the small handhold on his backpack and slid out of the booth. He quickly palmed the flash drive into Aiden's hand. "Don't lose this. It may be the only solid proof we ever get."

Like a professional, Aiden closed his hand around the device and shoved it into his pocket. Kevin's dad approached him like a linebacker in a suit. He swerved his way between tables and teens, and his lips formed a thin line across his face as though he were preparing to tackle someone.

Dad made sure his back was to everyone but Kevin and Aiden before he asked in a low voice, "Why didn't you answer my call?"

"Sorry." Kevin shrugged. "Why are you here?"

"I was looking for you and—"

"Maybe I didn't want to be found."

"Then you should have gone someplace you don't frequent."

Kevin glared. "Give me a five minute head start and I will."

"Kevin," Aiden ground out the words.

He glanced at his friend. Aiden would never talk to his dad this way. Kevin knew he shouldn't. If his mom were alive, she would have created another black hole in the painted galaxy behind him for being so disrespectful. But in the year since her death, his relationship with Dad had deteriorated to a series of shifts between arguments and apologies.

Chapter 1

Dad peered around the room as if deciding the best course of action. "Let's go," he said in a calm, measured voice. In one swift move, he latched onto Kevin's arm.

Kevin twisted out of grip, causing himself to backpedal into a chair. The metal legs screeched across the tiled floor. His backpack slipped from his hand and skidded back to where Aiden now stood.

A meaty hand reached down to help him up. Kevin tilted his head up and met Dad's furious gaze.

"That's enough of the dramatics, Kevin." Dad hefted him from the floor and clamped the other hand around his forearm in a grip that would rival any superhero.

The owner appeared in Kevin's line of vision, his expression one of controlled anger. "Kevin, you're making a scene. You need to go."

Kevin's gaze swept over the shop; all eyes were on him. A few mouths hung open. And for once, Galactic Jitters was completely silent.

Aiden passed him his backpack. He hooked it on his shoulder as Dad propelled him out the door and toward the waiting Volvo.

"Get in." Dad shoved him into the backseat. The chill in his voice could've convinced any scientist of the absurdity of global warming.

Kevin pulled back his sleeve. One hour and eleven minutes. Time was quickly running out. "Where are we going?"

"Somewhere safe."

Safe? Kevin glanced up into the unreadable expression Dad's face had taken on. Like Dad cared about his safety. Kevin felt his own expression harden. "I'd be better off working that problem out on my own."

chapter 2

With a frustrated grunt, Dad slammed the car door and circled around the back. Kevin pulled on the latch, still determined to make his bus. Nothing happened.

Safety locks.

Kevin scrambled over the seat and reached for the passenger side latch just as Dad opened the driver's door. Pain ripped though Kevin's side. He gasped as Dad's burly hand bit into his ribs, pinching the skin. "Stop!" he yelled.

"Let go of the door," Dad said, his tone calm yet steely.

Kevin obeyed and the grip in his side loosened. Dad's other hand reached across his back and snatched the small black device clamped onto the waist of his jeans. Then Dad withdrew both his hands.

Stephanie M. E. Gallentine / refuge

"Now get in the backseat. You can have your Icom once we get you settled."

Kevin slid into the rear seat and frowned. The engine started and warm air blasted from the vents. Dad maneuvered the car into traffic. With the sleeve of his hoodie, Kevin swished the fog from the side window. He tried to figure out their destination, but without his Icom, even his glasses left his vision worse than the normal eye chart could measure. The Isolated Computer Optical Magnifier controlled two tiny computer chips in the lower portion of his glasses. Those chips magnified objects up to thirty times their size and then relayed those images directly onto his retina, increasing the basic magnification of his glasses.

Clenching his fist, Kevin gave the door a sideways punch. He yanked back his sleeve and pulled the watch close to his face. One hour and seven minutes. But now he had to somehow retrieve his Icom before making his final escape.

"Where are we going?" Kevin called over the seat.

No answer.

A few moments later, Dad's cell phone buzzed. With a quick tap of his earpiece, he answered the caller. "Yeah, we're almost there." Dad adjusted the rearview mirror. His gaze reflected and met Kevin's. "I understand. Thanks."

Within a few blocks, traffic thinned out in the residential area. Dad slowed the car and then veered left onto a side street. Kevin strained to read the street sign, but it blurred. Halfway down the block of two-story homes, Dad pulled up next to a familiar wine-colored Escalade. Prof's house.

Chapter 2

Prophyrios Papakonstantinou, a second generation Grecian-American, better known as Prof around their Texas town, not only served as the high school principal, but was also one of Dad's closest friends. Both he and Dad had spent many Saturday evenings at this house.

Maybe this was about nothing more than his recent truancy. He hoped. Then he could agree to his punishment, get his Icom back, and make his escape. At least it was a plan.

"Kevin," Prof acknowledged him as he stepped through the front door. The older man grasped his shoulders and smiled. "Come in. I'm glad you could make it."

"Like I had any choice." Kevin hesitated until Dad came in behind him.

"Are we ready?" Dad hooked his coat on the coat rack in the corner of the foyer.

Prof shook his head and led them down the hallway. "Mr. Tyke phoned and said there was a snag at the office. Both he and Mr. Damon should be here shortly to sign the waiver, and then we'll be off."

Kevin tensed. What was going on? Were they about to take him down to juvie? Why sign a waiver? He had to get out of there before Mr. Tyke and Mr. Damon showed up.

The antique grandfather clock chimed the four o'clock hour as they passed it in the hallway.

One hour until the bus left.

"I had hoped they would have come and gone by now," Dad said.

"That was another snag." Prof seemed to hesitate. "It seems Mr. Damon wants Kevin present."

"Do you think that's wise?"

"I said the same thing, but Mr. Damon was adamant."

Stephanie M. E. Gallentine / refuge

Prof's blurred hand swung out and motioned for them to take a seat on the dark brown couch. The sweet aroma of freshly baked *baklava* drifted in from the kitchen. "Can I get you something to eat or drink while we wait?"

Kevin shook his head and instead made his way over to the large aquarium Prof had built into a shelf unit, visible from both the living room and the hall. He leaned in close to see better. Brightly colored tropical fish of all sizes filled the tank. Prof said he had bought them to remind him of home. Kevin couldn't imagine living in such a place or why Prof would have wanted to leave it to come to McKeltic, where the most colorful fish was the catfish.

Prof and Dad spoke in low tones that Kevin couldn't pick up. That was fine with him. While they carried on their conversation, he kept up his intent interest on the fish and slowly edged his way to the end of the tank. He made the turn into the hallway, where he could view the other side.

He glanced at the door. A mere eight feet away, freedom beckoned him with a grip more enticing than Prof's *baklava*. He could still do this. Kevin crept toward the front door. The steady tick-tocking of the grandfather clock sounded more like loud bongs, calling the adults, and alerting them of his imminent escape.

The coat rack came into view. Kevin reached his hand up and quickly sifted through Dad's jacket for his Icom. He found it hidden in an inner pocket. A sigh of relief escaped him as he flicked the power button and clamped it back on his waist. Instead of a blurred door in front of him, he now made out the fine carvings etched into the wood.

Chapter 2

Kevin glanced over his shoulder. Nothing but the steady hum of voices from the main room. He latched onto the doorknob and eased the front door open. Beyond that, the screen gave a short screech. He stopped. Then carefully, he squeezed himself through the narrow opening and pulled the door shut.

Smiling, he released the door handle. Freedom.

"Hello, Kevin."

Kevin groaned and turned.

William Tyke, co-owner of The World's Gateway, stepped up onto the porch and blocked his path.

"What are you doing here?" Kevin panned the porch. Mr. Tyke's form blocked his escape. Thorny rose bushes, covered in a thin layer of ice, surrounded the rest of the wooden-framed porch. He needed Tyke to move.

Mr. Tyke glanced at the still closed front door. He kept his voice low. "What did you do to my laptop?"

"Who says I did anything to it?" He moved away from the door and hoped Mr. Tyke would follow him. Then he would dart around the man and be gone before anyone had a chance to react.

Mr. Tyke's brows furrowed into a deep scowl. "Don't play games with me, Kevin. I can make your life a lot more difficult."

"Really?" Kevin crossed his arms and glared. "And you don't think I could do the same?"

"Oh, I am fully aware of what you're capable of. I went over the security footage of my office today."

No! Kevin's eyes slid shut and then reopened. How could he have forgotten to disengage the hidden cameras?

Mr. Tyke chuckled and ran his gloved thumb across the tips of his fingers. He glanced over his shoulder at the sound of a car rounding the corner. "I want that flash drive."

"Afraid I'll get arrested with it?" Kevin raised his eyebrow. "I wonder what the police would say."

Mr. Tyke's eyes widened and then narrowed. "You would do well to remember there are far greater things to fear."

Kevin sucked in a silent breath. Well, he didn't plan on sticking around long enough to find out. He faked a move to the left and then darted to the right.

Tyke caught hold of his hoodie.

"Kevin?" Prof asked from behind.

He turned. Prof stood on the other side of the screen. All his hopes shattered in that moment. He'd have to find another way out of this mess.

Mr. Tyke pulled Kevin toward the door. "Looks like I caught an escapee."

Prof frowned and then pushed open the screen for them to enter. "Thank you, Mr. Tyke." He gave Kevin a stern look. "I guess the sooner we take care of this matter, the better."

The sound of another set of tires crunching on the rock salt-covered driveway drew their attention. Glowering, Peter Damon, the shorter and rounder co-owner of The World's Gateway, slammed his car door and stomped towards them. "This better be good."

Prof waved them inside. "Gentlemen, I'm glad you could make it. Why don't we head back to my office, and I'll try to take as little of your time as possible."

Mr. Tyke and Prof sandwich-walked Kevin down the hall toward a small office at the back of the house.

"I want to thank you both for coming out in such

Chapter 2

nasty weather." Prof seated himself behind a large oak desk and opened a manila file folder.

Face pinched with hard lines, Mr. Damon scowled and shrugged out of his long overcoat. He crossed his arms but remained standing. William Tyke leaned back in his chair and allowed his arms to drape casually on the armrests.

Kevin swallowed hard. His Adam's apple bobbed and struck the top of his throat with all the force of a Strong Man's game at a carnival. His gaze darted about the room as he slid his backpack to the floor and then lowered himself into the narrow, cushioned chair that faced Prof's desk. He smoothed down strands of static-charged hair and willed the pounding in his chest to subside.

Like a miniature courtroom, he faced them: judge, jury, and prosecution. From the expressions on their faces, it wouldn't take long for a conviction. Kevin longed for the frozen weather outside. The temperature inside seemed too warm, suffocating. It should have taken them longer to trace it back to him. All he needed was another—he glanced at a wall clock—fifty-three minutes. "Where'd my dad go?"

"He had an important phone call come in. He'll be along shortly." Prof cleared his throat. "It's been brought to our attention that Mr. Damon and Mr. Tyke now know who was responsible for the virus planted in their system two nights ago."

Kevin's breath caught in his throat. He kept his voice as even as possible. "Oh?"

"Yes. Fortunately, Mr. Damon had all the company's files backed up." Prof sat with his hands folded on the desk and scrutinized Kevin in the silence.

"That's good." Kevin nodded. He felt like a mouse cornered by a cat. Still, he forced himself to remain calm, even appear slightly confused. "Why are you sharing this with me, sir?"

"I'm giving you an opportunity to confess."

Kevin's fingers curled around the arms of the chair. His eyes flicked to his watch. Fifty-one minutes. He had to think of something.

Prof's eyes bore into him. "Mr. Ramsey, we are all quite aware of your skills. They are well above the average sixteen-year-old by any measure."

"Sir, I . . . I don't know why you think I did it." Kevin shifted in his seat as he struggled to maintain his neutral expression. He focused his attention on a painting of the Parthenon just over Prof's left shoulder, a trick he had learned in juvie to make the adults think he was looking them in the eye.

Mr. Damon pushed himself off the wall, his expression hardened even further. He pointed at Kevin. "I know you did it. What I want to know is why?"

Kevin didn't reply.

Mr. Damon growled. "I told you this was a mistake. I don't know why I bothered to listen to either of you. I should've called the police and let them handle him."

"Peter, you did agree," Prof said.

"Agree?" Mr. Damon snorted. "That's a laugh. You, Tyke, and Ramsey talked me into this." He pulled out a handkerchief and dabbed the sweat on his brow. "I should have known better than to allow full access to my computers to any company that employed this kid."

Prof gave him a sympathetic nod. "You couldn't have known."

"I know Rollings Security assured me this kid was

Chapter 2

only helping and had turned from his criminal ways." Mr. Damon scowled at Kevin, loathing coating each word. "But I guess once a juvenile delinquent, always a juvenile delinquent."

Kevin cringed inside. The label clung to him like Saran wrap. Mr. Damon didn't know—didn't care. When Kevin took the job at Rollings Security, he'd promised Aiden's father he would stay out of trouble. But trouble had come to him.

"That's why we feel this move might be beneficial for him." Prof straightened in his chair and looked right at Kevin, his expression unreadable.

"I'll move him, all right," Mr. Damon murmured. "Move him right behind bars."

Prof stretched over the desk and handed a cell phone to Mr. Damon. "Fine. Call the police. Press charges. It's all been done before. Last time they even suggested medication might be the answer."

Kevin grimaced. Now everyone would know the juvenile authorities thought he needed medicating to control his anger and family counseling to deal with what they called "conduct disorder." Dad had refused—the only thing Dad had gotten right during the past year.

Prof and Mr. Damon held a visual standoff. The edge of Mr. Damon's mouth twitched, but Kevin could only guess what kind of communication passed between the two. Prof glanced at the cell phone and then back at Mr. Damon.

A suffocating silence enveloped the room. Kevin lowered his head, afraid to look up again, afraid to even breathe. His future hung in the balance. Where he spent tonight had nothing to do with a bus ticket, but rather with one man's decision.

Peter Damon emitted a low guttural growl before he slammed the cell phone down on the desk, took the pen from Prof's hand, leaned over, and signed something. "Fine, give him his second chance. But if that"—he pointed a pudgy finger toward Kevin as he seemed to struggle for the right word—"kid so much as takes a peek at my systems, I'll press charges so fast, he won't see the light of day for a long time. I'll make sure the judge makes an example of him."

Peter snatched his coat and stormed out the door. Mr. Tyke gave Prof an understanding grin. "You and his father, you're making the right choice. He needs out of McKeltic and the negative influences here. Where did you say he'd be going?"

"Didn't his father tell you?" Prof seemed to hedge.

"No. But since we've decided not to file charges, I thought maybe you'd tell me."

Prof met Mr. Tyke's gaze. "This has been a rather difficult year for Steven and his son. I'm sure you understand his need for privacy. However, if you would like, I'd be happy to see you have updates on Kevin's progress."

Mr. Tyke flashed Prof an appreciative smile. "Absolutely. And forgive me; I should have been more considerate of the situation." Mr. Tyke slipped a pen from his jacket pocket and signed the same paper. "Nevertheless, we'll stand behind you. Who knows? This may yet turn out to be an answer to your prayer."

Answer to prayer? What did Mr. Tyke know about prayer? The man appeared so congenial. His mannerisms oozed integrity. No one suspected that all the money he'd convinced investors to put up for a new island resort was

Chapter 2

slowly being embezzled away. Mr. Tyke might deny it, but Kevin had seen the file. Unfortunately that wasn't all he'd seen in the file.

The door clicked softly behind Mr. Tyke. Prof strode over to the water dispenser near his desk. "You're blessed that one of Mr. Damon's pet peeves is that he can't stand the thought of kids being medicated as a means of behavior modification." With a flick of his wrist, he tipped the cup back and drained it.

Kevin tried to ignore the gaze trained on him, but it didn't work.

"You never answered the question." The older man spoke calmly. "Why did you do it?"

Several moments passed before Kevin blew out a long breath and shrugged.

"Who convinced you to do this?"

Kevin's gaze flew up to meet Prof's. He hadn't expected anyone to guess, not with his record. "No one, sir," he said quietly.

"I know you better than that. Lying is not one of your more practiced skills, Kevin. Please do not waste my time. I will ask you once more before I call the authorities myself. Who convinced you to do this?"

A long sigh emptied his lungs. He hated how all the blame fell on him. But he couldn't bear them knowing the truth either. "I can't say, sir."

"That's what I thought." A satisfied expression came over Prof's face. "Your father and I, however, have come up with a solution to your"—he cleared his throat—"problem."

Kevin stared down at the paper resting beneath Prof's folded hands and tried to make sense of what he had just been told. This was crazy. In fact, it was nothing short of complete and total insanity. "So I'm to be placed"—he paused, not even sure he had the correct word— "at some research center until I'm eighteen?"

"That's correct. The Pacific Aquatic Research Center. PARC for short, but everyone just calls it 'the Center.' "

"How long did it take you to come up with that one?" he murmured. What were these people thinking? A research center? Did he look like a mutant from one of his comic books? He shook his head in confusion. Someone must have slipped something into his latte earlier. At the moment, that was the only explanation he could think of.

"No. No way. Dad won't let you do this."

"Your father asked me to do this."

The words hung in the air.

Kevin stared open-mouthed. This couldn't be happening.

Prof used the silence to explain. "It's a live-in environment. They've assured me you'll have your own room. As far as your schooling is concerned, you'll participate in our Outbound program similar to when you were in juvenile detention. Aside from that, I'm sure you'll find the Center a fascinating place with plenty to keep you occupied."

Occupied? Doing what? Watching the fish swim by in some oversized aquarium? He rolled his eyes. Oh joy.

"Right now their primary purpose is the development of underwater engineering, but they also have a marine biologist and a few divers on staff."

"So what? I have no desire to be any of those things."

chapter 3

Prof leaned back in his chair. "And your father has no desire for you to become a criminal at sixteen."

Kevin stuffed his hand back into his pocket. The ticket, his only hope, waited. He couldn't miss this one opportunity. Moisture formed on the bridge of his nose, causing his glasses to slip down. "I need to talk this over with Dad."

"I already took care of that. He said he felt it was a great idea and might teach you . . . how did he put it?" After a short pause, Prof continued, "A much needed lesson."

"He did?" Kevin felt the blood drain from his face. The struggle to hide his true feelings intensified. Just like that—a situation he ended up in that went awry—handled.

Stephanie M. E. Gallentine / refuge

"Yes. In fact your father also volunteered to sponsor this placement." Prof spoke very matter-of-factly.

Kevin mentally told himself to breathe. Sucking in a deep breath, he put on his best front. "He's bribing you."

"No one bribed anyone. Your father wants to make sure you're well provided for."

"Yeah, right." Kevin pulled the phone from his pocket. Forty-nine minutes. If he could find a way outside, he could duck in some place until he could catch a cab to the bus station. He wished he could drive. Life would be so much easier. Kevin sighed. Stupid vision problems.

Still, no way was he going to be carted off to some research center. He needed an excuse. "I need some time to get some stuff together if I'm going to be staying there."

Prof gathered a stack of papers and tapped their edges on the desk . "It's already been taken care of. Your father delivered your things to the airport earlier this afternoon."

"How about a bathroom break? Did Dad take care of that too?"

"There's a bathroom on the plane."

"What?" Kevin jumped up from his seat. "No. I want to talk to Dad. You can't do this." He snatched up his backpack, flung it on his shoulder, and yanked open the door. It slammed against the wall as Kevin flew through it and into the broad chest of his dad.

"Dad! You can't let him take me. You can't."

Dad frowned. "I asked Prof to do this. It's for your own good. Prof knew how to get in touch with Adam."

"Adam? Who's Adam?"

Dad clamped down on Kevin's thin arm and pulled

Chapter 3

him back into the office. The door thudded shut behind them. "Adam is . . . "

"Director of the Center," Prof supplied while he and Dad seemed to share some silent communication.

Aloud, Dad said, "I hope you still planned on leaving soon."

"The plane is waiting." Prof moved to gather his things.

Dad nodded. "Then we better go before this one attempts another escape."

"No." Kevin clawed at Dad's iron grip. "Let me go."

"Stop it." Dad leaned in and whispered in his ear. "This is the Refuge."

Kevin froze. His stomach knotted. It had been a long time since he'd heard that phrase. Too long for it to be real.

After a car ride to a small landing strip, Kevin, Prof, and Dad crossed the barren airfield to a couple who stood under the wing of an odd-looking plane. Wheels jutted out from the bottom of what appeared to be giant fiberglass floats attached to the bottom of the aircraft. The insignia on the plane was a strange looking frog with wings and the words written in script, *The Flying Frog*.

As Kevin and the others drew close, the couple stepped out from the shadows. The woman stood about a head shorter than the man, bundled in a bulky coat that looked more suited for Alaska than Texas. The man seemed to be almost as tall as Dad's six-foot-two frame. Dark hair peeked out from beneath the knitted cap the man wore. An odd feeling of déjà vu came over Kevin, but he quickly dismissed it.

What he couldn't dismiss, however, was the man's eyes. The one on the right was the brightest blue he'd ever seen. The other eye was an emerald green. Both of the eyes held such an intensity that for a second Kevin couldn't look away. Then it came to him. A human chimera. He'd read something on the Internet about people whose body contained two distinct DNAs. Sometimes one of the tell-tale signs was the different eye colors.

"Kevin," Prof said, "I'd like you to meet Adam Hollandale and his wife, Dr. Chelsea Hollandale. They will act as both your guardians and mentors during your stay at the Center."

"What?" He gaped at the woman, who smiled at him like she had gained an adopted child. Kevin seethed inside. Foster parents. "Mentors" was nothing more than a sugar-coated way of saying it. He shot an accusing glare at Dad. No. No way, no how.

Adam kept up that intense stare from both his blue and green eyes.

Kevin took a half step back. What kind of freak farm was Dad sending him to? No telling what kind of Dr. Jekyll and Mr. Hyde issues came with two different DNAs. His fingers searched for the bus ticket one more time.

"Adam." Dad's arm dropped away from Kevin to shake the other man's hand. A congenial smile spread across his face. "I really appreciate you agreeing to do this."

Kevin sucked in a quick breath. Agreeing? So Dad had really sunk to having to beg someone to take him. Then it couldn't be the place his mother had always called the Refuge.

He scanned his surroundings. To the left of him just beyond the airfield lay a small neighborhood. Kevin

Chapter 3

glanced back at the men still deep in conversation. He'd only have seconds to make his escape. Adrenaline pulsed through him like a multitude of tiny internal rockets ready to be launched.

Darting off to the left, Kevin sprinted across the airfield, determined to outrun anyone who might try to follow. Behind him, several voices shouted his name. In response, he pushed himself harder, pumping his arms. The backpack bounced around, pulling at him. He wished he could chuck it. Already he felt drained by the extra burden. But he'd need the money and clothes in it.

"Kevin!"

The voice closed in on him. Kevin forced himself to run faster. He could do it. Not much farther. Once he reached the neighborhood, it would be easy to hide somewhere.

Something touched him.

Kevin darted to the right. In a dead run, he used the last bit of adrenaline to reach the field that separated him from the neighborhood.

Hands tapped his shoulders and sent him flying forward. Kevin landed hard, falling face first into a patch of snow. He gagged at the taste of dirt and dead leaves mixed with the slush. Out of breath, he rolled over and sucked in long deep breaths of cold air. The air seemed to freeze in his throat and lungs.

Sitting up, he glanced around and realized the world had gone out of focus. His glasses must have fallen off when he hit the ground. Kevin worked to push back the familiar fear. Although the remote Icom would magnify images, without his glasses the device was useless. He had to find his glasses and yet didn't want to admit how lost he was without them.

"What in thunder were you doing?" Adam demanded.

Kevin glared up at the blurry figure before him. "Isn't that," he sucked in another breath, "obvious?"

"Your father warned us you like to run." Adam took in several deep breaths. "I hope you enjoyed it. It'll be your last one."

"You think so?"

There was a slight chuckle to Adam's voice. "Not unless you can swim."

Kevin glared at him. "I'll do whatever it takes."

"I'd like to see you try." The snow crunched under Adam's feet. "Because you'll literally need a wing and a prayer."

"I don't pray."

"Then you're not ready to do whatever it takes."

Several feet pounded on the concrete and then slowed to a walk. Multiple voices spoke at once.

A woman's voice rose above the rest. "Are you all right?"

"Can I have a minute with my son?" Dad asked. "I'd like to walk him to the plane."

Adam answered, "Of course."

Kevin waited until Chelsea and Adam were distracted by their own conversation before he patted the ground for his glasses. Thick fingers latched around his arm and pulled him to his feet.

"I've got them," Dad's low voice spoke into Kevin's ear. "Let's go."

Kevin rose and held out his hand. "Not until I get my glasses."

Chapter 3

"Not until you're on the plane." Dad pulled him along.

Kevin looked at the landscape in front of him. Without his glasses, the ground and sky blended together to create a world of varying hues of gray that formed a dense fog his eyes couldn't penetrate.

He growled under his breath. *So unfair.* But he allowed Dad to lead him through the blur and across the airfield. Like the superhero Saphearon, Kevin had his own weakness he tried to keep hidden. Without his special glasses, he was legally blind, and he hated it. Hated he couldn't fix it. Hated how helpless and scared it made him feel at times like this. And he especially hated the way people could use it against him.

"Don't look so petulant." Dad leaned in close enough that Kevin could smell the coffee on his breath. "Can't you see I'm doing this to help you?"

"Help me?" Kevin couldn't keep his pitch steady. This was his help?

"Here we go again. You're forcing me to say and do things I always told myself I would never do."

"Oh, so all of this is my fault?" He tried to wrench out of the hold, but Dad held him firm. "Mom would never have—"

"Your mom is the one that originally set this up." Dad paused. "Remember when she told you about the Refuge?"

"You're lying." When he was younger, his mother told him if anyone ever found out their family's true identity, she had arranged a safe place where no one would ever find him.

Kevin refused to believe Dad. It was nothing more than another lie to get him to go willingly. That had to be it.

"I don't expect you to understand right now—"

"You're right. I don't." Kevin glared at Dad. Anger tainted every word. "Why don't you explain it to me?"

Beside him, someone caught hold of his other arm and pulled him back. "That's enough, Kevin," Adam's voice warned him.

Kevin jerked out of Adam's loose hold and glared in the direction he thought Adam stood.

"Adam, Steven, I think it's time we get going. It's a long flight as it is," Prof said.

Adam called out to someone else, whom Kevin assumed to be the pilot. "Let's get this bird in the air, Mark. I'd like to get home."

Home. A four-letter word for another prison as far as Kevin was concerned. After Dad handed him back his glasses, Kevin allowed them to lead him up the stairs into the hatch of the aircraft.

"Watch your step," Adam cautioned him.

Once inside, Kevin lowered himself into one of the two seats in the back of the amphibian plane. Chelsea and Prof took two of the remaining five. Adam stood and blocked the hatch, while he spoke quietly with Dad for several minutes.

Kevin ignored what he could hear of the conversation. Ignored everyone.

Adam pulled the hatch closed and took his own place beside Chelsea.

Kevin twisted in his seat and stared out the window as Dad made his way across the airfield and out of his life without a single parting word.

Throwing his head back, Kevin squeezed his eyes shut and forced back his emotions. Adrenaline coursed

Chapter 3

through his system. Every nerve was on edge. Like a madman, he longed to break free of his restraints.

But not here, not now.

By tomorrow morning, these people were going to wake up to the surprise of their lives. Kevin's mind whirred with plans—plans that would put him as far away from the Center as he could get. The *where*, he would worry about a little later, once he got a visual of the lay of the land. Besides, he wasn't the only hacker who had been forced into hiding for a time. And he was always good at finding places to hide. This time, however, he was determined that no one would ever be able to find him again.

Adam Hollandale settled back into his seat as the plane took off. Through the window, the city shrunk and faded out of view. He let out a breath he hadn't realized he had been holding. They were really going to do this. Adam felt the reassuring squeeze on his hand; he turned to his smiling wife across the narrow aisle.

She leaned over, her long windblown curls falling over the seat, and whispered, "*Esperanza.*"

Hope. It was a word David, one of their staff members, had taught his wife. David was always mixing his Spanish and English when he became frustrated, and he did that quite often. Chelsea had told him enough was enough, and she would just have to learn the language herself. After six months, she'd learned the basics.

He chuckled to himself. That was his wife: stubborn, yet always determined to meet the needs of others. It didn't

Stephanie M. E. Gallentine / refuge

matter if it were medical or personal needs. She'd work on learning a language just as quickly as she'd bake someone a plate of cookies. Personally, he preferred the cookies.

But what about now? Adam turned his head and let his gaze glide over the teen seated diagonally from him. Could they help him at all? Right now as he studied Kevin's lips pursed together in a thin line and the crossed arms, he could only wonder if they'd made the right decision. Decision? Thinking back, Adam wasn't sure he had much to do with the decision process. Staring out the window of the plane, he replayed the conversation with Prof in his head.

"You want us to take some kid for the next two years? Prof you've made some pretty wild requests before, but this takes the cake. This is crazy." He tossed the pen down and adjusted the sound on the LinkWay, a conference call site on the Internet.

How did Prof expect them to take on some troubled teen right now? Didn't he remember the entire facility was ensconced in a project? A project that Prof himself had helped them acquire.

Prof, however, didn't seem put off by his skepticism. "Adam, there's a sizable grant that comes along with it."

"Baby-sitting money, you mean."

"I'm serious." Prof plopped some papers down in front of his own LinkWay. "You know we've been in danger of having to shut the program down for quite a while now."

"Yeah, I know." The Center had a lot more competition now than in the past. It wasn't as unique as it once had been. Adam sighed and reached for the other stack of papers on his desk, the dreaded financial records.

Chapter 3

"Adam," Prof said. "Kevin Ramsey's father practically begged me to talk to you. He's—"

"Kevin?" It couldn't be. He swallowed hard. "Staci's son?"

Prof dipped his head forward. "You know that's part of the reason I settled here, took the job I did, and the reason I've gotten so close to this family."

"Prof, I . . . I didn't ask."

"I know, but I wanted to help."

"I know but . . ." Raking both his hands through his hair, Adam studied the tiles on the ceiling as if he'd find the answers there. None appeared.

In his memory, Staci's small, desperate voice pleaded with him. *"Promise me if there's ever a time we ask, you'll take him."*

Funny how easily promises were made when you didn't think you'd ever have to fulfill them. How difficult the decision was when reality slapped you in the face.

Adam halted and peered down into the LinkWay. "You know we're in the middle of trying to secure a contract on the biggest engineering project we're ever had. Somehow the time doesn't seem right."

"But it is for Kevin." Prof's voice softened and filled with emotion. "He has so much potential, but I fear he's leaning too far in the wrong direction. Since his mother died a year ago—"

"I know when she died," Adam snapped.

"I know you do. But since that time, neither Kevin nor his father has been the same. Would you rather I have him sent back to juvenile detention? They can't give Kevin what he really needs."

Stephanie M. E. Gallentine / refuge

Adam didn't miss the pointed look Prof gave him. Pinching the bridge of his nose, Adam let his thoughts wander. Prof was right. How many times had he and Chelsea prayed they could do more for God? Guess he would have to file this one under "be careful what you pray for."

Although he still needed to talk to Chelsea, he knew without a doubt they would take Kevin. "So if I remember right, Kevin should be halfway through his sophomore year in high school?"

"Among other things."

Oh no. His eyes slid shut. There just had to be other things in the equation. "Define 'other things' if you don't mind."

"He's a computer whiz."

"Translated, means 'hacker' right?"

Adam noted a slight pause on the other end of the LinkWay before Prof answered. "That's probably a fairly loose translation."

"Right," he replied. "What'd he do?"

Prof sighed. "We had hoped the part-time job at Rollings Securities would encourage Kevin to redirect his talents to more ethical hacking. Instead he used that access to plant a virus in the computers of one of the companies they were completing a penetration test on."

"Penetration test?"

"Don't feel bad. I had to ask too." Prof grinned. "It's where one company hires a security company to break into their computers and find any breaches."

Adam's eyes slid shut. Maybe that kid did belong in juvie. He didn't even want to think of the havoc Kevin

Chapter 3

might wreak here. "So why does Steven Ramsey think this is the best option for his son?"

Prof reached for something beyond the edge of the screen. "Steven told me Kevin's made some new friends. He's not sure Kevin set the virus just to prove he could do it. He's afraid one of his new friends might be using Kevin for his own criminal purposes."

"Have you questioned these friends?"

"You know how many tall, lanky, brown-haired kids live in McKeltic?" Prof grinned. "We're hoping by putting some distance between Kevin and these 'friends,' he might open up and tell us why he really set the virus."

"All right." Adam nodded. That was enough reason for him. "I guess I'll see you tomorrow then." Adam flicked off the LinkWay and leaned back in his chair. Maybe he could help Kevin and in the process also get some answers to what happened to Staci and who had her so scared. Maybe this would be his chance to ease the guilt that still lingered within himself. Maybe he could save her son the way he could never save Staci.

chapter 4

"Run!" Aiden's voice shouts.

Kevin whips his head over his shoulder. A familiar face looms in the distorted world. Gone was the friendly façade, stripped away by the alcohol and need for revenge. Kevin stands paralyzed. Behind him, the embodiment of his fears; yet in front of him, an emptiness, which seems to stretch forever.

"Run!"

The man inches closer. Each step echoes in the fog that separates them.

Kevin's breaths come in quick succession. His entire frame shakes. There is no way to run from this man. He's tried it before.

He closes in on Kevin, now not four feet away.

Kevin runs into the silent void. Fear pushes him

forward. The only sound he hears is his own feet as they slap on some unknown surface.

A hand appears out of the void. It grips him.

Kevin tries to yell.

Nothing. No sound.

He is trapped.

Soft hands shook him. Kevin jerked back in his seat and sucked in a deep breath. His instincts took over. He glanced wildly around, for a moment unsure where he was. He slowly let his breath out as his heart hammered. Another dream.

"Hey, it's okay." The voice near him sounded unexpectedly soothing and feminine. She quickly withdrew her hand. "We've landed."

"Landed?" Kevin sat up and slid his fingers under his glasses, still trying to wake up. Memories of the last few hours came back to him in a rush.

The Center.

The plane rocked a little as Prof stepped back inside. "Have a nice nap?"

Kevin glared at the wide grin on the older man's face.

Chelsea handed him the backpack he had tucked under the seat in the small storage space. "Starting a collection of rocks in there?" A soft, teasing smile played on her lips.

Kevin snatched his backpack and muttered a quick thanks. He stood and waited for her to pass. The plane rocked beneath him. He steadied himself with the back of the seat across the narrow aisle. A single glance out the small window opposite the hatch caused him to lean forward, plant his knee in the seat, and adjust the magnification of his Icom. But no matter how much he adjusted

Chapter 4

the device, nothing changed. On the other side of the window was water—miles and miles of water. Nothing else except for a sky so wide and uninterrupted that the whole world before him seemed endless.

Where have they taken me?

He glanced back out the window as if the scenery would somehow change.

It didn't.

Weak, he twisted around and fell back into the seat. He chanced a look out the opposite window but all he could see was what looked like some sort of metal deck.

Prof called back to him. "Coming?"

Kevin took a minute to form the darkest glare he could. "This is no airport. Where are we?"

"Come out and see for yourself."

"No." His voice sounded wrong even to his own ears. He tried again, stronger this time. "No, I'm not staying here."

Prof grinned. "Kevin, you don't even know where 'here' is."

"I know where 'here' is *not*." He squeezed the thick cushioned vinyl seat until his knuckles turned whiter than his already pale skin. "There's nothing out here."

"Of course, there is. Just not what you're used to."

Kevin still didn't move. He planned to stay in his seat until this plane took off again if he had to. Once more he glanced at wide expanse of water out the window and frowned. The joke had been on him. No wonder Adam had laughed at the thought of his running away. He was trapped. But where exactly was he? His Icom had a GPS imbedded inside of it, but that wouldn't help him if he had no means of transportation.

Stephanie M. E. Gallentine / refuge

Prof crossed his arms and took on his stern Principal Prof look. "I need to warn you if you go back today, I will have no choice but to call the authorities and have you arrested as soon as the plane lands. Then again, you'd make Peter Damon a happy man. It took a long time to convince him to keep from pressing charges."

"Is there a problem?" a male voice called up through the hatch.

Prof turned to Kevin. "Is there?"

Kevin blew out a frustrated breath and stood. He slammed his fist down on the top of the seat and then slipped his backpack over his shoulder. Nerves amassed in his stomach. They multiplied and twisted into tight knots. As he stepped off the plane and onto the metal deck, he felt as if he had let go of his last connection with the real world.

Prof moved to block the entrance to the plane. "Welcome to the Center."

Kevin crossed his arms. The Center was nothing more than a huge metal deck. A two-story cylindrical building jutted up from the middle of the metal island. It looked more like a lighthouse than a research center. On the other side of the building, several boats rested in slips at the edge of the platform.

Prof pointed out into the water to a couple of islands maybe a mile or so away. "I inherited both those islands years ago from my Uncle Alexander. They're small—nothing but a beach and a few dozen palm trees. The one on the right has a small freshwater pond on it. The one on the left is mostly a giant rock pile. But I decided this would be the perfect location to build my dream: an underwater research facility."

Chapter 4

Prof's dream.

Kevin's nightmare. In all of his imaginations, Kevin would have never guessed Dad would send him to such a remote location. What was he going to do without Taco Bell or Galactic Jitters? Good grief, even Wal-Mart would seem like heaven right now.

He stood motionless and watched the waves as they lapped up onto the deck. This couldn't be happening.

Chelsea stepped up beside Kevin, her voice gentle and calm like the warm ocean breeze that blew over them. "Why don't we go inside? I'm sure everyone's tired."

Kevin forced himself to follow the others up the narrow flight of stairs that led up to a set of double glass doors. Each step felt as if he dragged cement blocks up the stairs instead of size seven Pro Jams. This was so crazy. But unless he could convince someone otherwise, he was stuck here for the next two years. Until he was eighteen, Prof had said.

Under his breath, Kevin growled. "Life is so not fair."

At the top of the stairs, Kevin peered through the double glass doors and wondered for the first time where they expected him to sleep on this floating prison. The small cylindrical building didn't appear large enough to house a research center, much less private living areas.

When the door opened, a guard stood from his place behind a desk and greeted them, while Adam walked over to what appeared to be a locking mechanism beside the elevator door.

How much trouble could they have out here in the middle of nowhere?

Kevin moved two steps to the right and pretended to study a painting that hung on the wall. He slipped his hand under the hem of his hoodie and adjusted the setting on his magnifier.

On his job at Rollings Securities, he and Aiden performed this task often during a penetration test: shoulder surfing. The goal was to watch over another person's shoulder for passcodes without anyone realizing it.

Adam punched in a set of five numbers in quick succession: 45839.

Kevin smirked. It always amazed him how many people would type in their passcodes without any concern about who might be watching. Adam could now be counted among them.

Pushing his glasses up on his face, Kevin followed the group into the elevator. Maybe Dad hadn't been so smart sending him here after all.

A swift glance at the numbers on the elevator control panel told Kevin more than he wanted to know. Seven floors and a single-lit arrow pointed down.

Great. Not only was he going to be in the middle of nowhere, he would be living several stories underwater. Who did they think he was? Hydroman?

Kevin put his hand against the wall as the elevator jerked to a sudden stop on the first floor. The doors slid open and a cool breeze rushed into the cramped space. He waited for the others to exit before he followed them across the hall to what appeared to be a reception area of some kind. Looking past the numerous cushioned chairs surrounding a large, square coffee table, Kevin took in the expansive glass wall that stretched across the width of the room.

As he moved closer, he could see light from the surface sparkle against the brightly colored tropical fish that

Chapter 4

swam by. For several moments, he stood mesmerized by the scene before him. It was like Prof's aquarium on a whole new level.

Kevin turned when Prof excused himself to get something to drink, leaving him alone with Chelsea, Adam, and another man who had joined them. He clinched the straps on his backpack and wished for an excuse of his own.

"I understand you worked with computers before you came here," Adam said.

Kevin dipped his head forward in acknowledgment.

"Good. I'd like to introduce you to our own computer guru, Paul Martinson."

Kevin tilted his head back. From his five-foot-three vantage point, the man seemed like a giant. His cropped hair was a mixture of white and gray, his skin a pasty white that reminded Kevin of a statue.

"It's good to meet you." Paul smiled and put out an ashen hand. "But just to let you know, around here, most people call me Rev."

"And you're telling me this . . . why?" Kevin folded his arms across his chest and left Rev's waiting hand hanging mid-air.

Adam blew out a frustrated breath. "He's telling you this," he punctuated, "so you will know who to call when you have a problem."

Kevin couldn't stop the eye roll. Call when he had a problem with computers? "Like that's ever gonna happen."

Lips pressed together in a tight line, Adam moved toward him. Both his blue and green eyes flashed in obvious anger.

Stephanie M. E. Gallentine / refuge

Kevin backed up until he felt the coolness of the glass wall behind him. His eyes searched for an exit. Suddenly, it was as if he were in one of his comic books. Any moment the villainous Human Chimera would extend his arms, use his powers, and blast him though the wall. Splintered glass mixed with warm, green seawater would gush in and flood the room. Arms flailing, he'd push himself upward. Even now, he could almost feel his lungs burst from lack of oxygen.

Adam halted; his gaze softened and then seemed to try to connect with Kevin. "Not as tough as you try to make us think, are you?"

The comic book world vanished. Kevin glared. "Ya think? I wouldn't put it to the test."

Adam's eyebrows shot up. "Really?"

"Adam, this isn't the time. We're all tired." Chelsea gently pulled at his arm. "And you did promise Staci."

Staci? Mom? Kevin stood in shock. The backpack now seemed weighted. At the airport, Dad had said this was the Refuge, but he hadn't believed him. How could it be? No one had mentioned that phrase since Kevin was ten. Even then his family had lived in safety for almost seven years. It seemed impossible that someone could find them after so long. Dad would've told him.

No, this was Dad's way of taking care of what frustrated him most—his own son.

Well, he wasn't going to stick around long enough to find out what was really going on. He planned on getting out of here. Tyke and Mr. Damon had already signed papers saying they wouldn't press charges. All those two men wanted was Kevin out of town, and he'd be happy to oblige them as soon as he got back to the States.

Chapter 4

Rev broke the tenuous silence. "Adam, why don't you and Chelsea go get some rest. I can show Kevin around and get him settled."

Adam shook his head. "Nah, I got it."

Chelsea stepped between Adam and Kevin. "You know it's not too late to put him in the spare bedroom of our apartment."

"No way," Kevin declared. He'd rather sleep outside—more specifically, on the plane.

Adam gave him a dark look, but Chelsea nodded. "It's all right. Your dad told us you preferred to be alone. I just wanted to leave the option open."

Options? The only option Kevin wanted was the one that took him out of here.

"Ready?" Adam asked him.

Kevin glared and stomped past the adults toward the elevator. "I'm leaving." He headed toward the elevator. He needed to get back on that plane, and nothing would stop him. Kevin punched the up button on the wall.

"They're already gone."

Kevin froze but didn't acknowledge the declaration.

"The plane just took off. Prof thought you needed time to get settled, and there was someone he wanted to visit on one of the islands a couple of hours from here."

"What?" Kevin's fingers balled into a fist so tight around the straps of his backpack his short fingernails bit into his skin. The elevator door slid open and he stepped into it, determined to see for himself.

Adam slid in beside him and blocked the control panel. His hand snaked behind his back and selected a button of his own. "I guess we'll head downstairs."

Stephanie M. E. Gallentine / refuge

Kevin didn't answer. The realization hit him. There was no escape. He was trapped—again. And freedom lay further away than ever.

chapter 5

"So how have you been since your mother died?" Adam asked as the elevator door slid shut behind them.

Kevin tilted his head toward Adam. A thousand thoughts flashed through his mind. None of them good. "As opposed to what?"

Adam rubbed the back of his neck. "Um . . . since before she died?" He swallowed and looked a little sick. "Never mind."

The elevator door slid open on the second floor. The aroma of Italian spices flooded the small space. Kevin stepped out into hall where the soft florescent lights lined the ceiling and worked with the intermittent paintings to tone down the bright white walls.

Adam led him down the hall as it rounded the interior of the circular structure. They stopped outside a set of glass doors that led into a cafeteria. "Hungry?"

A whiff of freshly baked bread captured Kevin's senses. His stomach grumbled. But the thought of eating dinner with these people tonight might give them the impression he accepted his circumstances, maybe even wanted to be friendly. Not even close. Kevin shook his head.

Adam nodded and guided him farther down the quiet hallway. He stopped when they passed a door labeled "Chapel." "I forgot to tell you, but we hold church services here every Sunday."

Oh no. Kevin groaned. Church? Not that too. How much more blood could they possibly want for this one mistake? Kevin glanced back down the hallway. What else had Prof and Dad gotten him into?

Adam grinned, as if amused by Kevin's reaction. "Don't worry. You're not required to come, but pretty much all of the staff do."

Good. He had no need of religion. What did God care about him? Not at all, as far as he could see.

They stopped in another area much like the glass room upstairs. A window stretched the width of the wall. The water appeared darker without the sparkle sunlight gave it closer to the surface. Several table games were spaced throughout the room with the furniture. Air hockey, foosball, Ping-Pong, and a few others Kevin didn't recognize.

Adam walked across the room to the far wall. "I figured this might pique your interest. This is our rec room of sorts." He pressed a button on a remote. "And this is David and Rev's personal favorite."

A wooden cover split apart to reveal a massive screen above a series of shelves packed with all kinds of games, movies, and players.

Kevin shoved his hands in the pocket of his hoodie

Chapter 5

and pushed back a grin. At least this place had one redeeming feature.

"David and Rev told me if they were going to live and work out here, we needed all the latest stuff in gaming to keep boredom at bay. They even offered to pitch in and help pay for it if they had to." Adam bent down on one knee, pointed to the five different gaming systems. "I agreed to purchase the screen and have it installed. David and Rev bought the first system. After that, it turned into a free-for-all. Now every time Mark makes his monthly flight drops, someone has usually ordered something new."

Adam glanced up at the wall clock. "You know, if we want to wait a few more minutes, this place'll fill up with people ending their shifts."

"No."

Adam nodded and they continued their track back down the hall. "So how long have you lived in McKeltic?" Adam asked.

"Obviously too long or I wouldn't have been sent here." Kevin followed Adam back into the elevator.

Adam hit the fifth floor button. "That's not true. Your dad said you made a new friend who he felt was leading you into trouble. He thought some distance might help."

Kevin crossed his arms. "Care to tell me how much distance?"

"Enough that won't be a problem any more."

The elevator opened and Adam led him down the long circular hallway identical to the other floors. All the doors ran along the outer wall.

"So tell me about this friend?"

What was this? An inquisition? "You mean my dad didn't fill out the questionnaire? I'm shocked. Your price of admission should have covered that."

Adam stopped and turned to him. His eyes narrowed. "Look, I know you're angry."

"Really? Did I say something to give you that impression?"

The blue and green irises darkened. Adam's jaw twitched. "That's enough." He walked a few more steps and opened the door to one of the rooms.

Kevin huffed and pushed past Adam into the room. He looked around and couldn't hold back a look of disgust on his face. The small, rectangular-shaped room reminded him of an enlarged walk-in closet. The walls were a hospital white that screamed for someone to turn the lights down. In front of him, a LinkWay videophone, a laptop, and an electronic reader sat on some cheap tabletop desk that looked like it had come from a garage sale.

To his right, a bed was shoved against the far wall. No headboard or footboard. Just a glorified cot. A partially open door revealed a small sliding-door closet. Kevin's eyes slid shut. Compared to his home in McKeltic, this room was practically a homeless shelter.

"Your dad insisted that we make sure you had a LinkWay so he could contact you."

Kevin nodded. At least that was one device they didn't take from him.

"But be forewarned. All of your calls will be monitored—and screened, if necessary."

Kevin sneered. So they thought they would monitor him on the LinkWay? Yeah, right. Everyone knew the LinkWay didn't archive calls, only chats and text. They had to be bluffing.

Chapter 5

Adam handed Kevin a small earpiece with a thin microphone attached. "Here, you'll need this. It's one of our personal internal communicators. If you don't know where something is or you need anything, call me. The radio's voice activated. All you do is press this button and say the name of the person you need to call."

Kevin turned the device over in his hand. Like he'd *want* to have contact with them.

"We tried the Bluetooths awhile back, but everyone kept dropping them into the water. We finally found one that is waterproof." Adam pushed on a door on the left side of the room. "There's a small half-bath though here. The showers are down the hall on your right. Mark already unloaded your things from the plane." He pointed to three boxes stacked in the corner.

Kevin nodded and then sat down at the desk to check out the laptop. While he waited for it to boot up, he twisted around to face the man who stood in the doorway. "Thanks." He hoped Adam would take it as a dismissal and not an invitation to further conversation.

"Well, I guess if you don't need anything else, I'll meet you in the galley at six. We can have a hot breakfast, and then I'll show you where you'll be working."

"Working? I wasn't sent here to work."

"Everyone works here. No exceptions."

Kevin narrowed his eyes. "And if I won't?"

"Then you'll lose your private room. I'll have your things moved to our apartment until things change."

"You'd regret it."

"Maybe. But so would you." Adam met his glare. "Want to find out?"

Stephanie M. E. Gallentine / refuge

Kevin didn't respond. Although he hated being here, he wasn't going to chance losing his privacy either.

"Then I guess I'll see you in the morning." Adam stepped out into the hallway before adding, "I know you can't believe it right now, but I'm really glad you're here."

"Well, that makes one of us," Kevin murmured.

As soon as Adam left, Kevin turned back to the computer. He hoped there would be something of interest on it.

Nothing. No networks and no WiFi. He clicked on the programs. A word processor, a media player, and, oh yes, he certainly couldn't forget to mention their generosity at including Solitaire. He twirled his finger in the air. Oh boy. Wasn't he lucky?

Prof and Dad must have warned them. Kevin unzipped his backpack and pulled out his own laptop. Thankfully, he practically never went anywhere without it.

He turned it on and searched for any active wireless networks. Being this far out, he would have to depend on satellite service. At least it wasn't dialup.

There it was. Perfect. Now all he needed was their password, and he would have his Internet up and running. But on the off chance they were monitoring their systems, he decided to wait till another night to try anything. Might as well let them think they had nothing to worry about with him.

Instead, he dug in his backpack and pulled out a can of Energy X. After popping the top, he tipped it back and guzzled the entire can. Then he squeezed it until the can was a mangled piece of aluminum.

He should have refused to plant the virus in the computers of The World's Gateway. Tyke's laptop was a dif-

Chapter 5

ferent story. But refusal hadn't been an option. Not really. Well, that wouldn't pose a problem any longer. Not out in the middle of nowhere? Kevin blew out a frustrated breath and decided to see if Aiden was at home. He typed in the contact number in the LinkWay.

Aiden's narrow face appeared on the screen almost immediately. "Where are you? I've been waiting for hours." The older teen leaned forward into the screen, as though trying to see where Kevin was. "You didn't make it did you?"

Kevin shook his head. He pulled a pen and paper out of his backpack and began doodling unrecognizable objects, a habit he'd picked up years ago while bored in class. "Simply put, I got caught."

"Well, you're obviously not in jail or you wouldn't have the LinkWay." Aiden paused and then added, "Unless you're calling me for your one phone call."

"It's not far from it." Kevin explained where he was.

Aiden's eyes grow round, his mouth dropped open. "Some research center in the Pacific Ocean? You're kidding."

"I wish I was," Kevin said, his tone dismal. Part of him felt bad for calling. Aiden looked horrible. His nose was red against his pale skin. A stack of wadded up tissue sat at the edge of the LinkWay screen.

"What exactly happened?"

"Exactly?" Kevin leaned back in the chair and was rewarded with a loud squeak. "Got caught, got exiled. But hey, at least Dad won't have to deal with me for the next couple of years."

Aiden gave him a sympathetic look. "What's it like there?"

"Let's see." Kevin counted off on his fingers. "Small room, junk for a computer, no Internet, about five floors beneath the ocean, and, oh yes, a couple of private, uninhabited islands to play on if I can ever get up there long enough to enjoy the fresh air."

His friend grimaced. "Ouch. But you have your laptop, right? So you know how to fix that."

Kevin laughed. It was the first laugh he'd had all day. "Hey, I've only been here an hour or so. Give me at least till morning to break in."

"I'm thinking in priorities here," came the pseudo-serious response.

"I know what you mean. If I get out of here and off the island, I'll be lucky. They have this place locked up tight. There's hardly an office or door that doesn't have to have someone's code to let me in."

Aiden smirked. "Like that's ever stopped you before."

Kevin reached for another can of Energy X. Usually he stopped at one, but tonight he was wrecked. The nap on the plane hadn't helped either.

Aiden excused himself, but was back within minutes with what looked like a glass of orange juice.

He must have really been sick to pick juice over his usual Energy X.

"You know, I still can't believe it." Aiden took a large drink and then reached for another tissue. "I get sick for a few days, and my best friend ends up as an unused extra on *Lost*."

Kevin smirked. "Yeah, well, the moral of the story is never let sickness keep you down. You miss out on so much."

"No, the moral of the story is never let people push you to do something against the law that you don't want

Chapter 5

to do." Aiden shook his head. "Man, I told you not to do it."

"I know." Kevin had berated himself enough over the last few days. "What was I supposed to do? I had no choice in the matter. I'd exhausted my other options."

"You always have a choice."

"You don't understand." Kevin twisted his watch around on his wrist and pretended to be interested in the time. He didn't want to admit he should have been stronger. But he couldn't explain that to Aiden right now. "There are consequences. You know that."

"And you're facing them right now."

"You know what I mean." Kevin glanced over to the boxes neatly stacked in the corner of the room. There sat his life—or what remained of it anyway—packed away in three medium-sized boxes. He was almost afraid to look inside of them. Dad probably phoned the part-time housekeeper and told her to throw some clothes together. "Thanks, Dad," he mumbled under his breath. "Thanks for everything."

The sound of Aiden's congested cough brought him back to their conversation. Aiden quickly downed the juice and then held up a flash drive with a slight grin. "I cracked the password on that file."

Kevin sat up in the chair, interested. "You did? When?"

"While I spent the last eight hours wondering what happened to you. Besides, Mom was determined that I stay in bed. You know how she gets."

Kevin grinned. "So what did you find?"

"P Thomas is Patrick Thomas of AsericA Investments, which used to be located in California."

"Used to be?"

Aiden nodded. "Patrick Thomas was known for his

Stephanie M. E. Gallentine / refuge

investments in the Asian markets. A couple of years ago, he took on a partner, and they started generating investments for an Asian company that made fake flowers like they sell at Wal-Mart.

"Anyway, Patrick apparently said he put all the money in an offshore account and set up individual accounts for each of his investors so the money would be protected against taxes or something like that. I guess at first, some of the people got returns for their investments. But after that, something happened. His partner claimed Patrick had duped him and transferred the money into yet another account."

The whole scenario sounded a bit too familiar for Kevin, but he waited for Aiden to finish.

"Patrick claimed it was the partner who was the guilty person, but his partner, Sean Griffin, apparently showed enough proof that Patrick was arrested. But then he got out on bail until his trial."

"So what happened? Did they ever find the money?"

Aiden shook his head. "No, that's just it. The night before the trial, Patrick Thomas suffered a major heart attack and died."

Kevin screwed up his face in question. "What?"

"Yeah, that's what I thought, too," Aiden said. "Get your Internet up, and I'll send the file to you."

"Will do." A thought hit him. "Did you find a picture of the partner?"

"No, but I'm still looking."

"So it's possible Tyke was his partner?"

"I doubt it, unless Tyke has the ability to change identities."

"Changing identities isn't that uncommon," Kevin said cryptically.

Chapter 5

"Like you would know anything about that." Aiden chuckled. "It's probably someone he knew. I mean, we run in hacking circles. Tyke runs in investment circles."

"You really believe that?"

"No, but my dad always says someone has to be the voice of reason, and it's not gonna be you."

"Ha. Ha."

Kevin grinned. Until he met Aiden, he hadn't really had any friends classified beyond the term of acquaintance. Aiden was so much like him, and yet so different. On the Internet, both of them were well-known hackers. But in real life, Aiden was the only one who saw him not as some weird teenager or some guy with secrets to keep, but as a friend.

"So how long do you have to be there?"

"Till I'm eighteen." He groaned. Eighteen seemed an eternity away.

"Wow." Aiden made a face. "Do they know?"

"No. And I don't intend on sharing any time soon."

"I don't blame you," Aiden said. "But then again, it might actually be to your benefit."

"Maybe."

"Are you relieved?"

The look he gave Aiden was a mixture of disgust and disbelief. "Relieved to trade in one adult over me for who knows how many?"

"Ouch. I'm glad it's you, not me." There was a pause before Aiden mused aloud. "Still, it might be different."

Kevin glanced away from the screen. "Yeah, but at least at home I knew how to deal with . . . things." He stumbled over the words "Dad's alcoholism," but couldn't choke it out. With as many problems as that created, that life was normal to him. He knew how to react, how to survive. What was he supposed to do here with a bunch of religious freaks? Instead of blaming their actions on the booze, they could blame them on their God.

"Too bad your dad didn't."

"I got to go." Kevin ended the connection. Some conversations didn't need to be had.

Ever.

chapter 6

Kevin paced the room. He wanted—no needed—out. His muscles tensed as though revving for a one hundred-yard dash. The room, however, barely allowed him five steps in either direction. No way would he last another eight hours in the cramped space.

Someone rapped on the door.

Reluctantly, he cracked it open.

Chelsea stood over the threshold, her arms outstretched. In her hands, she held out a plate heaped with food. Spaghetti, French bread, corn, and a bottle of orange juice. She smiled. "I thought you might like something to eat before you went to bed."

Kevin opened the door enough to take the plate. "Thanks." Afraid she would try and worm him into a conversation, he didn't say anything else.

Stephanie M. E. Gallentine / refuge

Chelsea must have taken the hint. After another brief smile, she turned and left.

Scents of garlic and spice from the spaghetti sauce filled the small room. He sat down and shoved the laptop out of the way. Within minutes, nothing remained on the plate except a few saucy trails mixed with corn juice.

He glanced at the LinkWay to check the time and then compared it to his watch. Kevin let out a tortured moan. He'd gone back seven hours. Suddenly, this had turned into the longest day on record.

The need to escape the room returned with a vengeance. He decided to return the plate to the galley before checking out the alternate exits.

Kevin crept into the narrow hallway that circled the interior of the Center on each floor and then took the elevator up to the galley on the second floor. He pulled open the double glass doors and entered the now dimly lit eating area. Behind the stainless steel serving line, he found a three-compartment sink where he quickly rinsed off the plate.

A soft glow from the dark kitchen caught his attention. After making sure no one was around, he made his way back to the lone computer in an almost hidden alcove. Clicking on the Internet Explorer icon, Kevin waited while the home page loaded.

He grinned when he was able to access the email Aiden had sent him. Leaning over, he searched for a flash drive. As usual, someone had left one poking out of the USB slot in the computer. Kevin transferred the file and then stuffed the device into his pocket. He'd return it later.

On his way out of the kitchen, the light suddenly brightened and a woman stepped in front of him. "What

Chapter 6

are doing in here?" she said in a heavy Southern accent. Arms folded across her chest, her suspicious gaze shifted from him to the computer and back again.

Kevin kept his hands in his pocket and nudged a shoulder in the direction of the sink. "Chelsea brought me something to eat. I thought I better bring the plate back and rinse it off."

"Oh." She dropped her arms and relaxed her stance. "Sorry. I guess I'm a little overprotective of my kitchen. You must be Kevin."

He nodded. "I gotta go."

"Sure. I'll see you later," she called to his receding back.

In case she was watching where he went, Kevin took the elevator back down to his floor and then followed the hallway around until he found an exit sign. A stairwell located behind the interior elevator had to be their emergency exit. Excitement surged through his system, tingling in his hands and feet. He pushed open the door and sprinted up the five flights of metal stairs that led up to yet another exit.

Kevin yanked on the door, but it wouldn't budge. He stared at the now familiar locking mechanism and tapped in Adam's code. If anyone questioned him, he could tell the truth. Adam entered his code in full view. Someone else he saw, on the other hand, used a swipe card. Maybe Adam had lost his or left it at the Center for the duration of their trip. Who knew? Who cared? Adam's mistake was Kevin's reward.

The lock popped and released. "Yes." He pulled open the door and stood for a moment, mesmerized at the sight before him. This door exited on the backside of the

Stephanie M. E. Gallentine / refuge

Center. Kevin dug in his pocket and pulled out the identity papers he'd created. Right now about the only use for them he'd have was origami. He folded the paper into a small but thick rectangle and then wedged it into the door so that the lock wouldn't engage until he got back.

Small, white-capped waves rolled in and slapped against the boats docked around the fifteen-foot metal deck. A stiff breeze blew over him and expanded in his hoodie like a balloon. Several boats rocked in the water alongside the platform. Above him the sun cast a burnt-orange glow on one of the tiny islands Prof had pointed out earlier.

Kevin leaned back against the Center and let his mind drift back to one week ago when the whole situation with Peter Damon and William Tyke had begun.

Aiden's father, Mr. Rollings, had assigned Kevin and Aiden to work with another employee on The World's Gateway penetration test. Part of the system had been a cinch to break into. Before the first night ended, they had taken complete control of the company's computer system and uncovered a number of problem areas.

While scrolling through Mr. Tyke's files, Kevin found the only encrypted one in their system. Out of curiosity, he set the password program to run. He cringed after he was able to open the file.

"Kevin, we've got to tell my dad," Aiden said.

"No." He needed time to think. Before him, the open file indicated that a lot of the money from overseas investments had disappeared. A name kept popping up throughout the document. CPA for The World's Gateway. Steven Ramsey. Dad.

Chapter 6

Kevin let out a long breath. "Just give me a few days. Let me talk to him. Maybe we can clear all this up."

Aiden shook his head. "We can't."

"My dad didn't take this money. I know it. Someone's setting him up."

Aiden gave him a sideways glance. "Are you sure?"

No—Yes. Dad might be many things—made Kevin angry more times than not—but Dad wasn't a thief. But why would Tyke want to frame his dad? "I'm sure. Give me a chance to talk to him. Then I'll explain the situation to your dad. If anyone gets fired, it'll be me."

"I don't know."

"Please . . . " Kevin's knuckles turned white as he clamped the edge of the desk. He had to think of something. Hadn't his world caved in enough in the past year? No way could he bear the thought of being the one responsible for seeing Dad arrested and possibly convicted for something he couldn't have done. No, there had to be another way.

"All right," Aiden agreed. "I'll give you a week, but then we have to tell my dad. Otherwise, Rollings Security might be blamed for withholding information on a possible crime."

"Don't worry. I'll think of something, and then we'll be the heroes. Mr. Damon will thank us and my dad . . . " Kevin's voice trailed off, the weight of the situation bearing down on him. "He'll go to the police and explain everything. Then Tyke will go to jail for fraud."

At least that's the way he had hoped it would work.

Glancing back at the boats, Kevin decided it was time for a little road trip—well, water trip. Anything to give him at least a temporary sense of freedom. Hotwiring wouldn't be a problem. He'd studied videos on the Internet. But he still had to get past the video surveillance camera stationed above his head.

The camera slowly panned the deck area. Kevin pushed up his sleeve and timed the rotation. Each swing took thirty seconds and then paused for fifteen seconds before panning back. He timed it again to be sure. As the camera made its journey in the opposite direction, Kevin bolted across the deck and then hoisted himself over the side of one of the smaller boats, similar to one his mother had let him practice on a couple of summers before.

He ducked as the camera swung back and used the time to access the boat's wires. Several minutes later, the boat started easily. Kevin loosed it from its moorings and backed out.

"And Dad said he didn't trust me to drive his car." As soon as he cleared the Center, he whooped and gunned the engines. Water parted and sprayed the sides as the boat sliced through the waves.

What a rush!

It felt so good to be free.

"Thought I'd check and see if you made it out of Kevin's room alive," Rev said.

Adam grinned from his prone position on the couch in his and Chelsea's apartment. "What? You think I can't handle a teenager?"

"Ah, so I see you're still in denial." Rev plopped down into the vacant recliner. "Where's Chelsea?"

"She went to Kevin's room to take him a plate of

Chapter 6

food." Adam leaned his head back on the sofa. Reaching up, he slipped off his radio ear bud and laid it on the end table. Someone else could answer calls tonight. "You know Chelsea. She thinks outside of God, there's nothing that food and medicine can't fix."

"What about you? What do you think?"

Adam closed his eyes and tried to think of something positive to say, but then settled for honesty instead. "I don't know. I'm hoping once he gets into the routine of life here and gets to know us, things will be better."

"Yeah, that had to be awkward for Kevin, being forced to live with someone he had only heard about."

Adam snorted. If only that had been the case. "That's just it. He knew nothing of this place until just before coming. He still doesn't know who I am beyond my name."

"That's impossible."

"Prof told me on the flight home." Adam sat up and grabbed his bottle of water sitting on the glass coffee table between them. "Apparently, Staci never told Kevin anything about her past."

"I wonder why." Rev leaned forward and planted his elbows on his knees. "Did you ask his dad?"

"Yeah, I called him when Kevin fell asleep on the plane." Adam tried to keep the steel out of his voice, but he was still angry over the answer he received. "Told me Staci had her reasons and to remember the other part of my promise to Staci: I'd take Kevin, no questions asked."

"No wonder the kid's angry." Rev frowned. "When do you plan to talk to Kevin about this?"

"Tomorrow afternoon."

"I'll be praying for you."

Adam nodded. "Thanks, I'll need it."

Rev chuckled. "You never know. Kevin may surprise you."

"Yeah, but with what?"

Kevin stood up and dusted the sand off his jeans, wishing he could have stayed longer. But he needed to get back before it got too dark and he couldn't see to dock the boat. Already the sun was making its final descent into the horizon. He wished he could sail off and never look back, but he had no desire to get lost in the middle of an ocean. No, his escape from here would take more time to plan. Until then he needed to get back.

Grunting, he pushed the boat out of the sand and back into the ocean. Knee deep in water, the white-capped waves crashed into him. Kevin stumbled and then splashed in the water. Sand crumbled beneath him as the ocean sucked the water back out before the waves returned. Reaching up, he gripped the side of the boat and hoisted himself over the edge.

Kevin turned the key in the ignition. He smiled, hearing the engine come to life. Then, without warning, the engine sputtered and quit altogether.

He tried again. The engine whirred, but never turned over. Time after time he tried, his desperation growing with each failure.

"No!" He punched the steering wheel. "Stupid boat. All I need is for you to start one time. Come on." He tried once more. Again, nothing happened.

Chapter 6

The sun seemed to have increased its rate of descent to the rhythm of Kevin's heart. Instead of the slow leisurely fall, it now seemed to tumble from the sky into the ocean below, leaving him shrouded in a darkness lit only by the stars. In the distance, he spotted the bright spotlight that swung in slow circles at the top of the Center. Would that be enough light to get docked in the right spot?

It was a chance he'd have to take. Sifting through the contents of the boat, he located an oar strapped to the side. He dipped the fiberglass paddle in the water and pulled it back. The boat moved forward until the strength of the next wave pushed him back toward the shore.

The sequence repeated itself several times. Then, as his untrained muscles quivered under the exertion, the wave caught the oar and swept it away. He scrambled to get it, but another wave quickly carried the paddle out of reach.

Kevin slammed his fist on the side of the boat. After several more unsuccessful tries to start the engine, he gave up and reached for the radio Adam had given him. "Adam?"

Silence.

He wondered if the signal would pick up at this distance. "Adam Hollandale. Chelsea? Rev?"

Still no response.

"Oh come on," he complained. "Don't tell me I'm the only one here who's awake."

He twisted the key one last time and gave it lots of gas, or at least he thought he did.

Nothing.

"Well, somebody better be up, or who knows where I'll be come morning."

Stephanie M. E. Gallentine / refuge

All right. He needed another name. David. Hadn't Adam mentioned something about a guy named David? It was worth a try at this point. Sucking in a deep breath in an attempt to steady the growing fear within him, he activated the radio once more.

"David?"

"*¿Mande?* Excuse me? Who is this?" a heavily accented voice answered.

"Kevin. Kevin Ramsey."

"The new kid who came with Adam?" The accent made the word *kid* sound more like *keed*. "Why are you calling me?" A long pause. "Do you know what time it is? Aren't you supposed to be in your room or something?"

"Or something," he mumbled under his breath. "Is Adam there?"

"Of course, have you called him?"

"Yes, but he didn't answer."

"He's probably asleep. What do you need?"

Kevin could hear the impatience on the other end of his earpiece. He rolled his eyes. Maybe he should have waited. "I need some help. I can't get back to my room."

"Where are you?"

He paused. "The island. I would've been fine, but the boat wouldn't start and—"

"What?" David yelled, causing Kevin to jump. "*¡Dios mío!* Does anyone know you took the boat?"

"I don't know." At least that was partially the truth. Someone could have seen him take it.

"So you stole our boat and now you are stuck?"

"Not exactly." Kevin looked around and gulped. The boat rocked in the waves. He knew he was still close enough to get out of the boat and swim back to shore, but

Chapter 6

in the dark he couldn't see what he was stepping into. Did jellyfish come this close to shore? And stonefish? Hadn't he read once how painful their stings were when they were stepped on? "Look, I can't get the boat started. Can you help me or not?"

The response came first in the form of a long growl, followed by a string of words for which Kevin wasn't sure he wanted to know the translation. Then the tirade ended.

"Don't move. I'll be there in a minute."

It seemed like forever before Kevin saw a spotlight and heard the roar of an engine approaching from the opposite direction. David's irritated voice carried through the dark, arriving even before the stocky Hispanic pulled up next to him. Rev frowned and hopped over the side of the boat. Silently, he checked the motor in the back, and then held up a gas can. "And here I was hoping we could at least get through the night."

Kevin groaned inwardly. "You'd do better hoping I get sent home."

chapter 7

A little after five in the morning, Kevin gave up on any thought of sleep. Between the nap on the plane, the energy drinks, and fear of what would happen once Adam found out he'd taken the boat, he was keyed up. Not even going through the files Aiden had sent him on Patrick Thomas helped. Those files were useless by themselves. What evidence could an obituary, newspaper article, or a picture contain? He needed more information. Frowning, he threw back the blanket and let it slide to a crumpled mess on the floor.

He sighed and let his gaze roam over the bare white-textured walls and then down to the mushroom-colored laminate flooring. The room was too clean. Hospital room clean. He hated hospitals. Gathering up yesterday's shirt, he tossed it into one of the barren corners. The socks, still soaked and sandy from last night's activity, he shaped into two awkward balls, pulled back his arm, and pitched them across the room. Each water-laden sock thudded against the far wall and then slid down to their new home on the floor.

The wall protested with a pounding from the other side.

"Oops." A mischievous grin pulled at the corners of his lips. His neighbor must not care for his early morning target practice. After a deep yawn, he fished his laptop out from under the bed. Who knew? If he kept this up, they might send him back on the first available plane after all.

Moments later, Kevin pulled up all his family pictures on his laptop. As he scrolled through them, he marveled how different life had been when Mom was still alive. She had been like a magnet that kept their family connected and happy. When she died, it was as if someone had removed that connector, leaving the remaining two magnets repelling each other.

Kevin let out a long sigh and continued the slideshow. One photo in particular stood out. Mom and Dad were playing a game of Monopoly, and Mom was gloating over the motel she had just put up on Broadway and Park Place.

Kevin stopped. How had he forgotten? Mom had shown him this picture a few months before her death. She had hidden information about the Refuge within the redundant data of the picture file so that no one would know how to find it unless they knew the information was there.

Chapter 7

Maybe that would be his ticket out of here. He pulled up a program that would allow him to read any data hidden within the picture the naked eye couldn't see. Slowly, he made out what appeared to be a phone number. But whose?

Kevin sucked in a deep breath. He grabbed the LinkWay, typed in the information, and waited for someone to pick up. By the fourth ring, he feared that after all these years, the number might have been changed or handed over to someone else. On the sixth ring, he reached up to disconnect. It had been a dumb idea anyway. It wasn't like anything would change. No one was going to fly out here and rescue him.

"Hello."

There was a slight pause. Kevin stammered as he tried to decide whether or not to hang up.

"You've reached Adam Hollandale at PARC Place International. I'm not in right now, so if you'll—"

Kevin hung up and let his head fall back on the chair. He slipped his fingers beneath his glasses and rubbed his eyes. No matter how hard he tried, he couldn't believe it. This was actually the place his mother had told him about. But why here and how did she know Adam? One of her hacker friends? Nah, he didn't look the type, and Adam had told him Rev was his techie.

His stomach grumbled, reminding him how long it'd been since he'd eaten. He hoped the cafeteria would have some strawberry pop tarts in stock. At home they, along with chicken-flavored ramen noodles, were a staple food of sorts.

A short walk later, Kevin peered though the glass doors of the cafeteria. Two people sat side by side, sipping from steaming cups at a table not far from the entrance. His gaze moved through the room until he spotted the coffee carafe by the far wall. A nearby table sat with the chair pulled out, as though the coffee itself expected him, welcomed him, even had saved a spot for him.

The door made a slight whoosh as it opened, but it went unnoticed. Although the couple sat with their backs to him, he recognized the heavy accent from the man who answered his call the night before. Next to him, the woman who had busted him last night listened to the irritated man. Her long copper braid hung over the back of her chair like a jumble of thick electrical wires twisted together.

This morning her drawl seemed thicker. Kevin shook his head. Between this woman's and David's thick accents, he'd need subtitles to understand. Not that he would read them anyway.

The woman waved her hand in the air. "Oh well, Lord knows it's probably the first time you've been to the surface since you started this whole project."

"*Pero* . . . I don't have time to be chasing some crazy kid who doesn't have the sense not to go running off when he knows nothing of this place."

Kevin stiffened against the wall.

"David," the woman said.

The man pointed to his chest. "I am an engineer, not a lifeguard. I don't do rescues." David slammed his cup down on the table. "The kid would have been better off locked up somewhere. But I guess we're desperate enough to take in juvenile locos to pay the bills now."

Kevin's breath caught in his chest. Is that what they thought? He was their meal ticket? Didn't anyone care

Chapter 7

that he didn't want to be here either? Anger and embarrassment volleyed within him like a professional tennis match. His stomach rumbled and growled. But how could anyone expect him to eat with these people? He turned and fled.

Last night's accident had been just that—an accident. Yeah, it had been dumb not to check the gas. So what? And now this idiot felt the need to not only broadcast it, but also insert his own erroneous opinions. At this point Kevin wished he had spent the night in the boat or swam back to the Center.

Fuming, he stormed down the hall, hands jammed in the front pocket of his hoodie and head tucked. All sorts of malicious ideas of how he could get even with David ran through his head.

"Whoa!" Rev stood in the way. He wore a smile that made Kevin feel like he had entirely too much joy for that time of the morning.

Kevin glared, hoping to put a dent in Mr. Happy's grin. It didn't work. He tried to sidestep the man, but Rev wouldn't let him past.

The giant statue of a man towered over Kevin like a broad wall that matched his every move.

"What?" Kevin nearly yelled. Didn't anyone remember the three-feet-of-personal-space rule? He blew out a frustrated breath.

Rev didn't move. Instead, he stared at Kevin as if to calculate his response. "Did you already eat breakfast? I'm going that way myself."

"Not hungry," he lied. Then he darted to the right.

An arm shot out and caught the sleeve of his jacket. Kevin tried to yank it free, but Rev locked his fist around the fabric and then continued with the conversation as though nothing had happened. Kevin swore the man must have taken lessons from Prof in how not to argue.

"Chelsea and Adam had an early meeting. I told them I'd get you started. And since I'm hungry and the person Adam wants you to work with today is in the cafeteria, I guess we'll head that way." Rev lifted an eyebrow and waited.

Kevin tromped back toward the cafeteria, glaring at every person he passed. Partway down the hall, he peeked over his shoulder. Rev kept close pace behind him, and soon they were back where he started. In the time since he left, the room had filled with people.

Rev led him over to the buffet station where the woman with the long braid stood, refilling a long metal pan with fresh pancakes. David stood behind her, still talking but in much lower tones.

Kevin suppressed a groan. This couldn't be the woman Rev meant him to work with. That meant he would go from working with computers to working in the kit—. He refused to even complete the thought. No way would he spend his mandatory work time washing dishes or cooking. Like he could cook anything anyway. Back home the fare of the day consisted of take-out, microwave, or strawberry pop tarts.

"Kevin, this is Anna Lisa." Rev seemed to hesitate. "And as you know this is—"

"Jesús David Juan Guillermo Castillo-Pérez." The stocky man from the night before stood and stared down his nose at Kevin. "You may call me Señor Pérez."

Kevin glared. *Señor Jerk is more like it.* Aloud he said, "Am I supposed to be impressed?" He didn't care how rude it sounded. This man did not deserve any courtesies.

Chapter 7

David moved to stand in front of Kevin. He ground out his words. "About as impressed as I am about . . ."

Kevin wondered why David's voice trailed off until he turned and caught the warning look Rev gave David. Kevin turned back to David and held his gaze. He refused to allow this man to intimidate him.

A large hand clamped down on his shoulder from behind and squeezed, the message clear. Kevin twisted out of the grip. Rev's hand reappeared. Kevin spun on his heels. "Don't touch me." He punctuated each word.

Rev dropped his hand, took a step back, and gave Kevin an extra foot of distance before he made another attempt to diffuse the situation. A lopsided grin on his face, Rev said, "He goes by David. His family just had more girls than boys, so they gave the boys longer names to compensate."

"And this is supposed to make a difference, how?" Kevin spun back around to David. The man stood stiffly in front of him and thrust a hand forward to shake. Kevin let his gaze travel from the man's hardened eyes to the waiting hand and back again.

Rev cleared his throat.

David nodded and his stance relaxed slightly. "*Lo siento*, I'm sorry."

All conversation in the room stopped. The way everyone focused their attention on them reminded Kevin of the day before in Galactic Jitters. He frowned. For all his desire to keep his life private, it had the most uncanny ability to publicize itself. With extreme reluctance, he took the offered hand. The shake between them was anything but firm. It must have been enough though. Conversation slowly restarted around them, followed by the clink of silverware on plates.

Stephanie M. E. Gallentine / refuge

Rev again acted as though nothing had happened. "Anna Lisa, did Adam tell you he wanted Kevin to work with you?"

She nodded. "Yeah, he called me last night." She stood and smiled down at Kevin. "Hungry? There's still plenty of time to eat before we get started."

It was then Kevin noticed a mole right above the left side of her lip. He watched, fascinated, as it moved when she spoke. For a second, he wanted to laugh at the picture his mind conjured up: Mole Woman, the newest superhero from the South with her braid of doom. She had the power to entrance a villain with her hypnotic mole. Then when she had him where she wanted him, whack! That thick, waist-length braid would knock him off his feet, coil itself around his neck, and choke the very breath out of him until he surrendered. With a sideways glance at David, aka Señor Jerk, he envisioned the perfect adversary.

"Kevin?" Anna Lisa said.

"Uh . . . yeah . . . I'll . . . um . . ." He motioned with his thumb towards the food and quickly piled a plate high with pancakes and bacon. If he had to work around all this food, he might as well eat as much of it as he could. Before he sat down, he poured himself some coffee and dumped in several extra sugar packets to give it an extra punch. Otherwise, he might fall asleep in the dishwater. How he longed for a Galactic Jitter's quadruple shot mocha. Still, he thought, as he took his first sample sip, not bad.

Chapter 7

While running the dishes through the industrial dishwashing machine, Kevin kept glancing over his shoulder. Anna Lisa seemed to be watching his every move. It was eerie, feeling as though he were being stalked by Mole Woman. Maybe one of the labs here was where she acquired her superhero status.

Good grief, this must be the sign that he'd read too many graphic novels. But it was fun to imagine. It kept his mind off other things.

"You'll have to ignore David," she said. "Sometimes he can be a pig."

Kevin tilted his head and smirked. "That wasn't the animal I was thinking of."

Mole Woman crossed her arms. She pursed her lips and narrowed her eyes. "Ya know, in David's defense, he has been pretty stressed about a project he's been working on."

Kevin lifted his eyebrows in question. "Am I supposed to feel sorry for him? Not gonna happen."

Both stood silent for several moments. The mole on Anna Lisa's face twitched. Was it a tick or a sign of readiness to strike? Her shoulders stiffened.

He imagined this time she appeared ready to use her scorpion move where the stiff copper braid came over her head, administering a serious blow to his head.

A strange, hummed melody drew their attention to the door. A small Asian woman walked in. As she came closer, Kevin realized he must be at least four inches taller than she. At his relatively short height of five-foot-three, it wasn't often that he towered over anyone.

She nodded in his direction but then turned her focus on Anna Lisa. "Did you get them?" she asked in a delicate voice.

"Yes, I put all your requested ingredients on the top shelf in the walk-in refrigerator." Anna Lisa's voice seemed a little tight as she introduced him to the smaller woman. "Kevin, this is Tuyen Phan. She's an Oxygen Tech here temporarily from GiOx Industries to help with David's project. But tonight she's offered to cook us some authentic Asian food. Tuyen, this is Kevin Ramsey."

The woman smiled and tipped her head forward. "It's nice to meet you, Kevin. You look very much like your mother, I see."

That got his attention. "What?" Kevin's gaze moved from Tuyen to Anna Lisa, and then back to Tuyen. "How do you know what my mother looked like?"

"They showed me . . . I mean I heard someone say . . ." Tuyen blushed and lowered her eyes. "I'm sorry. I didn't mean to . . ."

"Forget it." His gaze shifted to the blurred peripheral edges of the left side of his glasses. Anger rode just beneath the surface. He hated this feeling that someone knew something he should know, but didn't. "So do you have any more probing or embarrassing observations you'd like to make before I get back to work?"

"Kevin." Anna Lisa drew his name out, the warning clear.

He jammed his hands into his front pockets. "Sorry."

Anna Lisa led him past all the kitchen equipment to the computer in the back alcove. "We got our shipment in, so I thought I'd show you how to receive our new inventory in the computer and then how to enter new recipes in the database."

"Recipes?" Kevin curled his lip. Who did she think he was? Betty Crocker? "I'm capable of more."

Chapter 7

"So I've heard." Anna grinned. "But it would not only help us out but also give you an opportunity to prove yourself. This computer's not networked, so you shouldn't be able to cause too much trouble."

Not networked? He doubted that. But right now wasn't the time to prove her wrong. At least it beat washing dishes. He nodded, followed her to the computer, and waited while she logged in. 45851. Kevin was tempted to smile. A personal challenge formed in his head. He decided to see how many of their passcodes he could get by shoulder surfing. At least that would give him some entertainment during his incarceration.

A wicked grin emerged. *Then, when her back is turned . . .*

chapter 8

Kevin closed the door to his room and set his lunch tray on the desk. Maybe if he ate something, the nagging headache sitting just behind his eyes would go away. He dimmed the lights to fifty percent and pulled his laptop out of hiding. While he waited for it to load up, he dipped the corner of his grilled cheese sandwich into the steaming bowl of tomato soup. The hot soup slid down the back of his throat, soothing the slight soreness that had developed during the morning.

The LinkWay chimed.

Kevin wiped the grease from his hands onto his jeans and then pulled the LinkWay closer. The instant he read the caller on the readout, he froze. The bite of sandwich stuck in the back of his throat. Kevin swallowed some tea to clear his throat while he hit the receive button and glared at Dad's image.

"How are you?" Dad asked.

Kevin worked to keep his temper in check. "How am I? You've got to be kidding. You know as well as I do, I shouldn't be the one punished here. I'm the one who tried to help."

"And you did," Dad assured him. "But then Tyke threatened me—us. He *knows*, Kevin."

"Knows what?"

"Who we really are."

The words sunk into his mind like an anchor. "How?"

"The New Year's Eve investors' dinner I attended. A man I knew in college came up to me while I was visiting with Prof and Tyke and called me by name—my real name. Nothing but a stroke of luck on Tyke's part," Dad explained. "I had no choice but to call on Adam's promise to take you."

"We could have changed identities again. Mom made sure I knew how to do it."

Dad frowned. "I wasn't ready to take the chance."

"Why?"

"You've already been in trouble, and I have no guarantee that won't happen again. If we did run, we'd be found the first time you did get in trouble."

Kevin clutched the edge of the desk, struggling to accept the fact Dad and he couldn't run because of him. Didn't Dad understand Kevin didn't want to be in trouble?

"I sent you to Adam for your protection."

"Protection?" Kevin glared at the image on the screen. "Imprisonment is more like it. Why till I'm eighteen?"

"You know why. Until you're eighteen, they can make you go back to them, and I promised your mother I'd never let them have you back. I won't let anyone hurt you."

Chapter 8

"Let me go! Don't make me stay here." Kevin banged his fist on the table. He squeezed his eyes into angry slits. "You know, I could just tell Adam you were the one who made me set that virus and not some 'friend.' Then we'd see who went to prison."

"But you won't."

The confidence in Dad's words infuriated him. Dad was right. Kevin wouldn't tell. As much as he hated to admit it, he was more like Dad than he wanted to be. Most of his life Kevin had been trained to keep secrets. So many secrets. He'd never felt the freedom to be honest with anyone but his mother. Since her death, the secrets had darkened. Shame covered him at the thought of anyone finding out.

"Trust me, Kevin. This was the best solution to everyone's problem."

"No, it was the easiest solution to *your* problem." Kevin thumped the disconnect button. Anger boiled within him. His hand curled around the glass of iced tea. The cool beads of moisture soaked into his palm while he struggled futilely to quell the emotions that fought to erupt. With a quick thrust, he chucked the plastic glass against the far wall. The brown liquid splattered and slid down the textured wall like lava down the jagged rocks of a mountainside.

Pain pulsated in the middle of his forehead and radiated back. Kevin cradled his head between his hands and wished for some Ibuprofen—another thing he couldn't get without having to interact with Chelsea or Adam.

Kevin reached up under his glasses and rubbed his eyes. Lack of sleep must have caught up with him. He fished out his backpack from underneath the bed, dug out one of the four remaining energy drinks, popped off the top, and downed it. Maybe the caffeine would ease his headache, at least temporarily.

An unfamiliar beep sounded in his ear. He reached up to his ear and answered his radio. "Uh . . . hello?"

"Kevin, this is Anna Lisa." She sounded hesitant. "I just wanted to remind you that lunch was over ten minutes ago. Adam has a paper he wants you to work on."

"Be there in a minute." He tossed the now empty can into the trash on top of his half-eaten lunch. Only Dad could ruin a good lunch.

Clack, clack, clack, clack, clack. Kevin pounded the keys on the keyboard with all the passion of a concert pianist. His headache now abated, the crescendo of the pummeled keys drowned out any thoughts that tried to hound him.

"Are the keys sticking?" Anna Lisa hollered from across the room, an irritated scowl on her face. "No need to beat the things to death. I wasn't the one who wanted you to work on that assignment this afternoon."

Kevin gave her what had become his blanket response for the afternoon. "Nuh . . . um." If Anna Lisa had any sense at all, she would translate the nonsensical word for whatever answer she wanted and leave him alone.

Later in the afternoon, Kevin glanced up as Adam stepped through the doorway and panned the room. Anna Lisa sat at her desk, her expression now relaxed as though oblivious to the racket. Tuyen stood against the counter beside the stove, a deep frown marring her oth-

Chapter 8

erwise flawless skin. She chopped vegetables with the efficiency of a chef, muttering under her breath.

Kevin let up on the keys and listened.

Adam approached the small Asian woman first. "Everything okay?"

Tuyen tilted her neck back and glowered up at Adam. Pointing with her butcher knife, she rattled a few sentences in her native tongue, slammed the knife down on the stainless-steel counter, and stormed out the door.

"That challenging, huh?" Adam asked to her retreating back. He turned to Kevin, a frown of his own set in place. "I think you've set a record. You haven't been here twenty-four hours, and already you've caused two people to revert back to their native tongues. Good thing everyone else's first language is English, or I'd be in big trouble."

Kevin scowled and went back to hammering the keys, but peered over the monitor as Adam crossed the room to Anna Lisa.

Anna Lisa jumped and then proceeded to pull a set of earplugs out of her ears.

Kevin grinned. Maybe Mole Woman wasn't so dumb after all. He went back to typing.

Adam motioned for him. "Come on. We need to talk."

Kevin crossed his arms and huffed as he seated himself across from Adam. This must be his permanent place—the opposite side of a desk, in trouble. "You know if I'm ever going to finish that stupid assignment, I need to actually work on it."

"And pound my keyboards to death in the process?"

Stephanie M. E. Gallentine / refuge

Adam settled into his chair and opened a file in front of him.

"I didn't realize there was a policy against keyboard abuse."

"There's not. But there is one against theft and unauthorized field trips." Adam's gaze bore into him.

Kevin squeezed his eyes shut against the headache that had returned. With everything that had happened today, he had almost forgotten about last night. "I didn't steal anything. If the boat hadn't run out of gas, no one would even know I was gone. Besides, it's not like I can go anywhere else. You guys kind of made sure of that."

"It's my understanding your only other option was to be arrested. Seems to me this should be an answer to your prayer."

"I don't pray."

"Maybe you should start."

Kevin rolled his eyes. He hoped this wouldn't be the way every conversation would go for the rest of his time there. "Why don't you just send me home? We'd all be happier."

"Because I promised."

Kevin wanted to gag. Not that again. If it wasn't prayer, it was promises. "I know. I know," he said, bored. "You promised my mother. Well, in case you haven't heard, she's dead. I'm sure if she were here, she would release you from this promise."

Adam's expression froze. He glanced down at a small picture frame and then back at Kevin. Determination molded his expression. "I don't want to be released."

"That doesn't make sense." Was this guy a glutton for punishment? Surely he didn't want a teenager around for

Chapter 8

the next two years.

Rifling through some papers on his desk, Adam placed one in front of him. "A lot of things in life don't make sense. One thing in particular comes to mind." Adam pointed to the paper. "Your age."

"My what?" Kevin shoved his chair back and turned toward the door. This guy was nothing more than a whack job.

"How old are you?" Adam asked to his back.

Kevin didn't turn around. "Sixteen, but you know that already."

"That's what's on this paper." Adam paused. "But you know I keep thinking about the last time I spoke to Staci. Twelve years ago." Adam's voice took on a faraway tone.

Kevin didn't care. This conversation needed to end here and now. "You probably have your years mixed up. They say that's a sign of old age. Maybe you should see your doctor wife about that. She might be able to give you something to help."

"No, I'm sure of it. It was twelve years ago. I remember because it was a year after my own accident."

"Accident?" Now it was his turn to freeze. Kevin hated the word. The one-year anniversary of his mother's New Year's Eve accident had just passed.

"At the time, your mom said you were three." When Kevin didn't respond, he went on, "You're only fifteen, aren't you?"

Kevin sneered. "You're delusional."

"You forget. I knew your mother. You didn't randomly learn all those computer skills. Staci knew how to hack into almost anywhere without being discovered. I don't know why she did it, but for some reason she changed your birth certificate. And something tells me you know." Adam shuffled through the papers once more and pulled another one out. He planted his finger down on the paper. "Even your shot records don't correlate with your age."

Turning, Kevin said through clenched teeth, "Get over it. I'm sixteen years old."

Adam leaned back in his chair and crossed his arms. He gave Kevin a challenging look. "Are you afraid you'll have to stay here longer?"

"Well, duh!" Kevin said, but then stopped short, realizing what he had admitted to. "How do I know you even knew my mother? Maybe you were just some random stalker who—"

"Staci was my sister."

Kevin stopped, his mouth dropped open. He quickly closed it. Adam's sister? But that would make Adam his . . . No way. Lies. All of it. He pushed on the door, but it wouldn't open.

"Don't bother. I locked it."

"Is this some kind of joke? Lock me in this room and try for a confession?"

"No, it's insurance that you don't run when you don't want to answer a question."

"Someone sold you a bad policy then." Kevin glared at Adam. "How do you really know my mother?"

"I told you. She was my younger sister."

"Then why didn't she ever talk about you? Why weren't you at her funeral?"

Adam's face hardened to match Kevin's. "I was there. Seems to me you were so anxious to go off with your friend that I doubt you had even the slightest clue who

Chapter 8

was there and who wasn't."

Leaning back against the wall, Kevin swallowed hard. It was still difficult to think of that day. Mom had been his friend, his ally. Then coming home from a New Year's Eve party with Dad, the car hit some black ice, throwing them into a skid. The car wrapped around a telephone pole, killing his mom instantly. Dad survived but had never been the same.

Kevin shook his head. "What do you want?"

"I want to help. But in order to do that, I have to have some information. Your age for starters. And after that we'll talk about what happened that got you sent here."

Help? So now the conversation had turned into a counseling session. He didn't think so. "That still doesn't explain why you never came around, why I never knew about you."

"I'll make a deal with you. I'll tell you my secrets when you tell me yours." The start of a grin pulled at the corner of Adam's mouth.

Did he find this amusing? Kevin seethed inside. Adults were all alike. They thought if they knew all your secrets, somehow it might solve everything. But they were wrong. The information could just as easily open up Pandora's box. And the one thing he remembered about Pandora's box—it was locked for a reason.

He glanced up at the man who claimed to be his uncle.

Adam waited.

Fine, I'll show this man how useless having information can be. "All right, you want to know one of my secrets?"

Adam nodded but didn't speak.

Stephanie M. E. Gallentine / refuge

Kevin turned once more to face the door. He reached up to the keypad, punched in Adam's code, and smirked when the door lock disengaged. With a single glance over his shoulder, Kevin said, "Your locks can't hold me."

chapter 9

"Ten more minutes," Kevin moaned when the alarm clock went off yet again. Just ten more minutes and maybe the headache would subside. He snaked his hand out from under the edge of the blanket and patted at the table with his open palm until he finally found the snooze button on the alarm clock. Then he pulled the blanket over his head, cocooning himself in the blue cotton comforter that seemed far too thin for his shivering form.

Last night he'd convinced himself the headache and nausea were due to lack of sleep and too much caffeine. After his talk with Adam, he spent most of the night wandering around the vacant sixth floor of the Center, refusing to answer calls on his radio. But then Adam had Rev ping his location using the GPS in the radio, which ended in another useless conversation. Couldn't Adam leave well enough alone? Didn't he realize Kevin didn't come here to open the doors to the graveyard of skeletons in his life? Some secrets were meant to remain buried. But Adam seemed intent on examining every last bone.

A loud thumping replaced the incessant jangling of the alarm clock. Kevin peeled his eyes open and reluctantly tossed the blanket aside. He groaned as he struggled to stand. Every muscle seemed to ache and moan with each movement. He shivered like a ninety-year-old man standing barefoot in the arctic as he opened the door.

David stood just over the threshold, hand still poised in the air, ready to continue his attack on the door.

With one hand, Kevin reached for the support of the wall. Then he glared. "What?"

"You're late," David declared, his face a contortion of anger and irritation. "Anna Lisa sent me to make sure you were awake. I suggest you get up there before we report you to Adam."

"Great. So I should add tattling to your list of endearing qualities?" Inside, his stomach churned like a washing machine. Kevin drew his arm across his abdomen. If David didn't hurry, he might end up dodging projectile vomit.

"That will be the least of your worries if you don't tell me what you did to my computer."

"What?"

"Rumor has it, you already have the codes to get into our systems, and then I go in this morning and find my files locked up," David said.

"Well, it wasn't me."

"Then who did?"

Chapter 9

"Like I know." Kevin shook his head. "And why don't you have backups?"

The mocha-colored irises of David's eye darkened and smoldered. "I do, but not on the files I drew up yesterday. And I need them for a meeting with GiOx Industries in thirty minutes."

"So why are you bothering me? Since you're so sure I did it, what makes you think I would fix it? I thought that's why you have your own IT person here."

"Rev and Adam are both already in a preliminary meeting this morning. That's why I came here first. I need those files." David clenched his fist at his side. "Forget it. I don't know why Adam's bothering. Your father doesn't have enough money to cover your baby-sitting costs."

Kevin snarled, "Get out."

"*Con mucho gusto* . . . with pleasure. But stay away from my computer." David's stubby finger shot out and planted itself in Kevin's chest. "And the next time you need a wake-up call, you better be in a hotel."

Kevin jerked away from the extended finger and gave David his version of the death glare. As soon as the arm retracted, Kevin wobbled a step backward and slammed the door.

David's arm shot out, preventing the door from closing all the way. He stood for a moment, as though trying to get control of himself. Taking a deep breath, he said in a calm voice, "Look, I really need those files. There are other details I can concentrate on early in the day with GiOx. I'll leave my office unlocked this morning. If you really did anything, I'll give you until lunch to fix it."

David backed away and hurried down the hall toward the elevator.

Stephanie M. E. Gallentine / refuge

With a long sigh, Kevin dropped back onto his bed and drew the comforter around himself. His thoughts bounced between helping David to prove he didn't do it to invading their systems and wreaking as much havoc as he could. Then they'd have every right to blame him for what they already thought he did.

As if to add insult to injury, the alarm clock once again blared its insistent wake-up call. Kevin smashed his fist onto the snooze button but missed. The clock bounced off the table and crashed to the floor. Its high-pitched wailing continued. Frustrated, he yanked the plug out of the wall. Too bad his other problems weren't so easily cut off.

"You're late." Anna Lisa glanced up from washing lettuce. She dried her hands on the bottom of her apron and crossed her arms. As she approached him, her braid swung over her shoulder.

"Captain Obvious at work again, I see," Kevin mumbled under his breath as he crossed the room. He tugged on the edges of his hood draped over his head and forced his eyes to stay trained on the floor. Without another word, he made his way to the small dish machine surrounded by tubs of dirty dishes covered with remains of scrambled eggs.

Anna Lisa let out a long, slow breath. "Did you want something to eat?"

Kevin shook his head as he hoisted the first grey bucket closer to the small sink with a long spray hose to rinse off the dishes.

"Chelsea should be down in a bit. She's going to take

Chapter 9

over your schooling while you're here."

Anna Lisa's words sounded as if they were drawing closer. Kevin grabbed a square dish rack from below to load the first sink full of dishes and concentrated on not hurling.

"She would have already been down here, but one of the divers conked his head and she had to stitch him up."

The next plate Kevin grabbed had the gross remains of eggs doused in ketchup. Nausea swept over him. Kevin dropped the plate into the sink. He clasped the edge of the counter and worked at breathing through the queasiness.

"Kevin? Are you all right?" Anna Lisa swiped her braid back over her shoulder and leaned in more closely.

"Fine." He forced a small grin as the feeling passed. "I guess I should have had breakfast."

Anna's face softened. The back of her hand brushed across his forehead.

Kevin recoiled from the icy touch. "I'm fine."

"You don't feel fine," Anna persisted. "I'm sending you to Chelsea. You need something for your fever."

"What are you, a nurse?"

Anna shoved the rack into the dish machine. "I'm many things. A nurse, a cook. Even won first place in a knife throwing contest before."

Kevin leaned against the counter and tried to imagine Mole Woman with a knife in her hand. Nah, he could do without that image.

"Chelsea's my cousin. After I graduated from nursing school, she invited me to come out here and help her. But when the Center's finances went south, they had to cut back on employees. I didn't want to go back home, so I decided to stay on as the cook, although I still help Chelsea if she needs it." Anna Lisa's lips upturned in a wicked grin. "Now go to the infirmary, before I feel the need to check and see if my knife throwing skills are still up to par."

Yeah. That was his cue to leave.

In the hallway, Kevin unclipped the Icom that controlled his glasses and adjusted the settings to black and white, hoping his head would stop pounding. The bright colors all around him dimmed to various shades of black, white, and gray. He paused at the elevator. There had to be something to do to avoid having to go see the doctor.

A glance at his watch confirmed he had plenty of time before David and Adam were out of their meeting. It probably wouldn't take long to look at David's computer. If he could fix it before David could show it to anyone, David would seem like the whiner he was. Besides that, if he could prove he didn't do anything to David's computer, maybe Adam would leave him alone.

The hall circled toward David's office. Kevin smirked. At least David couldn't bug too many people this far back. Kevin tried the door and found it unlocked, just as David had said it would be.

The soft glow of David's computer interrupted the otherwise darkened room. Shivering, he flipped the light switch. The room's million-watt lighting exploded behind his eyes with the force of a supernova. The fingers of one hand splayed across his face while his free hand swatted at the light switch. Darkness once again settled over the room. Kevin blew out a relieved breath. This must have been the morgue before David arrived. The room had all the components: tables, bright lights, and a temperature as cold as an iceberg.

Chapter 9

He rubbed his arms, both for warmth and to try to massage some of the ache out of them, while searching for the environmental controls. With his hands held out in front of him, he maneuvered past an angled table and an obstacle course of smaller tables lined with an assortment of drawings. Shivering, he adjusted the thermostat to ninety-five.

By the time he settled into the chair, he could hear the soft whoosh of the heating. He rolled the chair back a few feet so it was directly beneath the vent. For several moments, he reclined under the air duct as it delivered a constant flow of warm air upon his fever-chilled body. It would be so easy to close his eyes and sleep. He forced his eyes open. This was not going to fix the computer, nor would it find out what really happened to it.

Beside the machine, Kevin spied a half-empty bottle of ibuprofen. Finally, something that might take out his headache. Then there'd be no need to visit the doctor. Two of these and he should be able to function for the next few hours. He shook a couple onto his open palm and popped them into his mouth. The rest of the bottle he stuffed in the pocket of his hoodie. David owed him that much at least. Besides, with David's stress level, the man probably kept a closet full of this stuff.

Kevin turned his attention back to the computer. Now he only hoped it would be as easily fixed.

A rush of intense heat enveloped Adam as he stepped into David's office. He drew in a suffocating breath. Had the environmental controls malfunctioned? His hand searched for the light switch.

"Well, at least we know what happened to David's computer," Rev said from behind. "It melted."

Adam chuckled. He found the light switch. "What in thunder?" On the other side of the room, lying hunched over David's desk, Kevin slept. Even from where he stood, Adam couldn't help but notice the pink-tinged cheeks and damp bangs plastered to his head.

"Oh yeah, I haven't had time to tell you," Rev said. "Anna Lisa told me she sent him to the infirmary this morning with a fever." He swiped the beads of sweat forming on his own brow.

Adam crossed the short distance and knelt beside Kevin. "Stay in here long enough and we'll all have a fever." With his right hand, he pushed a lock of damp hair away from Kevin's face.

Kevin didn't as much as stir.

With the back of his palm, Adam felt Kevin's cheeks, relieved when they were only slightly warm. He silently berated himself for not checking on him this morning. But he still hadn't completely made up his mind how he wanted to deal with Kevin's behavior yesterday coupled with David's accusation. He'd brought Rev with him in hopes of not only fixing the computer, but proving Kevin wasn't involved.

"Kevin." Adam gently shook the sleeping teen.

Kevin opened his eyes and then unfolded himself from the awkward sleeping position. "Sorry," he mumbled as he readjusted his glasses and made for the door.

Adam pulled him to a stop. "It's okay. You're not in trouble."

Chapter 9

"Not yet." Rev sent them both a teasing grin, which earned a matching set of glares from both Adam and Kevin.

"What are you doing down here anyway?" Adam asked. "Weren't you supposed to check in with Chelsea?"

Kevin jerked his thumb in the direction of the computer.

"Trying to fix what you did?" Adam inquired gently.

Twin jade daggers shot out of Kevin's eyes. "Trying to fix what David did. Tell him to watch what email attachments he opens." He pointed to the computer screen. "This one contained a virus."

Rev's brows shot up. "Virus?"

Adam glanced over his shoulder to Rev. "You better check the rest of the computers and make sure it hasn't gotten into the network."

Rev nodded and disappeared out the door.

"I'm sorry," Adam began.

Kevin shrugged. "It's all right." He pulled at the fabric of his hoodie, fanning himself.

"Kind of reminds me of one of those triple-digit summer days back in Texas." Adam flicked the switch back to cool. "You know, if you take your jacket off, you'll feel better."

Kevin nodded and bent forward as he wrestled to dislodge himself from the confines of the sweat-dampened hoodie. As he pulled it over his head, the hem of his t-shirt crept up his abdomen, exposing a long, ugly bruise across his side.

Adam honed in on the bruise, which couldn't have been more than a few days old. "What happened?"

Kevin followed Adam's gaze. He yanked down his shirt. "A fight."

"With who?" The long mottled patch of blues and purples looked as though it had been caused by a metal pipe or maybe even a baseball bat.

"Someone," was Kevin's terse reply. After a long pause, he asked, "What? You gonna ask my dad since I won't tell you?"

"No. I'm waiting for you to tell me."

"Yeah, like that's gonna happen."

Adam sighed and decided to let Kevin have the last word—for now. He needed to call Steven Ramsey tonight. Was this one of the reasons Kevin's dad had been so adamant to get Kevin out of McKeltic? He suddenly realized how little he knew of Kevin's life before he came here, other than the teen's mischievous hacking. "Come on, I'll walk you up to see Chelsea."

"I don't need a police escort."

"Who said I was policing you? Maybe I'm protecting you."

Kevin strode toward the elevator ahead of Adam. "From who?"

Adam quickened his pace to match Kevin's. "You tell me."

chapter 10

"Protection," Kevin scoffed. Everyone thought he needed protection. What he needed was freedom. Then he could protect himself. Kevin's hand unconsciously went to his side, where he carried the only visible reminder of that night less than a week before. He let his head fall back against his bedroom wall. Maybe it had been his fault. If only he'd listened.

He thought back to the exact moment it began.

"Kevin, I'm glad you told me about this first." Dad had entered the living room in McKeltic. He swirled the glass of amber-colored liquid in his hand. Ice cubes clinked against the glass.

"I knew you were innocent and wanted you to have a chance to take it to the police."

Dad paused mid-step and stared at a picture of

Kevin's mother that hung over the mantle. "You know I can't do that."

"You mean you're just going to let this guy set you up?"

"Of course not." Dad walked over and leaned back against the front door. "You're going to fix it for me."

Kevin froze. That wasn't the kind of help he meant to give. Underneath his charcoal gray hoodie, his heart rate accelerated. "Then I'll help you prove it. We still haven't finished the penetration test. I can hack in and get as much evidence as you need." At least he hoped he could.

Dad chugged back the last of his drink, his bloodshot eyes a testament that this wasn't his first drink of the night and probably not his last.

"I need to go. Aiden's waiting on me." A cold sweat broke out on Kevin's face. His glasses slowly slid down to where they hinged on the end of his nose. Hands trembling, he pushed them back into place and then slowly backed out of the living room.

"I want you to plant a virus. One that will eradicate any evidence of that file and that you were even in there. You can do that."

Now was not the time for Dad to be expressing confidence in Kevin's abilities. "If I set a virus, it will wipe out all their files, not just that one."

"Then that's the price they'll pay for trying to set me up."

"I can't do it. I'll lose my job. Mr. Rollings warned me when he hired me. One mess up and I'm out of there. Then they'll send me back to juvie. I won't go back." Kevin took another two steps backward. The game room was a mere five feet away. From there, he could escape

Chapter 10

out the French doors.

"Then make sure no one finds out you did it."

"But—"

"I need you to hurry. Mr. Tyke and I are attending a party tonight. He's picking me up in an hour."

Like Dad needed another party tonight. Even now, Dad steadied himself on the doorframe. Kevin shook his head. "No way. If you want a virus, you'll have to do it yourself."

Squeezing his forehead between his fingertips, Dad blew out a deep breath that could rival a dragon.

Kevin turned and scurried through the hall and into the game room. The French doors were up ahead. To his right, Kevin caught a blur of movement. A computer chair careened across the tiled floor and into his path. He darted to the left but not quickly enough. His upper body flew over the chair.

Dad's heavy footsteps lumbered after him.

Kevin managed to regain his footing, but Dad had him blocked in. He backed up but stopped when he felt the pool table against his back. Shaking, he grabbed the closest thing he could find to defend himself—a pool stick.

Dad frowned. Then his left hand shot out and latched on to another pool stick. They faced each other like two warriors, their sticks raised in preparation for battle.

"Don't come any closer. Go to your party." Kevin eased his way along the pool table. Once Dad left, he would go too. He couldn't stay here anymore. Too much drinking, too many explosive arguments, and too many worthless apologies.

"Put the stick down," Dad said. "Now."

"No."

"Don't ever tell me no." Dad swung.

The sticks cracked together. Kevin's hand stung, but he held tight.

Dad swung once more.

Kevin darted. The pool stick caught him in the abdomen. "Aaagh!" He collapsed onto the floor. Pain burned in his side.

Dad dropped to his knees, his movements awkward but suddenly concerned. "Kevin, I'm sorry. Are you all right?"

The stench of alcohol filled the space between them. Kevin turned his face away. After the worst of the pain subsided, he allowed Dad to help him to his feet. At least this argument hadn't lasted as long as the others. Even the damage was minimal.

Kevin glanced at Dad, not sure what to expect.

Dad's hand swiped over his face. "Come on, we have to get this done. No one is ever going to put me back in a jail cell again."

Kevin stifled a yawn. After being confined to bed in his tiny "cell" for the past three days, he was bored. Beneath the blanket, he squirmed as he tried to get in a more comfortable position. A few of his newest comic book drawings fluttered to the floor amid the sea of clothes, shoes, and dirty dishes that now cluttered almost every inch of floor space.

"Kevin?"

He glanced up as Chelsea stepped into the room. "I'm fine."

Chapter 10

"I know you are. But I figured you might like these." She handed him several photo albums. "I know your mom didn't tell you about her past, so I thought maybe you'd like to see it."

Kevin opened the first album and stared at his mother as a teenager with Adam on his motorcycle beside her. His throat tightened. He hadn't expected this. "Thanks, Chel."

"Let me know if you need anything." With that, she left as if understanding he needed time alone.

He flipped through the pages. Beneath each of the pictures, someone had labeled them with dates and descriptions. Mom with her first car. Mom's first fender bender. Mom and her best friend, Sabryna. Adam and Mom. Then Mom disappeared from the pictures. That must have been when she ran away.

Kevin drank in memories of people he never knew existed. Grandparents, aunts, uncles. He turned another page and stopped. The description read "Adam's accident." Suddenly the pictures changed from a man in a car or on a motorcycle to a man after an apparent partial leg amputation. Kevin turned page after page. Mom never reappeared until the last page where someone had placed a copy of her obituary naming only two relatives: Dad and himself.

The LinkWay chirped. Kevin set the albums aside and pulled the videophone onto his lap.

Aiden nodded to him from the screen. "Just called to see how you were feelin'." His friend sat back and took a long drink from his Galactic Jitters cup.

"Well, compared to three days ago, anything's an improvement." Kevin gave his friend a wry grin and then stuffed an extra pillow behind his back.

Aiden laughed. "Trust me when I say, I know exactly how you feel."

"No, you don't. You have Galactic Jitters just down the road. You have a store where you can get energy drinks." Frowning, he held up the now warm orange liquid Chelsea so faithfully delivered three times a day. "I have orange juice."

"Surely they have coffee there."

Kevin snorted. "Sure they do. But Chelsea is the doctor and she thinks teenagers don't need caffeine for one reason or another." He rolled his eyes and readjusted his pillow. "So how are things going in your world?"

"Not too bad, I guess. Peter Damon and William Tyke made a deal with my dad. If Rollings Security's fixes the damage and closes up any back doors, their company won't sue us for the damage you did to their system."

"What about the file I found? Can you make sure it didn't reappear on their system?"

"No, that was another stipulation. Neither you nor I can be involved in any way." Aiden leaned back in his chair. "Without telling the guys working on their computers, I can't find out anything, and the guys don't know what to look for."

"What about Tyke's laptop?"

"What about it? No one's mentioned a laptop," Aiden said. "But then again, maybe he had them run the same fix on it as with their business computers."

Kevin hesitated. "That might be kind of hard."

"Why would it be hard?"

Kevin picked up his sketchpad and drew some random lines. Why hadn't Tyke mentioned the laptop? Did the man have someone else who could fix it? Or did the

Chapter 10

laptop hold information that would incriminate Tyke? "The virus I put on Tyke's laptop was different."

Aiden gaze turned suspicious. "Different how?"

"It just was," Kevin hedged. "You think you could convince one of the guys to leave one back door open? Or better yet, get a copy of their report? It might show another flaw in their system."

"Oh no." Aiden shielded himself with the palms of his hands. "My parents threatened to take away my car till I'm eighteen for that last incident. I'll do whatever I can to help, but I refuse to give up my car. What would I tell my girlfriend?"

Kevin groaned and slapped his forehead. "Girlfriend? Car? I'm worried about hundreds of thousands of dollars being stolen and hidden away, not to mention the hundred people who are investing in fictitious overseas property, and you're worried about getting your car taken away?"

"Then tell my dad about the file." Aiden leaned back in his chair. "Let them contact the police, find the evidence, and I'll get to keep my car."

"I can't. At least not yet." He needed hard evidence first and answers to why Tyke was framing Dad for the crime. And how did Patrick Thomas and the incident with his investment company AsericA have anything to do with Tyke and Dad?

Kevin pleaded with his friend through the LinkWay. "Come on, just a little more time to find some evidence against Tyke."

"All right." Aiden blew out a frustrated breath. "At least one thing is in our favor. If we can't access Tyke's files, then more than likely, neither can he." Aiden popped up out of his chair and retrieved a can of Energy X.

Kevin's tired gaze lingered on the can. "Sure would like one of those."

Aiden pulled the aluminum top back and a semi-clear foam spewed from the opening. He slurped up the excess and then turned back to Kevin. "I could ship some over."

"I wish. But knowing Adam, he'll search every package that doesn't come from my dad. A supply of Energy X would probably be automatically confiscated."

"Then have dear old dad send you some." Aiden's face held a mischievous grin.

Kevin scrunched up his brows. "Why would my dad send me anything, much less energy drinks?"

On the other side of the screen, Aiden held a marker in his hands, pulling off the cap and snapped it back together, a mindless gesture that seemed always to enhance Aiden's thinking process. Aiden's gaze met Kevin's through the screen. "You know my mom always said I'd make a great dad someday. Maybe you could ask 'dear old dad' to email Adam and ask if 'dad' can ship you some things he forgot on the trip over?"

Kevin stared back at his friend, his mind whirling as he finally caught what Aiden was suggesting. "It'd take a little time to set up. But you know, it just might work." He reached under his bed and pulled out his laptop.

"I can get whatever you need."

Kevin didn't respond. Aiden would understand his silence. For three days, his mind had been idle, too idle. Right now, all he could see were possibilities. His fingers steepled over the keyboard as he worked out the plan in his head. "First, I need to set up an alternate email account for my dad," he mumbled to himself, but Aiden must have heard him.

Chapter 10

Aiden had moved his laptop to the desk with his computer. "You got passwords?"

Kevin's head snapped up, his fingers ceasing mid-keystroke. "Do I have passwords?" Could he have heard his friend right? "Please. Which one do you want to check first?"

Aiden laughed, and Kevin could hear the clacking of keys from the other end of the LinkWay. "I'll take your father's. I'm already there anyway. What's the password?"

Kevin told him. After giving Aiden the password, Kevin concentrated on Adam's email address. The password gave him access, and he executed a search for any emails either to or from Dad.

"I'm not seeing any messages to or from Adam on this end," Aiden informed him.

"Big surprise, there," Kevin said, rolling his eyes. Dad had no need to email Adam. With Kevin out of the way, Dad could lead his life and not worry about calls from the truant officers, the police, or the principal. "Oh well, the less actual communication between the two, the better." Kevin pulled off his glasses and rubbed his face, unable to hide the expansive yawn that escaped from his lips. It seemed the longer he stared at the screen, the harder he had to work to keep his eyes open.

"Hey, you feelin' all right? We can always finish this up tomorrow."

Kevin waved his hand at him. "I'm fine. Just tired." He gave half a laugh before adding, "Which is why I need a shipment."

"Don't worry." Aiden grinned. "We'll get it as soon as we finish getting control of their emails."

"About the only thing I'm in control of right now," Kevin muttered.

Kevin disconnected the LinkWay and laid it on the floor next to his bed. Satisfied they would be able to fool Adam into thinking he was speaking with Dad, Kevin yawned and reached up to snap the lid of his laptop down.

Before he could, the laptop chimed, indicating someone had sent him an instant message. Aiden probably forgot to tell him something. In the upper right hand corner of the screen, user L@anon typed in a simple message.

"I know where you are."

Kevin couldn't stop the short intake of air. His fingers froze, poised over the keyboard. This had to be a prankster. Maybe someone from one of those online hacking rooms he often hung out in. But he didn't recognize the name. L@anon?

Quickly, he typed a message back. "Is this some kind of joke?"

"Are you laughing?" A skeleton's head appeared in the box. It tilted back and broke forth in evil laughter.

Ordinarily, Kevin might have found it amusing. Might even have sent back one of his own images. But not tonight. He waited for the person to identify himself.

Instead, another message appeared. "It's not over yet."

Not over? Confused he typed back, "What do you mean? Who is this?"

A chill blew over Kevin, causing the tiny hairs on the back of his neck to stand up. He tried to tell himself it was because his bed sat in the path of the room's air vent.

Chapter 10

R
E
V
E
N
G
E

The user signed off. Kevin snapped the lid shut and shoved the laptop under his bed. He needed a minute to think, to figure out what to do next. Like a bad tattoo you could hide from others but always knew of its presence, the last word seared into his memory.

chapter 11

Kevin reclined on his bed. Sketchpad on his lap, he shaded in the villain's shadow as he edged closer to the hero, Saphearon. Midway through the panel, he tossed the sketchpad aside. He couldn't focus. Everything was too quiet. He stared at the wall. Maybe he should pull out some drawings or posters to cover the otherwise barren walls. No, that would make it feel too much like home, and he wasn't staying.

Although he hadn't heard any more from L@anon in the past two weeks, Kevin couldn't stop the nervousness that attacked him every time he signed onto his laptop. Maybe it had all been a joke. But what if it hadn't been?

"So are you acting anti-social on purpose, or am I misinterpreting your reclusiveness?" Arms folded across his chest, Adam leaned against the now open doorway.

"Something like that." Kevin grabbed his sketchpad and made every pretense of drawing. How he wished he could schedule these impromptu discussions with Adam. Right now he had more important things to worry about.

"You know, at some point, you're going to have to get to know everyone."

"I already do. What do you want to know?" Why would he want to know them?

"Hacking into personal files doesn't count," Adam said. "And don't even try to deny it."

A slight grin emerged. Rev must be better than he thought. He was sure he'd hid his tracks. "I won't."

He heard a deep sigh and the door close. Kevin glanced up, disappointed to see Adam still standing there.

"I need to ask you something."

Kevin shaded in the lines around Zezima as the archvillain gloated over his apparent victory over Saphearon. "I thought you just did."

Another sigh came from Adam, but this one was deeper and seemed slightly more frustrated. "I need your help."

Kevin rolled his eyes Adam's way. "And you're asking me, why?" He figured Adam was trying to find a way to ask more questions about his past or his mother, and Kevin didn't feel like being polite about it tonight.

"You're not going to make this easy, are you?"

"Any reason I should?"

"It'd be nice."

He shrugged. "Too bad for you, I guess."

Adam raked a hand through his short dark locks. "Why don't I start over?"

"Only if it means you leave and decide not to bug me."

Chapter 11

Adam must have decided to change tactics. The taller man leaned over and studied one of the panels Kevin had already finished. "Your dad never told me you could draw."

"Then maybe that's who you need to be bonding with right now." Kevin had to give him points for persistence, but enough was enough. Couldn't Adam tell he wanted to be left alone?

"I thought that's something you'd rather be doing seeing as how he sent you some more of your stuff."

"What?" Kevin chucked the tablet aside and bounced off his bed. His boxes from Aiden were here? He hadn't really expected them for another week or two.

"Mark, our pilot, has another stop to make out this way, so he brought our stuff a bit early. There're three unloaded boxes from your dad waiting in the hallway. But if you'd rather pick a fight . . ." Adam let the words hang in the air.

"I'm sorry. Just feeling grouchy, I guess."

Adam narrowed his eyes, examining him. "Any reason why?"

"Ya ever think it could be I'm tired of living here on this island of misfit toys? I'm ready to go home."

"Sorry, no can do." Adam stuck his head out the door and motioned for someone to bring in the boxes. "But at least now you'll have a little bit of home closer to you."

A uniformed man with close-cropped hair wheeled the boxes into the room on his dolly. The man greeted him, leaving Kevin to wonder where his accent came from. It almost sounded as if he came from one of the islands, but then again, Kevin had spent most of his life in McKeltic, Texas, before coming here. What did he know about accents? The only thing he wanted to know right now was if those boxes contained a fresh supply of Energy X drinks.

Kevin waited until the man left the room. "That didn't look like Mark."

Mark was known for his overly cheery disposition and laughter that seemed like a long explosion of joy. A little over the top, Kevin thought, but better than the alternative. It seemed in his life he often met extremes in personalities. Except for Aiden. Aiden was that middle ground.

"It wasn't. Mark brought some trainee co-pilot with him this time." Adam paused. "Now, can I ask you?"

Kevin nodded, eyeing the boxes in front of him.

"I need you to play a video game and win."

"Okay." Kevin drew the word out as if to ask, *Have you had your meds today?*

"David's been feeling his oats lately," Adam explained.

Kevin snorted. "And this is different, how?"

Adam surprised him with a low chuckle. "Which is why I saw tonight as the perfect opportunity to take him down a notch. I told you we were having a game night, right?"

He nodded. Adam had mentioned it that morning, but Kevin hadn't been interested. Still wasn't.

"And this little ploy to get me to attend your little family fun night isn't going to work either." He stared at the boxes, anxious for Adam to leave.

"I'll give you two weeks off work if you beat him."

That gave him pause. Two weeks off would be nice. "And if I lose?"

"I'll still give you a week for playing." Adam paused. "But you'll have to attend church with us in the morning."

Kevin's eyes narrowed. What kind of game was Adam

Chapter 11

playing? "No thanks." The last thing he wanted was to sit in some chair and listen to Rev drone on about one thing or another. Didn't he get enough of that from everyone on a daily basis?

"Three weeks if you win," Adam offered. "And you can choose to take them all at the end or sporadically."

"Three weeks?" Kevin had to make sure.

"Three weeks. Two if you lose, but you still have to come to church with us tomorrow."

It wasn't like he could lose. And how could he pass up three weeks of no work. Kevin nodded. "Give me ten minutes to check out what's in my boxes first."

"Done." Adam pushed off the wall and exited the room.

Kevin ripped the packing tape off and then pulled back the flap on the box. Rolled inside pairs of jeans and other clothing was can after can of Energy X. He popped the lid on the first one and tilted it back, draining the contents in a matter of moments. He smirked. It never hurt to ensure a win. Once the caffeine began circulating, his fingers would tap dance over the controller. For once, he would defeat David. And that was worth even having to attend family fun night.

"Ready, set, fight!" the computerized voice in the game console called out to them.

Kevin sat perched on the edge of his chair next to David. Energy coursed through his system like a raging river pushing everything else out of the way. Combos, one after another, pummeled his opponent. Like a fast-moving current, his fingers blurred over the buttons of the keypad.

David fought back, his character shooting a surge of energy at Kevin's character.

Kevin's character reeled on the screen but then recovered. Finally, he landed the blow that defeated David's character.

By the end of the night, he had won all but two matches.

Sullen, David mumbled something in Spanish under his breath. He frowned at Kevin. "Kid, that's the only time you'll ever win. Next time prepare for total domination."

Kevin grinned. "Yeah, mine."

"Good job." Adam sided up to him. "You sure you don't want to come to church anyway?"

Kevin rolled his eyes. "I'm *so* sure."

Adam nodded. "All right. But don't forget I'll be praying for you."

"Pray for David. He's the one who needs it. Not me."

The next morning Kevin's anxious breath left a patch of fog on the glass wall in the game room. He swiped at it with his bare arm, shivering at the chill from the water on the other side. Once again, he focused on the scene playing out before him.

A huge fish hovered in the deep water. Silent. Deadly. It watched a school of fish as they swam by, oblivious to its presence. Without warning, the larger fish darted forward, his jaw open, ready to clamp down on as many fish as he could capture. The smaller fish scattered, but not before a handful of them met their end.

Chapter 11

Kevin shuddered, glad for the safety of the Center. But it wasn't like he planned on going swimming here anyway.

"Don't see something like that every day."

Kevin jerked around. Behind him stood the man who had come with Mark, his arms akimbo.

With that same island-like accent, he said, "Sorry. I did not mean to frighten you. Actually, I came to see if I could solicit your help."

"Help?"

"Mark wants to leave right away. Something about wanting to get back to the missus," the copilot said in a deep baritone voice.

After a quick nod, Kevin followed the man down the hall past the elevator before Kevin gave him a strange look. "I thought we needed to go up. You passed the elevator."

"The elevator is not wide enough. I had to get the items up the stairway."

Kevin nodded. The elevator was small. Still it seemed odd. If the item being transported was that large, why wasn't someone else helping this man with it? It didn't take but a glance at Kevin's short frame and skinny arms to see he wouldn't be the one to give the best help.

The man's olive skin scrunched up in confusion. "Is something the matter? You do not wish to help me?"

"No. It just seems funny to be lugging something up the stairs when the elevator is there."

"Funny? Yet you are not laughing." When Kevin didn't immediately respond, he added, "I see. Perhaps it is some joke I have missed it. Forgive me." He threw back his head and laughed.

Stephanie M. E. Gallentine / refuge

Kevin froze. Images flashed through his mind. The short conversation with L@anon replayed itself in his mind. *I know where you are. Am I laughing? It's not over yet. Revenge.* He shook his head. This couldn't be that person.

"What did you say your name was?"

"I did not say." The bulky man's demeanor suddenly changed. He now stood erect, his head bent slightly forward, gaze intent on Kevin. Muscles bulged beneath the cotton fabric of his work shirt.

Kevin swallowed. The scattered puzzle pieces in his mind began to fit together one by one in a frightening way. "I—I need to go." He took a small step backwards. Maybe sitting through a church service wouldn't be so bad after all. Safety in numbers and all that.

"Landon." The man relaxed his tense muscles and hooked his thumbs in his back pockets. "My name is Landon Swift."

Kevin gulped. The admission should have put him at ease. But it didn't. The heavy accent made the name sound more like Lanon. L@anon.

"I . . . I really need to go. Adam just called me on my radio." Kevin pointed to the earpiece. "Needs me for something." He didn't give Landon a chance to respond. Instead, he turned on his heel and power-walked back toward the elevator.

Pain erupted at the base of his neck, and Kevin fell forward. He thrust out his hands to break his fall. It only lessened the impact. Loose strands of carpet stuck to his tongue as his open mouth hit on the floor.

Landon's boot nudged him in the side. "Get up."

Moaning, Kevin sucked in air against the pain and

Chapter 11

imagined what his bruise would look like after today. He planted his hands on the floor. Once he was partway up, he prepared to bolt.

"Move it." Landon yanked the back of Kevin's hoodie and hauled him to his feet. He shoved Kevin toward the back stairwell door.

Kevin twisted, attempting to free himself from the man's bone-crunching grip.

A deep growl emerged. With one fluid movement, Landon's foot swiped the back of his knees.

Kevin threw his arms out as the floor rushed up to meet him.

Landon stopped his fall, jerking Kevin to him. Like a python, the man's arm slithered around Kevin's neck.

His air supply cut off, Kevin clawed at Landon's arm. He twisted, kicked, anything to get free.

Landon didn't budge; his grip was sure.

Fear strangled Kevin. His life couldn't end like this. He was only fifteen. He struggled until his vision began to grey from lack of oxygen.

"Had enough?"

Kevin nodded as much as the awkward position would allow him. The grip loosened, but only enough that he could draw in air.

"That was your warning. Understood?"

Spittle sprayed the back of Kevin's neck as Landon spoke. Kevin winced but nodded again. His hand went for his radio. He wasn't quick enough. Landon's hand ripped the communicator out of his ear and flung it across the room.

Landon fished into his pilot's jacket and pulled out a small handgun.

Kevin's hope faded when he felt the cold steel of the handgun against his neck.

Landon twisted around and used his back to push open the door to the stairwell. As soon as the door shut behind them, he shoved Kevin to the floor and pointed his gun. "Move. Up the stairs."

Kevin pushed himself off the floor. "Where're we going?"

Landon smiled wickedly. "We have an appointment to keep."

Chapter 12

The man's searing gaze impaled Kevin to the wall like a thousand native spears slicing through his calm exterior, sending tremors throughout his limbs.

"Now I am only going to explain this once. You will go to the outside door at the top of the stairs. You will key us out. Then I will give you something to calm you for the trip."

Releasing a pent up breath, Kevin whispered, "No."

Landon acted as if he never heard Kevin.

A scream built in his chest, but everyone was still in the church service, where Kevin now wished he were too. He suddenly felt very social.

"You will then get in the plane. I have already loaded the large containers Mr. Hollandale needs transported back to the states. One of them is large enough to hold you."

"What?" Kevin's heart hammered in his chest. "But why?" His breath came in small gasps. He needed to think. His gaze darted in every direction, searching for anything that would help. Nothing.

The man crossed his arms and smirked. "You planted some sort of virus into Tyke's laptop. We need the information on that laptop to gain access to our account."

"Why not just hire someone to fix it?"

"Our computer expert was arrested the day before you planted the virus. We cannot risk anyone else happening upon the information. So I am afraid the task falls to you."

"Then why not bring the laptop here?" Kevin had to keep Landon talking while he tried to think of a plan. "I could have fixed it and had you out of here before their final prayer."

"You will have to ask Tyke. I'm simply following his instructions."

"I can't get your money back. I don't know anything about hacking into banks."

"Fix the laptop so we can open the file that contains the account information, and you will not have to."

"I looked on the laptop. The only file I found was for Patrick Thomas."

A low, guttural growl escaped from Landon's lips. He slammed Kevin against the wall. "What do you know of that man?"

Kevin clawed at the large hand pressing against his windpipe. "Nothing," he choked out.

"So you didn't find anything in the file?" Landon leaned in close. His aftershave made Kevin gag.

He shook his head.

Chapter 12

Landon released the grip.

Kevin's legs shook. No longer able to stand, he sank to the floor. "Prof wouldn't tell Tyke where I was going. How did ya'll find me?"

"Your location may have been a secret, but your flight plans were not." Landon checked his watch and then jerked Kevin to his feet. "Let's get this over with. Then we will contact your father. I'm sure he will pay dearly for your safe return."

"You hope," Kevin muttered.

Landon pointed his gun. "No, *you* hope."

Panic overtook all rational thought. With all his strength, Kevin kicked the man in his groin. He watched as Landon cried out and doubled over, his bulky form still blocking any escape upwards. Kevin raced down the stairs, taking them two and three at a time.

At the bottom of the next flight of stairs, Kevin slammed into the door with his palms. He peeked back over his shoulder, then groaned. Heavy footfalls echoed on the stairs. He opened the door, stepped into the hall, and hesitated. The hall was completely dark. He must be on the unused sixth floor.

Fear pushed him forward through the darkness. Kevin's only comfort was that it was as dark for his assailant too. The layout, he knew, was the same as the other floors—a single hallway running the inner circumference with rooms along the outer wall.

Partway around the floor, Kevin stopped. He leaned over and rested his hands on his knees while he heaved in some deep breaths. His lungs burned from exertion. The sound of his breath pounded in his ears. Kevin forced himself to take slower, quieter breaths. He no longer heard the footsteps behind him.

Something wasn't right. Slowly he turned and backed up. His palms felt first for the wall. Then they glided along the wall, searching for an entrance to one of the rooms. He needed some place to hide. Somewhere he could lock himself into.

"Kevin, don't make this harder than it has to be."

Don't breathe. Don't react. Chances were the man had no idea exactly where he was. He continued to edge his way along the wall.

A thin beam of light cut through the darkness and shone into his face. "There you are."

Kevin lifted his left arm to shield his eyes from the flashlight. With his other hand, he continued to grope along the wall for a door. There! He twisted the handle but couldn't get a grip with his sweaty palm.

In front of him, Landon advanced like a hunter. It was as though the man knew he had trapped his prey. The need to hurry was no longer present.

Kevin hastily rubbed his palm on the front of his jeans. He put his hand behind his back once more to turn the knob. This time it turned easily, and Kevin backed into the room. "Come on," he panted frantically as he tried to lock the door.

Landon burst through the door, sending Kevin sprawling backwards to the floor. A booted foot crushed into Kevin's chest, anchoring him in place. He clawed like a madman at Landon's foot. Kevin swung his leg up and tried to kick.

"Now let's get you calmed down. We have to get you settled before they're out of church." Landon drew a

Chapter 12

syringe out of his jacket pocket. He held it up, flicked the side of the syringe, and depressed it long enough for a tiny bubble of the clear liquid to form at the tip of the narrow needle.

"Oh God," Kevin said in a strangled whisper.

"Feeling a little religious now, are we?" Landon emitted a low chuckle. Harpooning Kevin's arm, he depressed the plunger.

Kevin cried out. The substance burned as it infiltrated the muscle. Fear wrapped itself around him like a body bag. The drugs waged war against his adrenaline, dulling his senses. This couldn't be happening to him. But it was.

Landon flung the syringe across the room. It pinged off the wall. Then he hauled Kevin to his feet.

Kevin's movements were stiff, his limbs uncooperative.

Together, they moved up the stairs. With each step, Landon's heavy shoe clanged against the metal stairs, but the sound seemed to echo and muffle at the same time in Kevin's ears. Once they reached the top, Landon shoved him up to the lock.

Kevin leaned heavy against the wall. He slipped his fingers under his glasses and rubbed his eyes. Maybe he could delay Landon by acting too drugged to remember the number. But that still left him trapped in the stairwell, and no one knew where he was. No, there had to be another way.

"Quit stalling." Landon shoved the butt of the gun in Kevin's neck. "No one can help you now."

Kevin punched in the first number and then paused and pretended to think. An idea formed. The security camera was just on the other side of the door. Help was now four numbers away.

Stephanie M. E. Gallentine / refuge

The lock disengaged and the door opened to a fresh breeze off the ocean. Kevin licked the salty beads of sweat off his lip and sighed. He stepped forward in view of the camera. "Help! Help!"

Landon chuckled and pointed the gun. "I might not have your computer skills, but I know how to cause security cameras to malfunction."

Kevin groaned.

At the edge of the deck, the seaplane rocked on the ocean waves. There wasn't much time. He had to figure out a way to get free.

"Listen up. We're going to walk over to the plane. You make any attempt to get away, and I will shoot you. Understood?"

Kevin nodded.

Landon replaced his gun into his pocket.

It was time to act. After a second's hesitation, Kevin did twice in one day the one thing he thought he could never do to another guy. He incapacitated his assailant with a single well-placed kick.

Landon doubled over.

Adrenaline flooded Kevin's system. He ran but then stumbled and fell.

Landon cursed and straightened.

Kevin struggled to get to his feet. Behind him, there was a click of a gun. He froze.

"I guess Tyke was right. That amount didn't quite knock you out. And here I was afraid of overdosing you." Landon waved his gun. "Now let's get on the plane before this gets ugly."

"You mean it's not already?" Where he found the courage to say that, Kevin didn't know.

Chapter 12

Landon growled and slowly, one step at a time, approached Kevin. "Oh no. You haven't seen ugly yet. Wait until I get you back home."

Another step.

Kevin blinked. Like pushing through a thick fog, he fought to maintain his focus.

Another step.

Kevin wobbled, struggling to keep out of Landon's reach. He glanced out into the ocean. A desperate plan formed in his mind. Hope renewed, he narrowed his eyes and spat out, "You'll have to catch me first." Kevin darted off to the left. Holding tight to his glasses, he plunged into the ocean. The water shocked his system alive.

He opened his eyes. The salt water stung, but as the bubbles around him faded, he spotted the blurred underbelly of one of the boats. Kevin forced all his focus on swimming to a hiding place. Already his lungs burned, desperate for air.

His hands reached for the bottom rung of the boat ladder.

I can't splash. He'll hear me.

Kevin pulled himself up and slowly let his head emerge from the water. Air rushed into his oxygen-starved lungs, reviving him.

"Where are you? I know you have to get your breath sometime." The voice now took on a singsong effect, as though Landon were hunting a frightened animal, luring it into his trap.

The footfalls on the platform sounded too close. Kevin grabbed another deep breath and sank back under the water. He swam around the stern of another boat. Near the dock, he spied a small crevice where he might go unnoticed long enough to catch another breath. If he could swim to the front of the Center, he could get the attention of the guard.

A shot fired into the water.

Kevin propelled himself forward. At his hiding spot, he broke the surface and opened his mouth to grab another breath. A wave crashed into the platform. Seawater rushed into his mouth. Afraid if he coughed it would give away his position, he cringed and gulped a mixture of oxygen and seawater.

Another shot fired. "You cannot win. Either the drugs will drown you, or I will shoot you. At least if you come with me, you will live."

Chills wracked him as the wind blew over him. Kevin clamped down on his jaw to keep it from chattering. Inside the drugs gained another foothold. His movements slowed.

He couldn't give up. Not yet.

He drew in one more breath and dove beneath the water. He had to make it. His life depended on it.

chapter 13

On his next breath above the water, Kevin heard another voice. Grasping the edge of the dock, he slumped in relief.

"Landon?" It was Mark's voice. "Did you fire your gun?"

"Oh, sorry. I thought I saw a shark."

"I thought you were from these islands," Mark said. "You should know that's the best way to bring more once the scent of blood gets into the water."

"I guess I was not thinking."

"It happens." Mark paused. "You ready to go?"

"Right now?"

Was that a hint of panic in Landon's voice? Kevin grinned. Good, it was Landon's turn to sweat.

"The missus called. Says she thinks my son broke his leg. I told her I'd get there as soon as I could."

"But—"

Another wave crashed into Kevin. This time it knocked him into the platform. Seawater filled his ears. He held on. *Just a little longer.*

Landon said something to Mark, but Kevin couldn't make out the words. Moments later, he heard the rev of the engines. Kevin shivered. His legs ached from treading water. On the dock, he noticed a shadow fall near him.

He froze.

Landon spoke in low sinister tones that carried on the wind to Kevin's ears. "Tell anyone about today, and I know someone who is still searching for you and your father, Kevin *Chandler*."

Kevin couldn't stop the sharp intake of breath at the use of his original last name. He cringed at the evil chuckle that followed.

"How eager do you think your father will be for such a reunion?" Landon bent down as though picking something up. His laughter caused Kevin's hair to stand on end. "Like I said, not one word."

Footsteps carried away his attacker. The water churned as the plane soon taxied down its watery runway. Once it was airborne, Kevin used what little energy he had left to heft himself out of the water.

Exhausted and unable to move any further, he hunched over on the dock and stared out across the water. Like a DVD, the events of the morning played over on the back of his half-mast eyelids frame by frame. It seemed impossible to believe Tyke would be so desperate for information that he would go to such lengths to retrieve it.

Chapter 13

A wave washed over the dock, soaking him again. He uncurled his fingers, opening and closing them several times to work out the cramps. Kevin pushed himself up. No telling how much longer he could fight the effects of the drug.

However, one thing bothered him more. How had Landon found out who they were and where they came from? His parents had worked years to hide that information. He wondered if Dad knew how much of their past had been unearthed and how unsafe this Refuge had become.

Kevin rubbed his eyes and clung to the metal banister for support. On sluggish legs, he climbed the steps to the front entrance of the Center. Inside, the guard greeted him with furrowed brows. Kevin decided to save the guy the breath. "I thought I saw something in the water. I guess I leaned over too far and fell in."

"Top heavy, eh?" The guard shook his head and chuckled.

Kevin forced a grin and stepped into the elevator. The fifth floor arrived and the door swished open. Head tucked, he barreled out of the elevator and instantly collided with someone.

"¿Qué está haciendo? What are you doing?" David backed up and brushed at where the water had penetrated his jacket. "Trying to get a shower and do your laundry at the same time?"

Kevin moved off the spot where he landed. Water had dripped from his clothes. A paper, still creased with folds, lay on the floor where he'd fallen. It was a picture drawn by what appeared to be small hands in washable markers. The blues, reds, and browns ran together, forming more of a collage than its original drawing. He scooped up the paper and handed it to David.

"Do you know what this was? It was a picture from *mi sobrina*."

His Sabrina? Kevin shook his head, confused. The drugs must be stronger than he realized. David had a girlfriend? "Your girlfriend draws you pictures that look like that? No wonder you have issues."

David's face tightened. "*Mi sobrina*, my niece." He yanked the wet paper from Kevin's hand. "And you have just ruined Christobell's picture to me."

"Christobell?" It had to be the drugs because things were starting to sound loopy. "Does she have a brother named Tacobell? Cause ya know, I miss Taco Bell. It'd be nice if they'd send us some nachos or maybe even a burrito supreme."

Red emerged from beneath the chestnut color of David's skin, mottling the colors and reminding Kevin of the ruined picture. With his free hand, David thrust his index finger in Kevin's chest and shoved. "Don't ever come near me again. *¿Comprende?*"

Kevin stumbled backwards, landing on the floor again. Too sluggish to get up, Kevin scooted back against the wall.

"That's enough, David!" Rev stormed down the hall. "Kevin?"

His eyelids strained to open. With heavy lids, he looked up from his prone position to see Rev bent over him, calling his name. How had that happened? Had he gone to sleep in the middle of the hallway? Kevin used his elbows as leverage to push himself up.

Chapter 13

Rev's hand kept him down. "Stay right there. I've already called Chelsea."

"Chelsea?" No, no, no, no. Chelsea was the last person he wanted to see right now. "I'm fine. David pushed me. That's it."

Rev shook his head. "I saw it, but it wasn't hard enough to knock you out."

"I wasn't—"

"You were unresponsive for a minute or so. You're also soaking wet."

Kevin glanced down at the clothes that still clung to his body. It took a second to remember. His brain seemed to be running in slow motion. "I slipped off the dock. I told the guard." Kevin shivered as the cool ventilated air blew down the corridor.

"David, get me a blanket," Rev ordered.

Chelsea's voice broke through the fog. "—vin," Something strong burned under his nose. "There, that's better. Rev, Adam, let's get him to the infirmary."

"No." Kevin jolted awake. "I'm fine. Just . . . tired. Haven't had my daily recommended dose of caffeine today." Inside his conscience reminded him he was getting smart with Chelsea, not David. David might play with his tinker toys, but the doctor played with harpoon-sized needles. He needed to use extreme caution.

Chelsea ignored him and proceeded to spread one of Kevin's eyes open and shine a pen light into it. "Rev said you fell off the dock and into the water. Did you hit your head? Something bite you?" She transferred the light to the other eye.

Kevin tried to swat it away. "Could you not do that?" To his right, Adam stared down at him, his face creased in concern.

"I'm a doctor. This is what I do." She slid her pen light into her pocket and checked his pulse "It's a little higher than I like. But since I'm sure you didn't plan to go for a swim, fading adrenaline would account for that." She ran the thermometer over his forehead and sighed. "No temperature. But your pupils are a bit dilated, and you never answered my question."

Question? He struggled to remember what it was. Oh yeah, something about hitting his head. "No. I didn't hit my head. I just slipped off the dock while goofing around." Kevin shrugged and forced himself to sound coherent. "I'm fine. Really. I probably stayed up too late the last few nights. Can I go change?"

Chelsea appeared indecisive as her hand pushed back the damp hair from his forehead. "On one condition."

There it was. The condition.

"You'll come to our apartment, have something to eat with us, and you can either sleep on the couch or in the spare room. I won't have you alone right now until I'm sure."

"But—"

"It's either that or the infirmary."

Rolling his eyes, he growled. "Fine."

Chelsea appeared far too pleased. "Adam, will you get Kevin a change of clothes? I'll take him up and let him get started on a shower. I'm sure he wants to get the salt water off."

Glaring, he allowed her to help him to his feet. A hot shower did sound wonderful. Too bad the memories wouldn't wash off as easily as the salt water.

Chapter 13

Kevin's eyes flew open. He couldn't stop the gasp as memories of the day's events flashed before him.

"Hey, you all right?"

Kevin inclined his head toward Adam's voice. Colors and images blurred together in one convoluted mix. He felt his face to adjust his glasses, but they were gone. He patted the soft comforter covering him but couldn't find them. "Yeah, I guess I was more tired than I thought."

"I'll say. You had Chelsea worried enough I can't tell you how many times I caught her counting your respirations."

Kevin turned away, not sure how clearly Adam could read his expressions in the dimly lit room. "Do you know where my glasses are?"

A book closed with a decisive pop. "They're on the table."

"Thanks." He lowered his head back down on the pillow. He needed an excuse to get Adam out of the room so he could search for his glasses. No way was he going to admit he couldn't see anything beyond moving blurs without them. "Uh . . . could I have some water?"

"Sure."

He listened to the sound of Adam rising from the chair and padding across the floor. Once he heard the squeak of cabinet doors in the kitchen, Kevin leaned over and systematically began running his fingers over the coffee table. His wire frames sported no color, making identification almost impossible. At home, he always kept them in the same spot.

Stephanie M. E. Gallentine / refuge

Bottle in hand, Adam stopped. In front of him, Kevin pressed a button on a small device no bigger than a pager. A steady but soft beeping could be heard near where the teen sat, perched on the edge of the couch.

With his free hand, Kevin slowly passed over the length of the square coffee table until his hand found the folded glasses. The beeping suddenly stopped, and Kevin slipped the glasses onto his face.

Adam rounded the couch and handed Kevin the bottle of water. He couldn't stop himself from staring. A million questions waited to be asked. He finally settled for the most obvious. "What is that?" Adam pointed to the pager-sized device Kevin had reattached to his jeans.

"Nothing." Kevin pulled his shirt over the object. "Just another crazy gadget I picked up somewhere."

Adam shook his head and sighed. He wondered if he and Kevin would ever come to the point where they could talk without walls flying up between them. "May I see it?"

"No," Kevin said quickly.

"Why not? If it's just a crazy gadget."

"I can't," the teen hedged.

"I don't understand. Is it a bomb?"

"No." His hand went to his side. "I can't see without it."

"Now I really don't understand."

"It's a remote device for my glasses," Kevin explained. "The bottoms of my lenses have a miniature computer chip that will magnify objects up to thirty times larger and place it on my retina for me to see." He held up the Icom. "This remote controls the magnification as well as the contrast."

Chapter 13

"But why?" Adam stared at Kevin, confused.

Kevin chewed on the corner of his bottom lip. "Because I'm legally blind without them."

Adam plopped into the chair. Legally blind? Why hadn't anyone told him, warned him? What would have happened if Kevin had lost his glasses when he fell in the ocean earlier? They could have lost him simply because he couldn't see to get back. "Why didn't we know about this?"

Kevin crossed his arms in defiance. "Because it's only need-to-know information."

"And no one thought we needed to know?"

"It's no big deal. As long as I have my glasses, I'm fine."

"That's too conditional. I can't believe your father didn't tell us."

"Why didn't you tell me you had a fake leg?"

"It's a prosthetic," Adam clarified.

Kevin glared at him. "Same thing. It's a fake leg."

Adam paced in front of the coffee table and ran both hands through his hair. He never thought he'd get into a verbal sparring match with a fifteen-year-old over disabilities. He had to give the kid credit. Kevin knew how to redirect the conversation even if it did infuriate him in the process. Maybe he should play Kevin at his own game. Adam sat back down in the chair. "Okay, I have a fake leg."

"How'd it happen?"

Adam glanced up at the baseball display Chelsea had set up for him. "I was in my senior year of college, dreaming of a long career in baseball. My parents were furious. They felt I was throwing away my education." Adam lifted the bat off the hook, pretending to swing it. "Anyway it was the last game of the season. Recruiters were supposed to be there. Staci had run away from home a couple of weeks before. She called me that morning and asked me to come pick her up. My car was in the shop, so I asked Prof to drive me. A deer ran out on the highway. Prof veered, trying to dodge it. The car ran off the road and rolled two or three times.

"Everything is hazy after that. The next clear memory I have is waking up in the hospital. They told me my leg was too badly crushed, and they had to amputate below the knee. My parents told me at least I had my business degree to fall back on. I was furious. After that, I pretty much shut everyone out of my life, except for Prof."

"Is Prof how you ended up here?"

Adam nodded. "He visited me every day at the rehab hospital. That's where I met Chelsea. She was an intern then. During this time, Prof started going back to church. Chelsea and I went with him. That's where we met Rev. I guess it was about a year after that we all moved here to work in the Center."

"And you've been here ever since," Kevin stated.

"I guess I have." Adam paused. "What about you? How long have you been legally blind?"

"Always."

Adam sighed. Back to one-word answers. He had hoped that by telling his own story, Kevin might feel comfortable to do the same. Maybe a topic shift would help. "How come—"

Kevin cut him off with a question of his own. "Do you ever talk to your parents anymore?"

Chapter 13

"Sure. I might have been mad at them at the time, but I got over it."

"Are they like you?" Kevin asked. After a slight pause, he added, "I mean are they Christians?"

Adam nodded, curious at the turn in the conversation. "They are now." He wondered what thoughts swirled in the mind behind those lightly-shaded lenses. A stiff silence hung in the air. Adam took the opportunity to ask a question of his own. "Did your mom never tell you about them?"

"No."

"I wonder why," he mused aloud. "So did she ever tell you that she called me when you were three?"

Again, Kevin shook his head. "She always talked about the Refuge. That's what she called it. She said it was best and to trust her if she ever sent me there."

"I wish I knew what had her so scared." He looked pointedly at Kevin, but the teen gave nothing away in his deadpan expression.

"I guess we'll never know now."

"Maybe." Adam wondered how much Kevin knew. Just by his initial reaction, Adam was sure Staci had never told her son about her family. But Kevin had to know more—much more.

"Enough already. Can't you just leave me alone?"

"No," Adam said in a voice barely audible.

"Is it really so hard to accept me without knowing every sordid detail of my past?" The teen didn't give Adam time to answer. Instead, he threw the next barb. "I've heard you and Rev talk about how people are supposed to 'come to God'—how did Rev put it—'bumps and all.' Rev said God accepts them and doesn't demand a resume or a pedigree. He also said Christians are supposed to act like God. So why can't you?"

Adam lifted an eyebrow in surprise. The kid was good. Kevin'd make a great lawyer someday . . . or a preacher. He'd obviously been listening more than he thought while playing games in the rec area. "That's because God already knows everything. I don't."

Kevin scowled. "Ever think there might be a reason for that? Stop trying to ease your conscience about not being close to your family by trying to extract every detail from me. You know if you'd leave it alone, maybe one day I'll tell you." He paused in his offered compromise and then clarified, "When I'm ready."

"Kevin—"

The teen rolled his eyes and blew out an exasperated breath. "I gotta go."

Adam stopped him. "Look, why don't you stay here for the rest of the night and have breakfast with us in the morning? Chelsea loves to cook." When Kevin hesitated, he tried again. "There's even a spare bedroom if the couch isn't comfortable."

"The couch is fine."

"Good, then there's no reason not to finish off the night here." And many more if Adam eventually had his way. He should have started Kevin out in their apartment instead of giving him a room as though he were nothing more than another employee. Somehow he was going to change that.

Kevin gave him a wary look. "No more questions?"

Adam shook his head. "Not tonight. Or tomorrow," he quickly amended.

Chapter 13

Kevin sank back down into the couch. He pulled the blanket up and turned his head into the couch.

Adam flicked off the light. The darkness offered a comforting refuge to think. Had he pushed Kevin too much with his insatiable desire to know about his sister and why she prepared a safe place for Kevin? Why would they ever need it? What had happened to his sister in those years after she ran away from home?

"Adam?"

"Yeah?"

"I need to see my dad."

Me too was what he wanted to say, but he didn't. Too many questions lay unanswered. Then again, with all this talk of family, Kevin had to be missing the only family he really knew. Maybe a short visit would be what the teen needed to help him resolve some issues with his father.

He turned to Kevin who waited quietly on the couch. "I'll see what I can do."

chapter 14

"Aiden, can you come in here a minute?"

Aiden Rollings halted and backtracked into Reginald Oscar Maklehaney's office, better known as Rom to those around Rollings Security. The twenty-one-year-old college graduate had come to work for Aiden's father's company six months before. Rom's shaggy dark locks seemed to mock the mandatory dress pants and button down shirt required for employees to wear.

"What's up?" Aiden caught a glimpse of the computer screen seconds before Rom switched to his desktop screen. In what appeared to be security footage, William Tyke stood in The World's Gateway reception area, his arm leaning on the secretary's desk while the other hand clutched a briefcase.

Aiden's brow furrowed and his gaze moved from the computer to Rom.

"Shut the door."

Aiden nodded. "Why are you watching Mr. Tyke? Is that some old security feed?"

"No. I've been looking for something." Rom wadded up a piece of paper on his desk and pitched it into a nearby wastebasket.

"I thought my dad had you guys close up all the existing back doors?"

"We did," Rom assured him. "But I made a new one just in case. From the couple of months I knew Kevin, he never struck me as someone to do what he did without a reason. And since you wouldn't tell me that reason, I went digging."

Aiden lowered himself into one of the vacant chairs. "Did you find anything?"

Rom's deep blue eyes seemed to peer into Aiden's mind. "You know it's funny. It's what I haven't found that strikes me as unusual. Tyke has very little outside communication, few files, works his eight-to-five and goes home."

Aiden glanced down at the floor. He wanted to tell Rom, tell anyone for that matter. He hated all this secrecy, especially from someone like Rom who might be able to help. But he promised Kevin.

"Until today."

Interest piqued, Aiden's gaze flew back to Rom. "What?"

Rom ran the mouse over an icon and the camera returned. "He was bragging to the receptionist about the deal he got on a new laptop. Seemed the other one acquired a virus, and he hadn't been able to recover the data. I also found it interesting that Tyke mentioned to the receptionist that he prefers to do his email off-site. It

Chapter 14

seems after the pen test, Tyke doesn't trust the security of his email at The World's Gateway. I guess he likes the anonymity of the coffee shop connection." Rom turned back to Aiden and waited.

The silent standoff continued until Aiden asked, "Why'd you call me in here?"

"Isn't it obvious?" Rom lifted an empty cup off the edge of his otherwise immaculate desk and squinted down into it. "I need some coffee." He pulled out his wallet, handed Aiden a bill, then fished something out of his drawer, and tossed it to Aiden.

Aiden easily snatched the object out of the air. He rotated the small device over in his hand and grinned.

"I take it you know what that is?"

He nodded, still grinning.

"Here's the deal. If you want to borrow it for a few days, feel free. If not, put it back in my drawer when you get back. But I still want my coffee. Get one for yourself too."

The chair squeaked on the cherry laminate flooring as Aiden rose to his feet. He appreciated Rom giving him an opportunity without demanding answers he couldn't give right now.

"Aiden, be careful. And remember I'd be glad to help. It's what I do." Rom volunteered in a local Cyberangel group called Guardian Angels that watched chat rooms and other places for people who used the Internet for nefarious purposes. Originally, Rom had worked with hackers who watched for perpetrators and then sent viruses into their hard drives to render their computers useless. Teenage vigilantes, Rom told Aiden, is what they called themselves at the time.

Both Aiden and Kevin had often stopped by to hear about the cases Rom had helped the police to solve. What Rom didn't know was that Kevin copied the virus he showed them one afternoon. The very one Kevin loaded onto William Tyke's laptop.

Aiden nodded and rushed out of the office. Within minutes, he arrived at the Java Hut and ordered himself a frozen coffee. From the corner of his eye, Aiden spotted Tyke seated in a booth, sipping a drink, his laptop open in front of him.

As nonchalantly as possible, Aiden made his way to Tyke. A chill ran through him, whether from the frozen coffee in his hand, the worry over what he would say to Tyke, or both, he didn't know. He slowly approached the table with only a partial plan in mind. "Mr. Tyke?"

Surprise colored Tyke's face. He snapped the lid of his laptop shut. An amiable smile replaced the scowl. "What can I do for you today?"

"I . . . I . . ." Aiden faltered as he tried to figure out what to say. "I just wanted to say I'm sorry. I never got the chance before."

"I see."

"I mean, I apologized to my dad and everything. I didn't know what Kevin was gonna do."

Tyke stared at him for several long seconds, his expression unreadable. The gray-haired man sipped at his latte and then motioned with his hand. "Take a seat."

Aiden slid into the opposite bench and placed his hands in his lap. He took a deep breath. "Anyway, I came in to get something to drink and saw you back here. I'm sorry if I ruined your thoughts of Rollings Security."

Tyke nodded. "I appreciate your initiative. Too bad Kevin didn't have your standards. I'd stay away from kids

Chapter 14

like him. No hope for them. Sending him away was the best thing his father could have done."

Blood drained from his face, but Aiden coughed to cover his shock. He should have ordered a latte so he could have tossed it in Tyke's face, show the man what it felt like to be burned by someone. But he couldn't. Not if he wanted to complete his mission.

With one hand Aiden took a long sip of his latte while he attached the device to the underside of the booth with his other hand. He glanced up at Tyke with sad, hopeless eyes. "That's what my dad said too."

"Your dad's right."

Aiden nodded. "I better let you get back to work." He slid out of the booth and after finding an empty one for himself, he pulled out his Electronic Reader and flicked through some pages of his comic book, though what any of it said he didn't know. Just a menagerie of colors and pixels. Something to do while waiting for Tyke to leave.

The older man didn't disappoint him. After another twenty minutes, Tyke gathered up his laptop and headed out the door. Aiden waited until he saw the dark sedan drive off before hurrying back to Tyke's booth. He slid his hand under the table and smiled as he retrieved the device. Hope washed over him. There had to be something here. Aiden shoved the thumb-size device in his pocket and smirked in triumph.

"Gotcha."

Kevin rolled another shirt and placed it in his carefully packed backpack. He zipped up the largest compartment and then reached into a drawer and pulled out his red sketchpad. A folded bus ticket, crumpled from being handled so much, lay between the pages.

For the past three weeks, Kevin had made a concerted effort to portray the reformed teenager. He couldn't count how many times he'd ignored David's snide remarks when he would have loved to take Adam's precious baseball bat off the wall and give the man an attitude adjustment. But if he wanted his last chance at freedom, he had to bluff them all into thinking they could trust him to visit Dad unsupervised.

As it stood, he would only have a two-day window to make his escape. He glanced at his watch. Three hours from now Mark would fly him, Adam, and Rev back to McKeltic. After accounting for the time difference, which would have them arriving early Friday morning, the plan was to spend Friday with Dad. On Saturday morning he would meet with Aiden at Galactic Jitters. He would spend Saturday evening with Dad, and then as soon as Dad went to his room for the night, Kevin would leave. The last bus left McKeltic at one in the morning. By the time Adam came to pick him up at six Sunday morning, Kevin would be long gone.

The LinkWay chimed behind him, and Kevin shoved the ticket into the smaller compartment of his backpack and then hit the connect button on the LinkWay. Aiden's worried face appeared in the screen.

"Kevin, I need your help."

"And it can't wait another twelve hours or so?"

Aiden lowered his voice. "I have something I need to do, but since my parents have restricted my laptop use to homework only, I'm stuck. It's already eight o'clock at night here. Mom said I get two hours to complete my

Chapter 14

essay for history. And to make matters worse, it's due first period."

"And you didn't already write the paper, why?" Kevin folded his arms over his chest in an effort to appear stern. Inside he chuckled. As much as he was known for getting into trouble for what he did, Aiden was known for what he didn't do.

Aiden rolled his eyes. "Ah, you know how it is. Mrs. Pathos can't understand why her entire class doesn't share her passion for history. Ugh. And what's worse is Mom said if I don't get that essay turned in on time, I'm grounded for the weekend."

"So what's so important that you can't work on it right now? Maybe I could help you out with whatever the other thing is while you write."

Aiden shook his head, lowered his voice even further. "Can't talk about it now. We'll meet once you're here."

Kevin rocked back in his chair. "Okay." He drew out the word.

"Just do it, Kevin. Save my behind. I promise you, it'll be worth it."

"Oh yeah? How so?"

"I'm thinking I might be able to save yours."

What was Aiden up to? How could his friend possibly have something to help him? But on the slim chance that he did, Kevin wasn't willing to pass up on the opportunity. He nodded. "Fair enough. Give me the details."

Aiden's sigh of relief was evident in his expression. From out of a folder, he pulled the instruction sheet and read it off to Kevin. "I need a two-page essay, typed, double spaced, Times New Roman, twelve-point font, on

Amelia Earhart and her last flight, the one where she disappeared."

"You don't ask a lot, do you?" Kevin said sarcastically. "The disappearance of Amelia Earhart? You do realize, I'm about to make a seven-hour flight over the Pacific Ocean? Not exactly the best preflight topic."

Aiden grimaced. "Sorry." He then inserted the small device into the USB port on his laptop.

"Is that a remote logger?" Kevin's eyes narrowed, curiosity mixed with interest.

Aiden shoved the small device out of the view of the LinkWay. "Look, I gotta get busy. Call me when you get the essay finished. Oh yeah, one more thing: don't forget to make it look like I did it."

Kevin burst out laughing.

Aiden severed the connection and the LinkWay went dark.

Kevin took another glance at his watch and sighed. Not a lot of time to get an essay researched and written, but he could do it. Aiden did tell him to make it look like he wrote it. So a few random thoughts and typos would be expected.

While he retrieved his laptop out of his backpack, he wondered why Aiden had a keystroke logger and what information could be so important.

chapter 15

Saturday morning Kevin jogged down the stairs past family photos that dotted the wall along the staircase of their two-story home. Three steps from the bottom, he jumped to the landing. Twenty minutes from now he was supposed to meet Aiden at Galactic Jitters. He couldn't wait. Six weeks at the Center had seemed like an eternity. Right now he could almost taste a steaming quadruple mocha latte.

Kevin hurried down the hallway, pausing to scribble a short note to Dad about where he'd be. Saturdays were Dad's half-work days, so Kevin's time was limited at best. He slid the edge of the note under a paperweight when the ringing LinkWay made him pause. He glanced at the caller id and groaned. Probably another telemarketer. The LinkWay had been on the market less than a year, and already telemarketers had honed in on new ways to drive people crazy. Kevin's hand lingered over the ignore button for a second and then hit the answer button instead. Maybe a little mischief would teach these people not to call back.

"Good morning," a middle-aged man dressed in a black suit and tie greeted him. "Is Steven Ramsey home?"

"No, he's serving life in prison right now."

The salesman blanched.

"I could give you his address. Not sure he could buy anything from you. Making license plates doesn't pay much per hour." Kevin's lips upturned into a wicked grin.

The salesman adjusted his tie and met Kevin's gaze. "Yes, well, perhaps I'll call back later. I'm sure the car wasn't for you anyway."

"Car? What car?" Kevin leaned in closer to the screen. "Look, I'm sorry. I thought you were a telemarketer. My dad gets off work in a couple of hours. I can make sure he gets the message."

"Early release, I take it?" The salesman's frown fell away, and he chuckled. "Well, I'm sure you're father will enjoy something to celebrate this new found freedom."

"Maybe."

"Of course." The salesman took a step back, allowing for a wider view of the showroom. "When Mr. Ramsey came to see us in December to get a replacement key for his car, he showed great interest in wanting to purchase one of our Mercedes SLL600 Roadsters. We've had an especially luxurious one come in, and we thought he might want to have a look at it."

Kevin's eyes bugged out. Why had Dad needed a replacement key? And since when was Dad interested in a

Chapter 15

car of that caliber? Sure, they had some money, but a large portion had been invested in the island resort William Tyke was supposed to be building. Another large amount had been donated to the Center in the form of a grant. Now he wanted to buy a high dollar car? Where was all the money coming from?

The salesman cleared his throat. "Would you like me to record a message?"

"Sure." Kevin pressed the record button on the LinkWay and waited for the man to rattle off his spiel of information. "I'll let him know you called."

The salesman ended the call, and Kevin hurried out the door to meet Aiden.

"'Bout time you got here," Aiden said.

Kevin slid into the opposite seat of the booth and took a long sip of his coffee. "When have you ever known me to be on time?"

Aiden laughed. "Never."

"So how did your essay go? Get it in on time?"

"Perfect. I got a C+. Any higher on a last minute assignment and my parent's would have been suspicious." Aiden grinned. "I even got my laptop back for the weekend."

"Good. Now it's your turn. What were you doing with that keystroke logger?"

"Saving your behind. What do you think?"

Kevin frowned, staring over the rim of his cup. He seriously doubted Aiden had anything that could help, and he didn't have much time to waste on cat and mouse games. "Feel free to clarify at any moment."

Aiden pulled out a flash drive from his own backpack and inserted it into the laptop. "It was Rom's idea."

"Rom?" Kevin blanched. "You told Rom?"

"No! Of course not. Rom's been watching Tyke since you left. He smells a rat. When Tyke bought a new laptop and took it to the Java Hut for coffee and Internet, Rom was suspicious. He offered me the remote keystroke logger. Rom doesn't know what's on it though. I erased all the information before I gave it back."

Kevin blew out a long breath of relief and fingered the flash drive, anxious to hear some answers. "Okay, what did you find?"

Aiden lowered his voice a notch. "I was able to break into his email account. From what I could gather, Mr. Tyke had an offshore bank account, but the bank closed down as of December thirty-first. He had to move his money. It looks like he had someone do it for him. I found an old email that told him that the new banking information was in the attached PT file and that after he opened it, he needed to delete the email."

"Patrick Thomas." Kevin nodded. So there really was something in that file, but what?

Aiden waited until some teens passing by were out of earshot. "But it looks like the person who sent the email forgot to attach the PT file the first time and ended up sending it twice."

"And all that information is sitting on the original laptop." Things began to click in Kevin's brain now. For some reason, Tyke had downloaded the file but not gotten the information before Kevin locked it up. Tyke couldn't access the account number to get at the money. No wonder he had been desperate enough to send Landon to try and kidnap him. Kevin shuddered at the memory.

"Which doesn't make sense. There was obviously a techie on board because Tyke mentioned this person set

Chapter 15

up all the accounts as well as created a new identity that he was going to mail to Tyke right after the New Year. Why not have that techie clean up the virus on Tyke's laptop or resend the attachment?" Aiden stared at Kevin over the top of his coffee.

"Because that person's in jail."

"What?" Aiden leaned forward on the table. "How do you know?"

"Even at the Center I'm not without my sources." He ignored Aiden's questioning look.

"So unless Tyke can get into his old laptop, he can't get his account number and password?"

Kevin nodded. "I guess so."

"Who do you think the money belonged to? Was Patrick Thomas innocent all along, or did Tyke find out about the account and take the money? You know with some offshore banks, you only need an account number and a password."

"I think the bigger question is what did we miss in that file?" Kevin sighed. He needed to take another look at the file before he left tonight. "What about the investors' money?"

"I don't know. It may have already been transferred to the offshore account. All I know is Tyke is desperate to get that information."

Kevin leaned back in the booth and sighed. "Which means I need to get out of here and soon."

"I thought you were leaving in the morning to go back to the Center. At least you'll be safe there until this blows over," Aiden said. "On the other hand, we could assume since Tyke bought a new laptop, he's not too worried about the first one. Maybe he gave up on getting rid of the virus."

"I wouldn't count on it." Kevin clamped his mouth shut. He slid out of the booth and tossed his cup away.

Aiden followed. "What are you talking about?"

"Nothing." Kevin shoved open the door and stepped out onto the busy sidewalk.

Aiden caught up with him. "'Nothing' is what you tell adults. Not your best friend."

"Let's just say Tyke hasn't quite given up trying to get rid of that virus." He poked fingers up beneath his wire frames and rubbed his eyes. "Look, can you pick me up and give me a ride tonight?"

Aiden shook his head. "What? To where?"

"I still have that bus ticket," Kevin said barely above a whisper.

"I can't believe you're still running. The Center is the safest place for you right now." Aiden wrestled his keys out of his front pocket. The locks popped when he pressed the button on the key fob to unlock his car.

Kevin sat down in the passenger seat, the heaviness of his thoughts weighing upon him. He couldn't risk telling his friend everything. Couldn't risk they might come after Aiden too. "I know what I'm doing."

Aiden sighed in frustration. "Do you?"

Surreal.

Kevin tried to think of another word but couldn't. Leaning against the pool table in their game room, he sipped at his soda and thought about the evening. No arguments, few awkward moments. Strangely enough, he'd been able to relax around Dad for the first time in

Chapter 15

what seemed like forever. A part of him didn't want it to end. It almost felt like before his mother died.

He set his glass down and reached for one of the pool sticks. He leaned over the table and decided to play a game against himself while Dad took care of the unexpected meeting with a client in the other room. Maybe he'd have better luck; he'd lost every game up to this point. He grinned. That was okay. If they had played video games instead, Kevin felt confident that he would have left Dad with nothing more than a box of tissue to ease the agony of defeat.

After successfully hitting two balls in the far corner pocket, he laid the pool stick across the table. Maybe he would offer to play just one more game of pool when Dad finished. For now, he wanted to curl up on the couch, sink deep into its cushions. He pushed aside the now empty pizza boxes and reached for the remote. He might as well watch something while he waited. It wasn't uncommon for Dad's business meetings to last in excess of half an hour. Glancing at his watch, he realized this would definitely not be Dad's night to prove him wrong.

In the middle of one of his favorite shows, Kevin heard the angry mumblings of his dad. Nervous, he scrambled out of the cushions into an upright position. A tangible silence followed. Kevin crept into the hall, pressed up against the wall near the door, and listened.

"Look, Tyke, I already told you no."

"But that was before we discovered the virus was set on December 31, and a large sum of money was also removed from an account. Peter Damon still has no idea someone managed to embezzle money from the business. And as I understand it, you came into a large sum of money that enabled you to pawn off your son to some estranged relatives."

Kevin gasped, then hoped they hadn't heard him. Embezzled money? Dad had paid the Center with embezzled money? His mind reeled. Now he understood how Dad had the money to invest in an expensive car.

Dad argued, "You gave me that money as returns from my investment."

"I recall no such transaction." Tyke paused dramatically. "But what I do recall is that unbeknownst to anyone, when Mr. Damon and I hired Rollings Securities to perform the penetration test, we also installed security cameras in our parking lot. Your car is on that film at 3:25 on the morning of January the first."

"That's impossible. And besides, if I was there, it would show up on the security camera on the inside."

"There's also evidence someone tampered with the interior cameras. Somehow, they were disengaged that night. Because of your son's involvement with the penetration test, there's high reason to believe he is to blame."

"You—"

Kevin didn't catch the end of the reply, but could easily guess as a fist slammed down on the table.

"You say that, Mr. Ramsey. But please remember I indicated I could make all this disappear. I only have one request. Seems reasonable, don't you think?"

Dad growled, low and deep. "You're bluffing. If you even think of blaming this on me, I'll show Peter Damon the file my son found, and you'll be the one arrested. So why don't we just call it a stalemate and be done with it?"

"That file—if it still exists—would only incriminate

Chapter 15

you further, Mr. Ramsey." William Tyke chuckled. It sent a chill down Kevin's spine. "Check. Mate."

Dad spat out a profanity.

"I'll be by in the morning to retrieve a disk that better contain the fix for the virus. I'd advise you to find a way to acquire it. Otherwise, I'll have no choice but to present this video feed to Mr. Damon. Do we understand each other?"

"I want to see the video first."

"Of course." There was a slight pause. "One more thing. In case you're still having doubts about convincing your son to get me that fix, don't forget I still have one more card to play."

A heavy silence followed. Kevin could only imagine the fear in Dad's face.

Tyke chuckled. "Surely you don't think I blew off that interesting reunion at the investors' dinner between you and your old college buddy, Steven . . . Chandler."

Tyke had played the ultimate trump card. Dad's worst fears were wrapped up in that identity. Kevin snuck up the stairs to his room. He had to get out of here. Family night was officially over.

The soft click of the bedroom door shutting seemed to echo through the house. He snatched up his backpack, hurried to the window, and climbed out onto the roof.

Outside, the night air felt thick and humid. Today had been unseasonably warm. The cool winds were kicking up a thunderstorm. In the distance, he could see bolts of lightning streak across the night sky like shards of glass. Seconds later, a deep roll of thunder rumbled. Rain wouldn't be far behind.

Kevin sized up the distance to the ground. The tree branches had been cut back after the last time he tried to sneak out. A landscaper had been called the next week to plant a cluster of rose bushes. The chances of falling into their dry thorny branches was too high to risk.

He crawled back through the window and tiptoed back down the stairs. The carpet muffled the sound of his footsteps, but not the pounding of his heart.

At the base of the stairs, Kevin halted at the sound of an interior door opening. He quickly ducked into the game room and tossed his backpack to the side of the couch. Like the comic book hero, Saphearon, he took a flying leap and landed in the deep couch cushions.

Breathe. Just breathe.

Moments later, Dad stalked into the room. Rage churned on his face, a storm about to let loose. He stumbled slightly as he tossed back the rest of his drink.

Kevin slowly pushed himself off the couch.

Dad swayed once more, straightened, then rushed forward and scooped up the eight ball from the pool table. He rolled the black ball over in his hand and squeezed it.

With his right hand, Kevin stretched over the side of the couch. Shaky fingers curled around the strap. While Dad was distracted, Kevin planned to run for it.

A roar broke loose. "Nooooooooo!" Dad pulled back his arm and pitched the eight ball across the room.

Kevin cringed as one of the panes in the French doors shattered. He took two steps back, then prepared to bolt. How many times had he watched this scenario play out? Drunken, explosive arguments. Scene by scene, he had it memorized. It was the part of life Kevin kept well hidden. In order to survive, he'd begun thinking of Dad as two people. One was Dad, the one with

Chapter 15

whom he could have fun, the one who all but disappeared after his mother's death. The other . . . well, some things didn't need a name.

chapter 16

Aiden strode up to Kevin's front door. Lightning streaked the sky behind him, announcing the impending storm. He pulled out Kevin's cell phone that he'd found lodged between the seats of his car. Although he wasn't sure if Kevin would actually take it since cell phone calls could be easily traced, it gave him an excuse to see his friend one last time before Kevin left, whether back to the Center or off on his own.

Aiden lifted his free hand to knock.

"No!" a man's voice bellowed from somewhere in the house.

Shocked, Aiden took an instinctive step back. Glass shattered around the side of the house. Thunder rumbled above.

Kevin's father. It had to be.

Aiden leaned into the door and listened. The house remained silent. Even the air seemed to stand still. Aiden walked over to the side of the house, searching for a light through a window. Anything to indicate everything was all right.

Take a deep breath. Maybe Kevin already got away and his father just found out he's gone.

But what if his friend was in there and needed his help? He remembered all too clearly the last time he visited after what Kevin termed an explosive argument between him and his father. Aiden couldn't imagine an argument so out of control that someone got hurt. Kevin had shrugged as though the small bruise was no big deal. That's what really bothered Aiden.

Afraid to knock again, Aiden carefully made his way across the yard to his car. A stray pecan exploded under his foot like a Fourth of July firecracker. He jumped, certain someone had heard him. His head pivoted back toward the house. Still nothing.

Kevin's cell phone felt heavy in Aiden's hand. How he wished he could call his friend, make sure everything was all right. He opened the door of his car and climbed in. He set the cell phone face up on the passenger seat. Hands curled around the steering wheel, he took one last glance toward the house, as though it would somehow reveal its secrets.

Large intermittent drops of rain splattered on his windshield like falling missiles. Lightning crisscrossed the starless sky.

Still the house remained quiet.

Aiden turned the key in the ignition, flipped on the wipers against the steadily increasing rain, and pulled out

Chapter 16

onto the street. "Coward," he accused himself. He banged the palms of his hands on the steering wheel. This was Kevin. His best friend. How could he just walk away? But what other option was there? He hit the gas.

At the corner he paused at the stop sign blurred by the rain that now fell in sheets. He toyed with Kevin's cell phone. One at a time, he scrolled through the names until he found Adam's. Dare he call? What would he say? How far did Kevin expect him to carry out his promise not to say anything?

How big of a chance was he willing to take that Kevin was still in there? Someone had to find out for sure.

Aiden drew in a deep breath and dialed the number.

Kevin stood, the backpack hung from his fingers like a weight, rooting him to the spot.

Move! But his legs seemed incapable of any response.

As the space closed between them, the pungent odor of alcohol filled the air, evidence Dad had probably been mixing his soda all night.

"Kevin." Dad's face had taken on a strange calm that was almost more frightening than the obvious anger. "I need you to get me the fix for that virus you put on Mr. Tyke's laptop."

"No." This time Kevin would stand his ground no matter what.

Dad's eyes narrowed. He swayed and grabbed the pool table for support. "You don't understand what this man is capable of."

Stephanie M. E. Gallentine / refuge

"All we have to do is call the police. If you let me, I can get you the evidence to prove Tyke is setting you up. You were their CPA, not their stooge."

Dad's face tightened. The knuckles on his fist whitened in their clenched state. "The police won't help us. They never did."

"Not everyone is like—"

"Don't say it!" Dad lunged forward.

The backpack slipped from his grip. Kevin dashed out of the room and into the hall. Heavy footsteps pounded the floor behind him and then faded.

As the door came into view, Dad appeared from a side room and blocked Kevin's escape. "You're not running this time," Dad said.

Kevin turned and ran for the back door. As Dad closed in on him, he sped up and darted into the bathroom, slammed the door, and turned the lock. All his insides shook. His heart had to have expanded to fill his entire chest cavity. Kevin's body pulsated with every heartbeat.

Kevin leaned back against the door. One foot lodged at the base, he planted his other on the tiled floor in front of him for balance. To further his barricade, he pressed the palm of his hand against the wall across from the porcelain sink.

The door thudded as Dad's weight slammed into it.

Kevin kept his muscles rigid against the door. He cringed at the string of curses that filtered through the wood.

Again, Dad slammed against the door.

Kevin tipped his head back. The only window in the room was a small rectangular sliding glass, barely big enough to shove his foot through. No, he needed another

Chapter 16

plan. The wood throbbed behind him. Kevin held his arms taunt, despite the ache. His muscles screamed for relief.

Then like the calm in the eye of the storm, it stopped. The ramming. The cursing. Everything.

Kevin relaxed his shoulders and legs, afraid to move, afraid not to. His head fell back against the door, and he sucked in a shuddering breath. He'd forgotten how different home could be since spending time at the Center. After tonight, if not for Landon, he might not feel the need to run anymore. But his mom had spent years reminding him of the importance of keeping their secret. He could easily be in a worse situation than this with no hope of escape.

Rain pelted against the side of the house like bullets from a machine gun. Branches scratched against the small window.

With trembling fingers, he dug into his pocket. Nothing but loose threads. He growled in frustration. Where was his cell phone?

The silence in the hall came to an abrupt halt. Something metal scratched on the doorknob. Beads of sweat trailed down his neck and formed a puddle at the base of his back.

The storm raged on.

Adam slipped a marker between the pages of the book he'd been reading and laid it down on the end table in Prof's living room. He yawned and arched his back while his arms stretched outward.

Prof held out a cup of coffee. "Kind of early for you to be so tired."

"Jet lag, I guess."

"Still?" Prof chuckled. "You're getting old."

"Speak for yourself." Adam stirred a generous amount of hazelnut creamer into his coffee. "So when are you going to tell me about Staci and Kevin?"

Prof took a long sip of his coffee. He sighed. "I don't know as much as I'd like."

"What can you tell me?" Always before, Prof would evade a direct answer. Tonight Adam wasn't going to let his friend off. Rev had gone to visit his own relatives and wouldn't be back for another few hours. There was nothing to disturb them.

"Something happened about twelve years ago, and they had to go into the Witness Protection Program."

"What?" Adam's coffee cup clanked on the glass end table. "Why didn't she call me? I would've helped—"

"She did, Adam. Staci called you. She wanted to make sure Kevin always had a safe place to run to."

"Prof, I would've taken them in." Adam was still trying to recover from the shock. "Wait a minute. You knew about their identity, so you must have known about Kevin's age."

Prof nodded. "I did. But I figured no one had figured it out in twelve years, I didn't see a need in telling you." The older man took another drink from his coffee. "Besides, we'd already asked you to take Kevin for the next two years. One more year seemed too much to ask."

Adam shook his head. "I'm not giving him up in two years unless his father insists. We need that year if we hope to—" On the glass countertop, his cell phone commenced its vibrating dance to the musical ring tone.

Chapter 16

"About time," Adam mumbled when Kevin's name registered on the display. He had told the teen to call and check in tonight, but so far nothing.

"Adam? Adam Hollandale?" the anxious voice of a young man asked.

Adam held up an index finger to Prof and walked into the kitchen. "This is he. Who is this?"

"Aiden. I'm Kevin's friend." The voice seemed nervous, reluctant. "I'm sorry to bother you. I . . . uh . . . needed to return his cell. He left it in my car." Aiden paused. "Is he there by chance?"

"No. He's spending time with his father." Adam furrowed his brows. "Did you try his home?"

"Um . . . well . . . yeah . . . I guess I'll try there." Another pause. "You haven't talked to him tonight, have you?"

"No. Should I have?"

"Well, I know you guys are leaving in the morning. And I know Kevin is always late." The words tumbled out. "Maybe if you called him, reminded him." The voice sounded hopeful.

After a rather abrupt click in his ear, Adam retracted his cell phone. He stared at it still in the palm of his hand. The entire conversation struck him as odd.

"Who was that?" Prof asked. He rinsed out the two cups and placed them in the dishwasher.

"A friend of Kevin's."

"Everything okay?"

He shrugged. "I guess Kevin left his cell phone in Aiden's car."

"Hmm. You look awful pensive for something so simple," the older man noted.

Stephanie M. E. Gallentine / refuge

"You ever talk to someone and feel as though half the conversation must've been subliminal? Because you're sure more was said than you actually caught?"

Prof flicked off the coffee pot and walked out of the kitchen. "Are you sure you're not reading too much into this? Aiden does tend to get nervous from time to time."

"Maybe." Adam excused himself for the privacy of a room and a LinkWay. "There's only one way to find out."

The soft whirring sound of an electric screwdriver filtered from the hallway.

Kevin grasped the doorknob. Felt it loosen in his hand. "No, no," he whispered, frantically.

The whirring continued.

The doorknob clanged on the bathroom's ceramic tile floor.

Kevin stiffened against yet another onslaught. The door buckled. His muscles quivered under the strain. "Dad, stop."

Thwack.

Kevin's foot slid. "Please, stop."

The door gave way. Dad stormed in the room and shoved Kevin against the wall.

The towel rack jammed into Kevin's back. He yelled and threw out his hands for protection.

"Why do you have to always make things so difficult? Why can't you just do what I ask?" Dad grasped both of Kevin's upper arms and shook him.

Kevin tried to wrestle free.

Dad swayed and stumbled against Kevin.

Chapter 16

Their heavy breaths mixed together in the small space. Kevin turned his head, the rank smell of alcohol causing him to gag.

Suddenly, like a bell in a wrestling match, the LinkWay rang, signaling a time out. Dad stiffened. "Let's go." He pulled Kevin into the den, shoved him on the couch, and gave him a warning look that dared him to move. Then after smoothing down the front of his shirt and straightening his tie, Dad answered the call

"Adam." The words no longer slurred. It was as if Dad had suddenly sobered.

Kevin felt sickened by Dad's uncanny ability to act as though he hadn't had a drop of alcohol. Why did Dad go through so much trouble for others and not for his own son? Anger and bitterness washed over him. Was he worth anything to Dad?

On the floor not far from him, he spotted his backpack and stood to retrieve it.

"Kevin," Dad called out in a tight voice. "Adam wants to speak to you."

Kevin shook his head. He couldn't talk to Adam. Not now. Not like this.

"Now."

After scooping up his backpack, Kevin swallowed and stepped in front of the LinkWay. He cringed under Adam's intent stare.

"You look a mess. Everything all right?"

"Yeah."

"That was a wordy answer."

"I charge by the word. You should be grateful." He grinned to offset the biting edge of his words.

Adam's face softened through the screen. "You do remember we'll be by to pick you up at six in the morning?"

Kevin groaned and rolled his eyes. "Yeah."

"Good. I'll see you then." He studied Kevin for several more seconds. "Don't forget I'm praying for you."

Kevin nodded. For once, those words didn't bother him. He craved them. "Thanks."

Adam's head tilted and his brows furrowed. Then he, too, nodded. "Get some sleep. You look awful."

The connection severed, and Kevin turned back to Dad. "I'm going to my room." He hefted the backpack on his shoulder and stormed out.

"You still have work to do." Dad followed him. "I need that fix for Tyke's laptop."

Kevin didn't stop. He hurried down the hall toward the stairs. Somehow, he had to get away from here. The night was far from over, and he feared what the rest would bring.

A loud boom of thunder detonated outside their home like a bomb. The house lights flickered. Behind Kevin, uneven footfalls followed.

"Kevin, wait."

Panting, Kevin headed up the steps. *God help me!*

Dad's hand slipped between the banister rails. It gripped, then tugged at his ankle. Kevin stumbled and threw out his hands.

The weighted backpack pulled him. He twisted, kicked against the air as he tumbled down the stairs. The tip of his left shoulder took the impact of the fall. Pain exploded in his arm. His body jackknifed at the base of the stairs. Jostled wire frames flew off his face and skidded across the floor.

Chapter 16

"Kevin!" Dad rushed over, pausing when Kevin's glasses cracked under the weight of his step. He knelt beside his son.

Kevin sat up. Streaks of pain flashed from his shoulder down to his arm He moaned and drew the limb close to his side. Black spots danced in front of him. He squeezed his eyes shut. *Breathe.*

So much for praying for help. His torso rocked back and forth on the floor. How had the night gotten so out of control? Why hadn't he just left earlier? If he hadn't been here, maybe Dad would have found a way to deal with Tyke on his own.

Dad slammed his fist into the nearby wall. Pictures rattled. A curse spewed from his mouth. "Now, how are we going to fix all of this?"

chapter 17

Kevin opened his eyes. Had he heard right? Here he sat, in more pain than he ever thought possible. The only pair of glasses he brought with him lay in a mangled mess, and Dad hadn't moved beyond the need to fix his own problems.

In that moment, he didn't know whom he hated more: William Tyke or his own dad. Right now they were both running neck and neck in that competition.

An uncharacteristic gentle hand helped him to his feet and steadied him when he stumbled on his first step. "Thanks," Kevin muttered.

"You're welcome. Now, how do we go about getting Mr. Tyke that fix for his laptop?"

Kevin sighed. This night would never end until he did what Dad asked. If he kept refusing, circumstances would eventually escalate again. There wasn't a prayer out there that could help him. He surrendered. It wasn't worth a fight he couldn't win. He clutched his arm close to his body. "All right. But I'll need to call someone to help me."

Immediately, Dad's defenses came out. "Who?"

"Just Aiden. I didn't write the virus. Aiden knows where to get the fix. He could spend the night, and we'll have it ready before Adam or Tyke gets here."

Silence hung in the air while Dad considered it. "Fine. Call him. But don't tell him anything beyond what is absolutely necessary. Got it?"

He nodded.

"What's his number? I'll dial it on the cell." Dad pulled his cell out of pocket and flipped it open.

"I'll just use the Link."

"No. He doesn't need to see you face to face before he gets over here."

That gave him pause. Kevin's hand moved instinctively to his face. No blood. Once he'd rattled off the number, he accepted the small phone placed in his hand. "Aiden?"

"Kevin! Where are you? Are you okay?" Aiden asked, his voice filled with concern.

"I'm home."

"You are? I was there. I heard the glass breaking."

Embarrassed, Kevin's eyes slid shut. This was his problem. He hated to bring Aiden into this, but right now, there seemed no other alternative. "I need a favor." He licked his chapped lips. "I need you to contact Rom and get the fix for his virus."

"What?"

Chapter 17

"I'm trying to make things right before I leave. This is the only way."

"Your dad's behind this, isn't he?"

Kevin clenched his teeth as much against the pain as in frustration. "Just do it."

There was a lengthy pause. Kevin feared he'd ask too much of his best friend.

"All right. But you owe me a major explanation."

"Thanks. Tell your dad you're spending the night over here." Kevin surmised Dad would be on his best behavior if Aiden were there. Dad was too well known in town as the owner of the top CPA firm in McKeltic. He couldn't risk letting his true colors shine through the well-constructed façade.

"Sure."

Kevin trudged back into the game room and allowed Dad to help him to the couch. He leaned into the corner of the overstuffed couch cushions.

"Want something to drink?"

Kevin shook his head but listened to the clink of glass on glass followed by the gurgle of poured liquid. Not even this could stop Dad from drinking. How did Dad function at work?

Three hours later, Aiden stood before him and handed him the disk. "Sorry it took so long. Rom was on a date. I had to wait until he got home, and—what happened to your glasses?"

"Broke." Kevin put his hand out, hoping he grabbed the right blurred object. "What did Rom say?"

"N-Nothing. Said he had to make some minor adjustments to the program. That's all."

"Why?"

Aiden shrugged. "I don't know. Something about a Cracker Jacks."

"Okay." Kevin drew out the word. "What did you tell him?"

Aiden paused a moment, and Kevin figured he must be glancing around to see if Dad was within earshot.

"I told him you were playing with the virus and accidently froze up your father's computer. You needed the fix before he found out what you had done."

"Thanks." Kevin laid the CD down on the blurred coffee table and told Dad they were going upstairs to talk and pack. He tried to act as if everything was fine. It lasted about ten seconds until he bounced off the doorframe leading into the hallway. He quickly recovered but kept his hand out to feel along the wall for direction.

Aiden sidled up next to him and whispered, "Kevin, can you even see right now or is something else going on I need to know about?"

"I'm fine. I told you my glasses broke, and I left my other pair at the Center. Things are just a bit fuzzy." They rounded the corner, and Kevin used the banister to guide him up the steps.

"What happened here tonight?" Aiden demanded as soon as the door to Kevin's room clicked shut.

"It's hard to explain."

"Let me guess. Your father wanted you to get that fix. You said no, and he beat you up. How am I doing so far?"

"He didn't beat me up. I fell on the stairs."

"I bet." Aiden sighed.

"No, I really did fall down the stairs. Dad and I were arguing."

"And the argument got out of control.

Chapter 17

"Um . . . sort of." The mattress sank in as Aiden sat beside him.

"Why didn't you ever tell me you can't see without your glasses?"

He glared at Aiden. "Oh, I'm sorry. Was I supposed to send out a public service announcement or something?"

"I'm your best friend. It would have been nice." Aiden's voice held an edge to it.

"Sorry."

The blur in front of him bobbed in what Kevin assumed was a nod. In a more controlled voice Aiden said, "You need to tell Adam about your dad. Let him take care of it."

"No. It'd be all over town. Everyone would know. I couldn't take that."

"But—"

"No buts. I won't become the next poster child for adults with alcohol and anger management issues. Forget it." Kevin picked up a book close to him and chucked it across the room. "Besides, Dad hasn't always been this way."

"But he is now." Aiden wouldn't let it go. "If the tables were turned, what would you do?"

"I . . . I'd . . . I don't know."

Aiden said, "Yeah, you do."

"Can we just drop it for now? My shoulder's killing me."

"Do you need to go to the emergency room? I have my car outside."

"No!" Kevin paused and tried to get his heart to stop pounding at the thought of going to the hospital and the questions they would ask. "They wouldn't treat me anyway without parental consent. But my dad has several bottles of pain relievers in the bathroom. If you could bring me one, I think I'll be all right."

Aiden sounded uncertain. "Are you sure? You don't know if they'll make things worse."

Kevin grinned. "At this point, I don't think things could get any worse."

Aiden returned a few minutes later. "I found a bottle of prescription strength Ibuprofen and Tylenol—"

"This is way beyond regular Tylenol. Hand me an Ibuprofen." He swallowed the large pill dry, forcing it down with what little saliva remained in his mouth. He stuffed the bottle of Tylenol into his backpack and told Aiden to set the other one back on the bathroom sink.

"Now what?" Aiden asked.

"We need proof. We've got to find the money."

"And how're we supposed to do that?" Aiden asked.

Kevin thought for a minute. Landon had said they hadn't looked hard enough. Later Kevin had studied the three items in the Patrick Thomas file but found nothing. Even the file sizes were normal—or were they? Maybe he had been looking in what he could see instead of what he couldn't see. "Aiden can you pull up that file on Patrick Thomas?"

"Sure, what for?"

Beneath the sound of clacking keys, Kevin explained, "Call it a hunch. I need to see if there was any information hidden in either the picture or the two articles that we can't see. Check the redundant data in the headers too." In the following silence, he could only imagine the look Aiden was giving him. "Just check."

"Oh, no," Aiden said a little later.

Chapter 17

Kevin grimaced. "What did you find?"

"A name and some numbers followed by a set of letters and numbers." Aiden read them off. "Deisldorf Banc. Kevin, I think we found the money."

Groaning, Kevin fell back on his bed. "And we just handed the money over to Tyke."

"About that—"

He wasn't listening. Another idea formed. "Aiden, you said this account had been set up recently?"

"Yeah, it was in an email. He also said that he was changing identities again."

"So we print those emails to use as evidence?" Kevin asked.

"One problem. I can't prove they came from Tyke. Emails are for the most part anonymous."

"What name did he choose? Maybe we could somehow link that back to him or even Patrick Thomas' partner for that matter."

After an ominous pause, Aiden replied, "SWRamsey@cpaworld.com."

Kevin's eyes slid shut. He groaned. Steven Wayne Ramsey. His dad. His nightmare.

"Aiden. Kevin." Dad's footsteps lumbered up the stairs.

Kevin stuck his head out the door as Dad reached the top of the stairway. "Yeah?" Behind him, Aiden zipped up the last of Kevin's stuff in a jumbo-sized suitcase. While Kevin had told him what he needed, Aiden had searched through closets, drawers, and packed everything.

"I think it's time for Aiden to go home."

"Go home? Dad, it's after four in the morning. Adam'll be here in two more hours."

"I'm sorry. I've already called his father. Mr. Rollings is waiting up for him as we speak."

"What?" Aiden's voice spiked up a notch.

Steven cleared his throat. "I had to call and tell him you two had snuck out. Wherever you'd been, Kevin came home with alcohol on his clothes, looking like he'd been in a fight and neither of you would tell me where you'd been. I thought it best if Aiden went on home."

Kevin felt the blood drain out of his face. "How could you?" But he knew how. Dad had a fear of going to jail—a fear that had grown to almost mythic proportions. The man took no chances. He should have never brought Aiden into this. But he couldn't have gone to Rom himself.

Beside him, Aiden groaned. Keys rattled as he fished them out of his pocket. "I gotta go. Somehow I've got to get my dad to believe the truth."

Kevin pulled on his arm. "You can't. I mean . . . make up something."

"Someone already did," Aiden said tersely. "Remember. I'm just working on damage control." He stormed down the stairs. Kevin tried to keep up. But even using his hands as a guide, it was hard.

Outside the storm had passed. Stray branches crunched under his feet as he followed Aiden out to his car. Kevin heard another groan followed by the slamming of the door.

"No, no, no, no, no. I forgot to lock my car." Another groan. This one deeper and more frustrated.

Kevin stopped just outside the open car door. Even

Chapter 17

from there, the overwhelming sickening smell of spilled alcohol assaulted him. Dad's handiwork, no doubt.

"I am so dead." He turned to Kevin. "If he finds the cup of spilt alcohol on my floorboard, he's gonna ground me for eternity. You have to come with me and tell my dad the truth."

"I . . . I can't." He shook his head, pinched the bridge of his nose. No matter what he did, the nightmare just kept getting worse.

"You have to. You can't let that man do to me what he does to you. Come *on*, Kevin."

Kevin hunched over, clutching his stomach. Nerves tumbled about his insides. Indecision plagued him, pulled him. He had to help, but he couldn't. Then everyone would know. "I'm sorry."

"Fine, you go back in there and wait for your ride out of here. I'll go home and do what you do. I'll play the martyr. I'll keep your secrets. But know this. I won't ever, *ever*, take the fall for that man again. No more promises to keep your secrets. I'm through." As if to emphasize his point, Aiden slammed the door to his Camaro, revved the engine, and sped off, tires squealing as he did.

Kevin stood in the stillness of the night, staring off into the black inkiness of the sky. Hopelessness became his only friend.

"Let's get you inside. You can at least get a couple hours sleep before Adam gets here."

Numb, Kevin allowed Dad to lead him back into the house. In a couple of hours, he'd allow Adam to take him to the Center.

What did it matter? He'd never be free.

Stephanie M. E. Gallentine / refuge

Voices.

It sounded like Dad's and Adam's. Muffled footsteps treaded up the staircase and stopped outside his door. The doorknob twisted. Kevin rolled to the edge of the bed, intent on getting up. His shoulder protested, sending sharp pains down his arm. An involuntary moan escaped his lips as the door creaked opened.

"I told you I thought he raided my liquor cabinet last night," Dad said to someone in the hall. "Give me a minute. I'll see if I can get him up."

What? Kevin's eyes flew open. What kind of game was Dad playing now? Taking in a deep breath, the smell of alcohol assaulted him, causing his stomach to churn. The smell seemed to be coming from the floor by his bed.

"Tell him to hurry. The pilot's waiting on us," Adam said.

Dad's blurry face came into view as Dad leaned over him. The smell of minty toothpaste and coffee barely covered last night's alcohol consumption. "Hey."

"Hey," was Kevin's tentative reply. This was how they always started "the conversation"—the one that always occurred the morning after a blow up. Kevin knew every line, every response, could quote it by heart, as if it were a rehearsed speech.

"I'm sorry." Dad's hand came to rest on Kevin's good arm. "For everything."

Kevin stared upward. It was his turn. He was supposed to say, "It's all right," even when it wasn't. It was his job to forgive Dad, make Dad feel like it was okay to go to work. Everything would be fine. But it wasn't. How could it be?

Chapter 17

In a moment of anger, Kevin shoved Dad's hand away. "You lied to him."

"Son, it's not what you think."

He glared. "Sure it isn't."

"Look, I can't control my drinking right now. I can't control my temper either."

Kevin rolled his eyes. "Oh, that's a real shocker."

"That's enough. Remember I have your best interest in mind. Why do you think I'm sending you back? To protect you. But I'm not going to jail for this. It was an accident. If only you'd listened to me—"

"So you're the good guy here?"

Dad never got a chance to answer. The door opened and both Rev and Adam walked in.

"Whew. Smells like a brewery." Rev whistled long and low. "You got a still hidden somewhere in here."

Adam answered in that quiet voice he reverted to when he was angry. "Rev, would you mind waiting for us downstairs?"

Pushing back the comforter, Kevin slid out of bed. As he stood, his foot stepped on what felt like a bottle. He stumbled, feeling someone's hand steady him.

"Here, let me help you." Dad put a set of clean clothes in his hands.

Once behind the locked door of the bathroom, Kevin eased off his shirt, surprised at the effort it took. His shoulder felt swollen and hot to the touch. With a growl, he thrust the used shirt on the floor and reached for a clean one.

So Dad wanted to put on a good show. Fine. Whatever. Kevin didn't have the time or desire to correct him. What difference would it make anyway? Who would believe him? Especially with the bottle of alcohol on his floor.

Stephanie M. E. Gallentine / refuge

He stood in front of the mirror. Nothing but an indiscernible reflection stared back. Pain and anger came together with the potency of one of Dad's mixed drinks. Dad would go to work as though nothing had happened. And Kevin would go back to the Center, never able to forget, and have to make up some story about last night. One that everyone could believe. No way would he tell them the truth. He could only imagine the response. A fifteen-year-old teenager letting his dad hurt him? No one gets hurt by your parent at fifteen. Maybe at five.

Shame covered him, the catalyst igniting his anger. So he was the disobedient son. The cause of all Dad's troubles. Fine. He opened the cabinet and grabbed the fullest bottle of shaving cream he could find. Using his good arm, he pulled back, channeling all his rage as he pounded the mirror in front of him with the can. It felt good to hear something else break for a change.

Shouts came from the other side of the door. He heard them, but it was like a shout from far away. The beating on the door like the beating of his heart, keeping time to the strikes on the glass, forming a cacophonous rhythm. A nightmarish song, a haunting melody, spurred on by a broken and beaten-down soul.

The rage crescendoed, then slowly faded to an end. Spent, Kevin leaned back against the opposite wall. Beads of sweat trailed down the sides of his face. He grimaced, feeling the physical pain resurface in his shoulder. It wouldn't be long before someone would get the doorknob off. Another thing Dad seemed to be gifted at.

Kevin popped another prescription Ibuprofen and then shoved the rest of the bottle into his pocket. He

Chapter 17

turned on the water, dipped his face under the spigot, and took a long drink to wash it down.

The doorknob rattled. Kevin decided to be merciful and save them the trouble.

Adam pulled him out of the bathroom as soon as the door opened. Everyone was speaking, but he didn't care. Instead, he waited as Dad surveyed the damage. Would he explode? Show his true colors? Then everyone would know him for the man he truly was.

"I think it's time you go," Dad said, a strange calmness providing a thin shield for his desired reaction. He spoke to Adam. "Now do you see why I ask you to take him?"

Kevin felt as if he'd been punched in the gut as he stared at the hardened man Dad had become. It was the one time he was thankful Adam had tightened the hold around his waist when he tried to move. Otherwise he might have fallen.

"Yes, I think I do."

chapter 18

Hours later, Kevin awakened to the jerking of the plane as it skirted the wave-filled waters of the Pacific. His stomach lurched. An acidic taste surfaced in the back of his throat and then disappeared.

He slung his backpack on his good shoulder and stepped off the plane. A soft wind blew over him and evaporated the cold sweat that covered his face. Again his stomach flipped and turned. As if on cue, his mouth watered and filled with saliva. He swallowed, took another step, and realized there would be no holding it at bay. Using the side of the plane to guide him, Kevin hurried to the water's edge, leaned forward, and emptied what little existed in his stomach.

Bags of luggage hit the deck. Arms came from behind and wrapped protectively around him.

"Come on, let's get you inside. You still look pretty green," Adam said, his voice level.

"Just a sec." He knelt down and cupped some seawater in his hands to rinse his face. The cool water felt good as it dribbled down his face and neck. With a firm grip on his backpack, he rose and then stumbled a half step to the side.

Arms tightened around him as Adam guided him in. Kevin would have fussed, but he didn't have the strength.

"You know he seems more drunk now than he did this morning," Rev murmured to Adam.

Kevin gave him the best death glare he could under the circumstances. What did they know? Had anyone checked his alcohol blood level? Had they checked Dad's? No! They just assumed because of appearances. Inside his anger coiled around him like a boa constrictor. Was there no one on his side?

As they entered the elevator, Kevin shook off Adam's arm. He didn't need anyone's help. Even without his glasses, he could still feel for the right floor button.

Adam intercepted him. "I got it."

The door slid shut and opened again within seconds.

"Not my floor," Kevin protested even as his stomach began to reel again.

"It is now." Adam propelled him forward when he didn't move. "Besides you're in no condition to be alone right now."

"I need my glasses."

"I'll send someone to get them, but the best thing for a hangover is sleep."

"Fine." Kevin allowed Adam to lead him to the spare room in their apartment. He placed his backpack on the

Chapter 18

bed. As soon as he heard the door close, he pulled the second bottle of pills from his backpack. The first ones made him too nauseated. But the pain in his shoulder had increased, and he was desperate for some sort of relief. He pulled the bottle as close as his eyes would allow him and concentrated on making out the larger letters. T-y-l-, he read. Tylenol. It must be, but it took too much effort to make out all the letters. He popped two of them and fell back into bed. Maybe this injury wasn't so different from a hangover. Maybe he could sleep it off.

Kevin rolled over in bed and cast off the blankets. His arms and abdomen felt on fire. The urge to scratch was relentless. Where were his glasses? He scooted over toward the nightstand in hopes that Adam had retrieved them. Relief washed over him when he felt the folded frames. He quickly slipped them on and sighed as the world came into focus once again.

Another need surfaced, and Kevin slipped into the small half-bath. Finished, he pulled back his sleeves and let the warm water run over his hands. It was then he noticed a series of small, angry raised spots on his arms accompanied by the desperate need to scratch.

He sucked in a deep breath and then bent over, clutching the counter, as a feeling somewhere between nausea and dizziness assailed him. He needed to lie down. That was it. Go back to sleep. Maybe this was nothing more than a nightmare. How many times had he had dreams that were this real?

The door swished open to his room. Adam called out to him. "Kevin?"

Kevin slammed the bathroom door and locked it. "In here." He couldn't believe it. For the third time in as many days, he was hiding out in the bathroom.

"How are you feeling?"

He rubbed at the welts. "Fine."

"Chelsea made some soup. Said you needed to get up and try to eat something."

"Okay, just give me a few." Kevin waited until he heard Adam leave before rummaging through the drawers and shelving behind the mirror on the off chance they kept some anti-itch cream. He opened the cabinet doors below the sink. Rolls of toilet paper filled the space. Good grief. How much toilet paper did they think it took?

Just in case anyone was listening, Kevin leaned over and flushed the toilet. Then he did a quick double search. Nothing but towels, soap, and gobs of toilet paper. He sighed, made sure his sleeves covered his arms, and after several more deep breaths to clear away the nausea, went out to join Adam and Chelsea.

The aroma of chicken noodle soup drifted through his nasal passages. His stomach must have caught wind of it because it turned as though daring him to try it—challenging him to see how long it would take before the soup reversed course.

"Have a seat." Chelsea set her spoon aside and brought Kevin a bowl of soup and a cup of hot tea. When he protested, she shook her head. "Just try a bit. You'll probably feel better once you have something on your stomach."

Chapter 18

Adam leaned back in the wooden chair. "How are you feeling?"

"I'm fine."

"I think you need a new blanket answer."

Kevin glared into his soup bowl, stirring his spoon along the bottom.

"I talked to your dad just a bit ago," Adam said.

Kevin rolled his eyes. What more could Dad possibly have to say?

"He said he ordered a spare set of glasses, and he'll send them on the next flight out."

He shrugged. "Whatever." Is that all it took to atone Dad's conscience?

"I would think you'd be more grateful considering you depend on them the way you do."

"I'm fine."

Chelsea interrupted. "How's your head?"

Confused and embarrassed, Kevin met her gaze. "What are you talking about?"

"I've always heard hangover headaches are the worst."

"I didn't have a hangover."

Adam scowled at him. "Then whose alcohol was in your room? Aiden's?"

It would be so easy to blame his friend right now. They were seven hours away from the nearest state. And although he couldn't fix what had happened last night with Aiden and his father, he could at least tell a small amount of truth. "No. Aiden didn't have anything to do with last night."

"Kevin, are you all right?"

Kevin yanked his sleeve down. Without even realizing

it, he'd been scratching at the irritation on his arm. He'd have to be more careful if he didn't want Chelsea to find out. "I'm going to go lie down."

"Kevin, wait."

He ignored her and charged off to his room.

A heavy hand caught hold of his left shoulder and applied pressure to stop him. Pain spiked down his arm. Kevin cried out. Unable to stop himself, his knees buckled and slammed into the floor.

Chelsea suddenly knelt in front of him. "Kevin, tell me where it hurts."

He swallowed back the nausea. Why was it people passed out from the pain in books, but he was fully coherent? In between breaths he whispered, "Shoulder."

"Can you tell me what happened?"

"Accident." Kevin clenched his teeth against the pain.

"Accident? What sort of accident?" She pulled back the sleeve of his hoodie, exposing the still spotted arm. A frown creased her lips. "You're having an allergic reaction. I need to know if you've eaten or drank anything out of the ordinary."

Kevin shook his head. Did they have to play twenty questions?

Chelsea's fingers encircled his wrist, took his pulse, and counted his respirations. After a long sigh, she pulled his face around to her. "This is important. Did you take something?"

Kevin sucked in a deep breath. "It hurt."

"I'm sure it did," Chelsea said, her tone full of understanding. She sent a questioning glance over to Adam before asking. "What did you take?"

Chapter 18

"Backpack." Footsteps pounded the floor behind him as Adam hurried to retrieve the pills. Kevin's eyes slid shut. Never in his life could he remember having a reaction like this. It frightened him, made him feel like he would die any minute and yet he remained.

Adam handed Chelsea the two bottles of pills. "Kevin, which one did you take?"

"Tylenol . . . here," he said. "Ibuprofen . . . before . . . coming."

She dumped the white pills from the Tylenol bottle into her hand. "These aren't regular Tylenol. Someone used the bottle and put hydrocodone in here instead. Couldn't you tell these weren't regular Tylenol by looking?" She stopped as it dawned on her what she had just said. "Never mind. We'll deal with that later. All right, it's probably a codeine allergy—very common." Her voice held a certain cadence to it that soothed his nerves. "Do you think you can walk or do you want me to call for a gurney?"

Kevin blanched. Gurney? Ohhhhh no. "I'm fine. I just need to sleep it off."

Chelsea shook her head. "I'm afraid you're beyond sleeping it off." She motioned for Adam. "Let's get him down to the infirmary. I need to get an x-ray of that shoulder and start some meds."

"No!" They couldn't take him. He didn't have a story yet. Didn't want her to see. Not now. Not like this. "Please."

"Not this time." Chelsea pulled him slowly to his feet. "I need to see what you've done to yourself."

What he'd done to himself? Too bad that hadn't been the case.

"Adam, make sure he keeps that arm folded across his chest. I want the least amount of jarring possible."

With help from Adam and Chelsea, Kevin slowly rose from the floor. How he wished, hoped, prayed he could pass out and forget this moment. It didn't work. Each moment found itself indelibly etched into his memory. He ground his teeth as Chelsea held his bent left arm over his chest.

She must have caught his reaction. Her eyes filled with concern, and she swiped his hair back from his forehead. "We'll get you fixed up. Just a few more minutes."

Kevin twisted his head to the side.

Chelsea heaved a heavy sigh as she and Adam walked him the short distance to the elevator and then to the infirmary.

Kevin closed his eyes, refusing to focus on anything except Chelsea who squeezed his hand as they helped him up onto one of the beds. He opened his eyes wide when he felt a tourniquet constrict his upper arm. "Can't I just take a pill?"

"It seems that's what got you into this mess in the first place." Chelsea patted his arm in search of a vein. "Now hold still. You'll feel a sting, but I doubt it'll compare to the pain you're already in."

He stiffened when the needle broke the skin, hating the way everything was tumbling down around him. Pretty soon they'd be asking questions. He still needed a plausible story.

Anna Lisa appeared in his line of vision. "Adam called and said you might need some help."

"Good. Would you get me the Promethazine and a syringe?" Chelsea asked.

Chapter 18

Kevin looked up, eyes wide. "What's that?"

"It'll stop the nausea. I'm also giving you some Diphenhydramine for your reaction." Chelsea paused, adjusting the flow of the IV, and then bent over to insert the drug into it. "As soon as we get your reaction and pain under control, we'll get an x-ray of that shoulder."

"Don't bother. I probably just pulled a muscle. I—" The rest of his protest was cut off by a burning sensation that traveled up his arm.

"The burning will stop in a moment. Trust me. The relief will be worth it." She smiled down at him. "Now, about that arm, why don't you let me be the doctor right now? Hmmm?"

He nodded. That's what scared him the most.

chapter 19

Like Chinese water torture, Adam's soft rhythmic snores threatened to drive Kevin insane. Glaring, he twisted his head to the side as if he could stare the sleeping man into silence. It didn't work. Adam slept on, and Kevin didn't have the heart to wake him. All through the night, Adam's murmured prayers had filtered through Kevin's drug induced haze. And like the hum of a ceiling fan, it comforted him.

He told himself they were just words, but the thought that someone cared enough to spend time praying for his well-being affected him more than he cared to admit. In contrast, Dad was more concerned about his own well-being than Kevin's.

"How are you feeling?" Chelsea appeared on the other side of the bed, a chart in one hand and a pen in the other.

Stephanie M. E. Gallentine / refuge

"Fine."

She smiled at him and then busied herself checking readouts on the IV drip machine. "Fine or well medicated?"

Kevin grinned. "Maybe a little of both."

"How's the nausea?"

"It's gone." He lifted his arm with the IV still intact. "Can we get rid of this?"

She nodded. "I don't see why not. Last night I wasn't sure what we were dealing with." Chelsea laid a fresh icepack on his shoulder.

Kevin hissed. "So what's the verdict?"

"Well, you had an allergic reaction to the Codeine. That you knew. You also have a bad AC joint sprain in your shoulder. I'm—"

Adam let loose a snore that could have registered a seismic reading of at least three point two. The man's head seemed to vibrate against the wall his head leaned on as he slumbered in a chair across from them.

"Somebody put a plug in that," Kevin mumbled under his breath.

Chelsea leaned over and peeled back the tape that held the IV in place. She giggled. "Don't look so irritated. You weren't exactly quiet yourself last night."

"I don't snore."

"But you do grind your teeth." With a quick tug, she pulled the plastic needle from beneath the skin and pressed a cotton ball and tape over the small puncture wound. "Reminded me of a rusty swing in some horror film." She imitated the high-pitched squeak and then plugged her ear as if the very thought brought on pain.

Kevin rolled his eyes. "I didn't ask him to stay."

Chapter 19

Chelsea's grimace softened into a smile. "You didn't ask him to leave either."

"I wouldn't have left anyway." Adam stretched out in the chair, arching his back, and scrubbing his face where patches of dark hair peeked out from below the pale skin of his lower face. "How're you feeling?"

"Fine."

Chelsea made a place for herself at the end of Kevin's bed and sat down. "Feel up to telling me what happened to your arm?"

"Not really." He had a story but wasn't sure if she'd buy it.

Adam glared at him. "She wasn't really asking."

"Why do you need to know? It isn't going to change anything."

"First, because I care." Chelsea reached for his chart in the holder at the end of his bed. "Second, because I'm required by law to ask and log it into your chart." After a slight pause, she asked, "Were you with your friend?"

"And be forewarned, I'll know if you're lying," Adam said.

Kevin scrunched up his face at Adam's remark. "What are you, a walking lie detector test?"

"Something like that."

He rolled his eyes.

"So what happened?" Chelsea asked.

The hours Kevin had been awake this morning paid off. At least he thought he had a plausible story. As far as he was concerned, his story would be more believable than the truth. Now he had to make it convincing. He turned to glance at Chelsea, bit his bottom lip, and did his best to appear hesitant. "It was a dark and rainy night."

"Kevin." There was a warning in Adam's voice.

"Well, it was." He shifted his gaze to the ceiling. "Aiden and I decided to go to the park and talk."

"And what possessed you to do that?"

"I don't know. We were bored, and it seemed like the thing to do at the time."

"So this all started because you and Aiden were bored." Chelsea grasped her forehead, shaking her head.

"Pretty much." Kevin paused.

"Then what happened?" she asked.

He blew out a long breath before a wave of pain hit him, causing him to clench his teeth. After catching Chelsea's observant eye, he quickly went on. "We got bored and decided to goof around on the merry go round."

Chelsea's eyes slid shut. She shook her head.

"We were horsing around, taking turns pushing one another. Had it going pretty fast too. The harder the rain pelted us, the faster we pushed it."

Something changed in Adam's expression. He chuckled. "Quite the rush, huh?"

Kevin played along with him. His face lit up. "Oh yeah. But then a huge crack of lightning lit up the sky. I kind of got distracted and lost my grip on the slick bars. The next thing I know, I went flying and landed on my shoulder." *There*, he thought, pleased with himself. That sounded believable.

Chelsea still looked unsure. "Is that how you broke your glasses?"

Kevin nodded, his breath catching when he shifted his shoulder.

"I think it's time for your next dose of pain medication." Chelsea handed him two small white caplets along

Chapter 19

with a glass of water. "Which brings me to another topic of conversation—self-medication."

He cringed and slumped into the bed. He'd wondered when she was going to bring that up.

"Your dad said he put prescription meds in the Tylenol bottle to take to work when his teeth were acting up. You were already here, and he forgot about doing it. But from this point on, any medicine you need will come from me. Understood?" Her cool hand brushed his forehead, sweeping back his hair. "You don't know how scared I was yesterday."

Kevin nodded, unsure of how to respond. It had been a long time since he had felt this cared for. He pulled the blanket up and allowed his eyes to close, willing the drugs to hurry and put him to sleep. Anything to escape the rush of emotions that threatened to break through his carefully constructed wall.

Four days later, Kevin threw down his electronic reader. He was sick to death of reading. Even the adventures of Cosmic Warrior couldn't hold his interest. He'd lost count of how many times he had read every issue. Of course, there was always homework to be done—like he could concentrate on that either.

Once again, he was the victim. This time the assailant was boredom. Every electronic device had been taken from him except for his reader. It had to be a conspiracy. Somewhere they were laughing. Didn't the adults realize they lived in a technological world? Taking away everything was the worst kind of torture ever. How was he supposed to function? No video games, no laptop, no Internet, no movies, no LinkWay.

It didn't seem fair. Both Dad and Tyke had gotten what they wanted, while Kevin and Aiden bore the punishment.

Aiden.

He needed to talk to him, to apologize. There had to be some way to fix this without dragging all his family skeletons out for viewing. He'd come up with one story for Adam and Chelsea. Surely he could come up with another that would satisfy Aiden's dad and get his friend out of trouble. It wasn't like he didn't have the time. All he needed was one phone call.

Kevin pushed himself up from the bed and padded into the living room where Adam reclined in his overstuffed recliner.

"Hey."

Adam looked up from his book. "Hey yourself. How's it going?"

"Fine." Kevin glanced around the room, trying to think of a way to ask. After several moments, he spit it out. "I need to make a phone call. Just one. I owe someone an apology for what happened that night."

"Your father?"

"No!" Kevin scrunched up his face. Adam had to be crazy to think he owed that man an apology. "Aiden."

"I see."

Silence engulfed the space between them. Kevin took the moment to explain. "I left some things in quite a mess. I just need to talk to him for five minutes. That's all I'm asking."

The recliner came forward as Adam sat up and heaved a heavy sigh, thinking.

Chapter 19

Five. The silent countdown began. Kevin had observed this too many times with Dad

Four. Adam raked a hand through his hair.

Three. Kevin felt confident enough to lean back on the couch and wait.

Two. Adam heaved another sigh, gave an almost unperceivable nod. Still thinking.

One. Here it was. Adam was about to cave. Kevin suppressed the smug grin waiting to emerge.

Adam rose from his chair and returned with an ink pen and spiral notebook. He handed them to Kevin.

"What's that?" As if he didn't already know.

"Your newest hard drive and printer."

"What?" Kevin shook his head. "No way."

"Mark will be flying in Saturday night and leaving right after the service Sunday morning. That should give you plenty of time to get a letter written. Mark can mail it as soon as he gets back to the States."

"Why can't I just call?"

Adam sat back down in his chair and leaned forward on his elbows. "Because your father and I agreed you needed the distance."

"Oh, and three thousand miles isn't enough?"

"I'm sorry."

"No, you're not."

Adam's eyes widened. "Oh, you want to talk about sorry? Sorry is part of the reason I won't give in." In answer to Kevin's questioning gaze, Adam went on, "You're sorry, but that's it."

"What more do you want?"

"Repentance."

Kevin balked. "Look, I didn't bring my church dictionary with me, and I already told you I didn't want anything to do with church."

"I'm not talking about church. It's true that repentance is an important step to salvation, but it's also important in our daily lives."

Kevin threw back his head and rolled his eyes. Here it came. The one thing he'd worked so hard to avoid. Religious conversations.

"You're sorry things didn't turn out the way you wanted them to. You're sorry you got caught. You may even be sorry your friend got into trouble. But not sorry enough to want to change."

"Maybe I'm not the one who needs to change."

"So said the man brought before the judge on murder charges. 'Judge, I'm sorry, but my hands squeezed a little too hard around her neck. If only she'd held her breath a little longer, she might not be dead.'"

Kevin grinned at the weird illustration coupled with the change in Adam's voice to one of a prisoner.

"The appalled judge continued to listen while the man even took it a step further. 'In fact, Your Honor, if you examine the situation, you'll find out it was really her fault. If she hadn't pushed me and made me so angry, I wouldn't have hurt her.'"

Like the darkness, eclipsing the sun, Kevin's face fell. How many times had his own dad said those words? If Kevin hadn't made him so mad, Dad wouldn't have hurt him. Anger shrouded him. A phone call wasn't worth this conversation.

"Kevin?"

Chapter 19

"I'm not the one you should be having this conversation with."

"Then who?"

"Just forget it." Kevin growled, snatched up the paper and pen, and headed to his room. Boredom now seemed a safe haven.

Steven Ramsey sat opposite his worst nemesis in the small alcove he used for his home office. The tension between them felt immeasurable

William Tyke's face contorted with an inner rage. "I warned you, Ramsey." He punctuated each word with an unspoken threat.

Steven met his gaze, giving away nothing of the nervousness the other man created in him. "And you got your CD. So we have nothing left to discuss."

"Was this your idea of a joke?" Tyke waved the CD in front of him. "Or are you so unaware of what your son is capable of?"

"Are you saying you're incapable of a simple install?"

Tyke growled and spoke through gritted teeth. "I know how to install a fix. I also know when I've been had."

Steven gulped. What had those boys done? "I had no idea. But I'm afraid Kevin's not here anymore to ask."

"But I know where he is."

The ominous tenor of his voice sent a shiver down Steven's back. He mirrored the frigidness. "Don't even think about it. You can't touch Kevin out there. I won't let you."

"Who says I haven't already?"

Stephanie M. E. Gallentine / refuge

The words hung in the air like a knife ready to plunge deep into Steven's heart. "What have you done?"

"Exactly what you do. I protect my reputation at all costs." Tyke rose from his seat and strode out the door.

The air in Steven's lungs came out in a rush. What had he done? Two sides within him argued, battled for dominance. He glanced at the now repaired French doors. Nothing but a memory remained of that night he had once again lost control of his temper in his desire to protect his reputation. But had the cost been worth it?

Somehow he had to figure out a way out of this mess. In the meantime, he'd have to find another safe place for Kevin.

Steven rubbed at his aching temples even as the headache escalated. As he blew out a long breath, he reached for a glass and a nearby bottle. He needed a drink if he were to calm down and think. Yes, he just needed a drink.

chapter 20

Sunday morning Kevin smiled when everyone left for church services and left him free of their ever-watchful eyes. After waiting another ten minutes, he hurried to Adam's office. Although Rev had changed everyone's passcodes, people in a hurry still didn't pay attention to who might be watching. Again, Kevin could boast of at least four passcodes so far—Adam's included.

Once behind the desk, Kevin pulled out the LinkWay. He let out a sigh of relief. Finally. For the past week Kevin had felt cut off from the real world. He desperately needed contact with someone outside the Center.

Within moments, Aiden's surprised face appeared on the LinkWay screen. "Man, I thought they had you on LinkWay lockdown."

"They do. But I had to find a way to call." Kevin paused. "I'm sorry for what happened."

Aiden nodded. "So you gonna tell my dad now and get me out of this mess."

"I wish it were that easy. I—"

"It is that easy, Kevin. If nothing else, stay on the line and nod your head while I tell him."

"I . . . I can't. You know that." Agony swept over him once more. "I wish you understood."

Aiden leaned back in his chair and glared at Kevin. "You wanna know what I understand? I understand that thanks to your father's lie and your silence, I'm grounded for the next month. That grounding also includes my car and my job at Rollings Securities."

Kevin's mouth dropped open in surprise.

"Yeah, that's right. My parents were furious. So furious that my car almost ended up with a 'for sale' sign on it."

"I'm so sorry."

"Doesn't matter. Mom stopped Dad from actually selling my car. Now I just can't drive it again until I'm thirty."

Kevin cradled his head in his hands. "Put your dad on the phone. I'll tell him you didn't know I had the alcohol. That it was all my fault."

Aiden rolled his eyes. "Don't bother. He's already certain if I hadn't become friends with you, I would have turned out a much better person."

"I'm sorry, so sorry."

"It's all right." Aiden took a sip from his drink. "I do kind of understand. I mean, I have no idea what I'd have done in your shoes."

"I hope you never have to find out."

Chapter 20

"I won't because my parents would never treat me the way your father treats you. Remember, my dad gave you a job in ethical hacking to try and keep you *out* of trouble. Your dad pushed you into more trouble."

"He's not that bad, you know." Kevin picked up a pen and began doodling on a scratch piece of paper. "It's cause he was afraid of going to jail for something he didn't do."

Aiden let loose a callous laugh. "Well, he's certainly not afraid of sending you, now is he?"

"What?" Kevin's heart felt like it stopped.

"You don't know? Oh man, they really do have you on communication lockdown."

Fear crawled up from the pit of his stomach, leaving an acrid taste in the back of his throat. Kevin waited for his friend to explain.

"Do you remember me telling you Rom had to tweak the fix?"

"Yeah. Something about cracker jacks."

Aiden stared down at the hands clutching his legs. "Rom didn't believe the story you gave me about your dad's computer. He wore me down. I finally told him about Tyke and what he was doing."

"What!" Kevin shot up from his seat and slammed his fist on the desk, causing the LinkWay to jump. His best friend had betrayed him.

"I didn't mean to. But he was right, Kevin. You need help." Aiden sucked in a deep breath and let it out. "Anyway, he installed a Cracker Jack virus to the fix."

The springs on the chair bounced as Kevin plopped back down. This was impossible. He wasn't sure if he wanted to hear the rest. But he continued to listen.

"He set the fix to run. But as soon as Tyke hit any key after the restart, another virus took over and connected him to the internet. Before Tyke could open any file, it condensed all the contents on Tyke's hard drive and emailed it to a file dump Rom created."

"So Tyke still never saw the file?"

Aiden shook his head. "No. But now we have it."

"You don't sound too happy about it."

"No," Aiden replied. "Tyke went to Damon and showed him some video feed with you in your dad's car in it. Tyke also showed documentation where a large sum of money had been removed." Aiden stared back down at the floor. "Your dad said you used your knowledge of their systems and hacked into the mainframe and did it while he attended some New Year's Eve party Tyke picked him up for."

So this was the addendum to his never-ending nightmare.

"Mr. Damon pressed charges. I guess you're due in court Tuesday morning. Your dad chartered a flight and should already be on his way out there to get you."

"And no one said anything, why?" Inside, Kevin fumed. Why hadn't anyone told him? No wonder Adam had been so adamant that he not have any communication with anyone from McKeltic.

"Don't ask me. I found out when I got a call from Rom. He wants to help, Kevin."

"Don't you think he's helped enough?" Kevin glared. "Rom should have just done what I asked."

"You still think this is all about you? Surprise, it's not." Aiden's eyes darkened. "Did you know I found out my dad invested a chunk of his retirement in Tyke's supposed

Chapter 20

resort? How about Prof? He bought a couple of shares. And Joe, down at Galactic Jitters, told us how he and his mom scraped together enough money to buy a share. What about them?"

Aiden didn't give him a chance to respond. "How do you think I'm gonna feel when I have to tell my dad that I knew it was a scam and I helped Tyke get to his money? And then you don't even want me to tell my dad the truth of why I did it? You know, Kevin, you can whine all you want. But remember you don't have to face everyone every day and know what I know. And I wasn't brought up to lie."

"Me either."

"Your whole life has been a lie. Your mom changed your age, your identity. You couldn't trust your best friend enough to tell me you are legally blind. You make up stuff or you don't answer. Everything has to be on your terms, cause if it isn't, your whole life is going to unravel." Aiden scowled at him. "No wonder you want to run away."

"Aiden—"

"Maybe my dad was right. I should have been more careful who I became friends with."

"I'm sorry. I—"

"Really? Are you? Apparently not sorry enough to do the right thing for once." Aiden curled his lip and shook his head. His hand reached up to the disconnect button on the LinkWay. "I gotta go. If I get caught talking to you, my dad really will put my car up for sale, and I'm tired of losing. Maybe after a year of juvie, you will be too."

The screen went dark. Shock, and then like a slow burn, anger engulfed him. With both of his hands, Kevin shoved the LinkWay aside. Who was Aiden to judge? What did he know?

Stephanie M. E. Gallentine / refuge

Kevin stormed out of the office. Like the roaring winds of a Texas tornado, emotions swirled about him. Anger, bitterness, betrayal, and pain. The broken remnants of his life flew past him like debris. Dad couldn't be satisfied that Kevin had borne the blame for everything thus far. Now he had to take it a step further. Why couldn't Dad stand up for him? Wasn't it enough that he'd sent his son away until he was of age?

Each step propelled him forward, the destructive power growing in the vacant hall. All the elements had come together in a violent mix. There could be no stopping it now. Either Kevin would have some form of release or implode.

Was this how Dad felt when rage overtook him? Maybe he wasn't so different from Dad after all. He was simply a younger mix of the same ingredients. So what did it matter anymore what he did?

The door opened to the apartment. Chelsea, Adam, and Rev sat around the dining room table talking.

"So you both plan to fly back with him?" Rev asked.

Adam nodded. "Of course. Hopefully we can be back before the end of the week."

Kevin glared as he stormed past them into the kitchen. It was true. Dad was on his way, and Kevin would be back in juvie in two days' time. With the force of a superhero, Kevin yanked open the door of the refrigerator and felt a small amount of satisfaction when it banged the cabinets beside it and rattled the knickknacks on a nearby shelf. Once he grabbed a water bottle, he slammed the door closed with an equal amount of force.

"Kevin!" Chelsea scolded him.

"What?" he yelled back.

Chapter 20

Adam's low voice held a warning. "Kevin."

"Oh, I'm sorry. Was I not supposed to be angry when I found out I was being carted off to juvie?"

"How did you find out?" Chelsea rose slowly from her seat.

"Does it matter? I did, but I'm not going back and you can't make me." Kevin didn't wait to hear their excuses. He didn't care. Turning on his heel, he headed for the door.

Someone caught up to him and caught the back of his hoodie.

Furious, Kevin instantly turned and shoved with all his might.

Chelsea's body landed on the floor in a heap.

Kevin sucked in a breath. His hands shook. "I'm sorry. I didn't mean to . . ." His voice trembled and trailed off.

From across the room, Adam and Rev approached, giving him death glares of their own. Fists curled at their sides, arm muscles tensed, they held the visage of henchmen on a hit.

After a glance at Chelsea as she pulled herself from the floor, Kevin slowly backed away. There was nowhere to go. If he ran, they'd catch him, and then what? The heartbeat in his chest increased in rhythm and intensity with every step. For a second, he allowed his gaze to travel around the room. They all stood back as though watching a scene in a book play out.

"Kevin, sit down," Adam said with his quiet authority.

He shook his head. "I'm not going back. I'll run before I do, and I swear this time you'll never catch me."

"Not this time. We'll help you all we can, but running is not an option," Adam said.

"You can't help me."

"But God can."

"Well, last time I checked, you weren't God."

Adam took a deep breath and then let it out. "Sit down, Kevin. We need to talk."

"No." With every step closer that Adam came, Kevin battled the hidden fear within himself. In his mind, he knew with certainty that Adam would never hurt him, but his nerves, his breathing, his heart rate, all the automatic responses had a mind-set of their own. Alarms blared inside of him.

Adam picked up his pace, closing the distance between them.

Defend! Defend! His mind had now joined his body. It shouted to him. His eyes darted around the room. In one fluid movement, Kevin located the bat and ripped it from the display hooks. He pulled it back in readiness to strike. "Don't come any closer."

The atmosphere changed. A heavy silence settled in the room. Adam halted, examining the situation. "Kevin put that down. No one's going to hurt you."

"That would be a first," he mumbled sarcastically.

It must have been loud enough though. His head jerked around at the sound of a gasp. Chelsea. Once more, he let his gaze travel around the room. What had he just done? This wasn't him. He kept everything inside.

Adam took another step.

After a hard gulp, Kevin tightened his grip on the bat. "I swear I'll pound anyone who comes near."

Adam stopped. He turned to Chelsea and Rev. "I want both of you to sit down." Once they complied, Adam said to Kevin, "Now I want you to put the bat down. Then we'll talk."

Chapter 20

"That's your answer to everything, huh? Let's talk. Well, I'm sick of talking." When Adam took a tentative step forward, Kevin swung the bat. As it contacted with the wall, one of Chelsea's pictures fell from the wall. Glass shattered.

Chelsea put her hand on Adam's arm, pulling him back. "Kevin, I'm not going to pretend I understand what's going on." She stood facing him, arms at her side. "I do know you won't hurt me. Your mother taught you never to hit a woman, didn't she?"

Kevin swallowed hard. The bat felt slick in his grip. He couldn't answer. All his emotions were too near the surface.

"Now, I'm going to walk to you, and I want you to give me the bat." She took two small steps toward him.

"No," he said, but without the same vehemence of before.

Chelsea edged closer, her voice smooth and tranquil, like a gentle stream in a forest. "Then if you need to take a walk, you can. No one will stop you. And when you're ready to talk, we'll talk."

"You say that now."

"And I mean it. If anyone tries to go after you, I'll hit them with the bat myself." Chelsea looked back on the two men as if daring them to try it.

Kevin couldn't suppress his grin.

"I imagine your shoulder's giving you fits right now."

He nodded. The ache had gradually morphed into pain. She crossed the room, got a few items, and returned. The bottle rattled as Chelsea tipped it in her hand and then held out two white tablets. Kevin eyed it with suspicion. "How do I know you won't drug me?"

Stephanie M. E. Gallentine / refuge

"Because I not only want the bat, I want your trust."

Kevin lowered the bat, but kept one hand in a firm grip. With his other hand, he reached first for the proffered pills and then the small cup of water. He quickly tipped his head, downing the water, appreciating her kindness after what he had done to her.

"Now, do you need some time alone?"

Once more, he nodded. After letting the bat clatter to the floor, he turned and ran.

chapter 21

Adam panned the room and surveyed the damage. Like the calm that descended after a storm, the room held an eerie stillness. Slivers of glass glistened in the earth tone carpet like spotlights shining on the picture of him and Chelsea that lay angled on the floor. The wall above it now sported a vacant spot with a partial impression of the rounded end of the bat. Not far from him, Chelsea bent forward and retrieved the bat. Not exactly the way he'd pictured his favorite memento would be used.

Rev broke the tenuous silence. "What just happened in here?"

Leave it to Rev to draw attention to the obvious. Adam raked a hand through his hair. Good grief, now he was beginning to sound like Kevin. Just what the world needed—two Kevins. "Rev, would you mind getting my LinkWay from the office?"

His long time friend nodded and left.

"Are you all right?" He stepped toward Chelsea, who stared blankly at the bat in her hand.

She nodded. "I feel like we failed him."

"It wasn't us who failed him." Adam could feel his eyes smoldering. He plopped down on the couch and threw his head back. Time was running out. Steven Ramsey was due here in a few short hours, and they needed answers. Answers he wondered if he was prepared to hear.

He arched his back, trying to work out the tension. He needed a massage, an aspirin, and probably before the day was out, a padded cell. Whether to beat *his* head against the wall or someone else's, he didn't know. The protective nature in him rose like an angry lion. Now more than ever, he hated the fact he hadn't searched harder after his accident. But he had only thought of himself and his loss at the time. He grimaced, not wanting to think about the possibility.

Rev returned with the LinkWay and excused himself. Chelsea sat down next to him on the couch. "Who are you calling?"

"Whoever Kevin called while we were at church." Adam powered on the device. While waiting for the system to load, he turned to Chelsea. "I'm hoping whomever he spoke to will have more information."

Chelsea folded her arms across her chest. "I think we have lots of information, but until today we didn't have the key."

Blowing out a deep breath, Adam glanced at his wife and then back down to the LinkWay. "I don't want to believe it."

Chapter 21

"I'm a doctor. I'm trained to believe anything." She twisted on the couch to get his attention. "But my training also tells me I don't believe Kevin went to the park that night or that he was drinking."

"Oh?" This was news to him.

"Kevin didn't sleep long after he got here. One of the first things I did was run a tox screen. I wanted to make sure we knew what we were dealing with. The test came back negative for anything except the Codeine, exactly what he said he had."

"But wouldn't the alcohol have filtered through his system already?"

She shook her head. "It depends on how much he had to drink. You said his father indicated Kevin had still been drinking in his room. You also indicated it was hard liquor, correct?" As soon as he nodded, Chelsea went on. "For the amount of liquor everyone thought he consumed, trace amounts should have still been present in his blood stream.

"Not only that. How would Kevin have gotten the liquor? Even if he managed to come by a fake ID, there's no way that baby face would pass for twenty-one."

"Maybe his friend," Adam suggested, but even he didn't believe that.

"Again, why?" She placed her right index finger on the finger of her upturned left palm. "Let's see if I have the story right. This friend—and I use the word loosely—called you and created enough anxiety that you called Kevin, who was obviously still at home. How was Kevin at that time?"

"The way he usually is. Sarcastic." He thought back to the LinkWay call, trying to remember details he might have missed. "I told him to get some sleep. He looked rough."

"Rough? How so?"

Adam shrugged. "Like I would have imagined him after the park incident."

"But Aiden hadn't gone over there yet. Was Kevin favoring his shoulder?"

"No." Adam remembered the hair that seemed to go in more directions than usual and seemed damp around the edges. "Like I said, he just looked rough."

"So his friend picked him up, bought him the alcohol, drove to the park, watched him drink it and showed no fear of being thrown up on while a drunk teenager spun on a merry-go-round. His friend is either very brave or very stupid."

"They're teenagers. Anything is possible," Adam said. "But it does sound a bit far-fetched now that I have time to think about it."

Chelsea snorted. "Far-fetched? That story has enough holes to sink a fleet of ocean liners."

"Why did Kevin lie to . . . ?" Adam didn't finish his own question. Kevin had told him he hadn't been drinking, but he hadn't believed the teen. So why would Kevin have expected them to believe anything else?

"That's our next objective—to find out why." She laid a hand on his shoulder and waited as the LinkWay called back the last contact.

Seconds later, a dark-headed teenager, much like Kevin except a little heavier, appeared on the screen. The teen's hazel eyes grew wide when he saw Adam's face.

For fear the teen would disconnect, Adam hurried to introduce himself. "Hello, I'm Adam Hollandale. And you are?"

Chapter 21

The teen glanced over his shoulder toward a door. He licked his lips before speaking. "Aiden."

Adam smiled, trying to put the boy at ease. Inside he was ecstatic. He'd hit pay dirt. "Ah, good, you must have been the one who called me that night on my cell."

Aiden nodded and cast another nervous glance over his shoulder.

"Don't worry. I didn't call to get you in trouble. What I need is some information." Adam paused. "When you called that night, you seemed awfully worried about Kevin, to the point I called his house."

Aiden shrugged. "I told you. I was worried when I found his cell in my car and knew he was leaving the next morning. You guys don't exactly live around the block."

"Not exactly." Adam grinned. "But then you spent the night with Kevin."

"No, Kevin called me later that night and invited me over."

"What time?" Adam hoped if he could get to the truth he'd have something to question Kevin with.

"I don't know. Ten, maybe?"

"Seems awfully late to invite someone over."

Aiden's gaze turned suspicious. He pressed his lips together into a thin angry line. "What do you want? If you want information, why don't you ask Kevin?" His finger hovered over the disconnect button. "I don't turn on my friends, like some people do."

"Who?" Adam asked, but the connection had already been severed. "That went well," he said with biting sarcasm. He frowned at the dark screen on his lap. "How many more teenagers do you think I can tick off before my work is done for the day?"

Chelsea grinned, but it didn't cover the determination he saw in her chocolate eyes. "As many as it takes."

Kevin peeked over his shoulder and breathed a deep sigh of relief. No one had followed him. As he whipped his head back around, he bumped into something wide and solid.

Mark, aka Mr.-Rogers-flies-a-plane, smiled down at him. "Hey, Kevin. How's it going?"

Kevin's brain scrambled for words. "Sorry. I . . . I didn't see you."

"Really?" The pilot chuckled. "I'm surprised you didn't hear me singing. Course that might be a good thing since my wife always says I sing like an alley cat under a full moon." He started to sing out a few bars.

Kevin forced out a thin smile. "Do you still have to leave today?" He hoped he didn't sound too eager. The wheels in the back of his mind were turning. A plan formulated.

"Yeah, in fact, I'm headed down to the galley to fill up my thermos, and I'll be on my way. The in-laws are having a family reunion this week, and I told my wife, Clarice, I'd fly out right after church." Mark rocked on the back of his feet, grinning so wide it nearly severed the top half of his face from the lower half. "I also promised my son we'd go bass fishing while the women catch up on the boring stuff."

Oh joy. So that was what went on in Mr. Roger's neighborhood. Kevin caught himself before he could roll his eyes. It was important to act natural if his plan was going

Chapter 21

to work. "I better get going. I'm kind of in trouble. Adam wants to 'talk' to me." Kevin formed quotation marks with his index fingers and let his eyes roll this time.

Mark chuckled. "What'd you do this time?"

Kevin shrugged. "Said more than I should've."

"Ah, that reminds me of what my mother used to say." The pilot reached up and adjusted the cap on his head. "A closed mouth gathers no foot."

"I thought it had something to do with a rolling stone and moss."

"Not in my house. We all talked too much. Mom had to adjust all the sayings to fit our smart aleck mouths." He nodded his head at Kevin. "You better get going. I'll see you next time."

A mischievous grin crept onto his lips as he waited for Mark to enter the elevator and the doors to slide shut. He doubted he had much time. Kevin hurried toward the stairs behind the elevator and flew up them two and three at a time. The clanging of the metal steps seemed to echo in the confined space.

Once he reached the door to the outside, Kevin punched in Adam's code and waited for the lock to release. He hesitated a moment and then activated his radio.

"Chelsea."

"Kevin?" There was a sigh of relief and then, "Are you all right?"

"Yeah. I . . . I just wanted to say I'm sorry . . . for everything." He hated it. Here he was using the "conversation." But it was safe.

"It's all right."

Stephanie M. E. Gallentine / refuge

Kevin cringed inside. No, it wasn't all right. Not today. Not tomorrow. Not ever. He sounded just like Dad. Another reason he needed to go. He couldn't allow himself to turn into the same monster his dad had turned into.

Her gentle voice brought him out of his thoughts. "Are you ready to talk?"

"Can I have another half hour or so?" He paused. "Please."

"All right, I'll let Adam know. And, Kevin?"

"Yeah?"

"I love you."

An unexpected knot formed in the back of his throat. Those words. She wasn't supposed to say them. It wasn't part of the conversation. Love? How could she love him after the way he lost it up in their apartment?

Kevin glanced at his watch. Mark would head toward the plane any minute. He hesitated. Maybe he shouldn't do this. But he had to. There was too much at stake.

"Thanks," he told her and shut off his radio. With renewed determination, he stepped onto the deck and breathed in his first breath of outside air in almost a week. The air had that certain taste and smell of expected rain. He leaned over the railing. The cool, brisk winds off the ocean rifled through the dark tendrils of his hair.

The wind beckoned him with the one thing it possessed that Kevin so desired: freedom. No one told the wind where to blow. It had the power to control everything in its way. If the wind so desired, it could call up a hurricane and destroy everything in its path or it could blow gently over a hot and dry land. No one could bind the wind.

Chapter 21

But Kevin could follow it—ride on it. Ride on freedom's wings.

After a quick glance below to make sure there was no one around, Kevin closed the door behind him. He took one last look at the Center, swallowing past the lump in his throat.

A sudden gust of wind blew past him. Droplets of ocean spray rained down on him. He swiped his hand over his face. Not more than a few feet away, the seaplane bobbed on the frothy waters of the Pacific Ocean. Freedom called.

Kevin ran. He had a plane to catch.

chapter 22

"It's been an hour." Adam paced the length of the apartment, stopping to glance at the wall clock every time he passed through the living room.

Laptop balanced on her lap, Chelsea smiled up at him from the couch. "You're the one who keeps saying to give him another ten minutes."

"It's just that . . ."

"And you were right. Give him plenty of space to calm down. The last thing we need is a repeat of earlier events." She typed something on the keyboard. "I'd really like to get to the bottom of this before his father arrives."

Adam nodded, taking another glance at the time. Two minutes later than last time he checked. He frowned and opened his mouth to say something when the LinkWay buzzed.

"Aiden?" he asked, surprised to see the teen's face on the screen.

Aiden nodded. "I'm sorry for cutting you off earlier. And I wouldn't have called back, but I really need to talk to Kevin."

"I see," Adam said.

"I know Kevin's not supposed to be on the LinkWay right now—me either, for that matter. But I really need to apologize to him."

A slow grin spread across his face. "Kevin said the same thing about you earlier this week. I take it he did that this morning."

"Yeah. But then everything blew up." Aiden sighed long and deep.

"Give me a minute. I'll get him." With a slight tap at the earpiece, Adam called Kevin's name.

No answer.

"Kevin," he tried again.

Still no answer.

"He's run off again, hasn't he?" Aiden asked from the LinkWay, having heard the exchange.

Adam chuckled to put the boy at ease. "I wouldn't say *run off*. There's no place here for him to go. You forget we're located in the middle of the Pacific Ocean."

Aiden's eye roll and shaking of his head told Adam exactly what the teen thought of his confidence. "You don't know Kevin."

Chelsea broke her silence and leaned into the LinkWay. "Then why don't you tell us."

Chapter 22

Kevin sunk into the back seat of the seaplane and stretched out his cramped legs while he searched for a set of earphones to muffle the loud drone of the plane's engines. As long as stayed deep in the seat, Mark wouldn't know anyone had come aboard with him until it was too late to send him back.

A satisfied grin emerged. He had actually made it. Granted, due to his impromptu departure, he had nothing on him. Not even a change of clothes or a bottle of water. None of that mattered anymore. Life had finally granted him his freedom.

His mind wandered back to the airfield in Texas before he'd come to the Center. After Adam had caught him from escaping, he told Kevin, "You'll need a wing and a prayer."

Adam had been wrong. Kevin didn't have to pray to find his way off that make-believe island. Once again, someone underestimated his determination. Maybe after this they would believe he didn't need anyone's help. In a few short hours, the plane would land, and he would prove it to them once and for all.

A shadow darkened the small cabin. Kevin glanced out the window. A dark cloud moved past them. At this height, the ominous cloud looked as if it could envelop the plane. This was a little too up close and personal for his taste. He swallowed and closed his eyes.

Just pretend you're already through it. Think of something else.

Chelsea's final words flashed through his mind. "I love you."

Those words would probably prove the hardest to run from.

"What do you want to know?" Aiden's cautious voice asked over the LinkWay.

Adam suppressed a knowing grin. Aiden didn't have a clue as to what he'd opened himself up to. Although used for a good purpose, his wife's melodic voice reminded him of the sailors' stories of the Sirens. Sailors found themselves mesmerized by both the beauty and voice of these mythical creatures and felt compelled to follow the sound.

Chelsea smiled gently. "How did Kevin injure his shoulder?"

The teen must have felt safe with that question. "That's all?"

"Unless you have something else you'd like to share," she said.

"No. Nothing."

"That's fine." Chelsea waved a reassuring hand. "So how did it happen?"

"Didn't Kevin tell you?"

"Yes, but I'm not sure who did most of the talking, him or the medication." She laughed softly and the teen chuckled in response. "Sometimes the medication can distort the story."

Adam continued to pace the floor out of sight of the LinkWay, listening, waiting for his wife to work her magic. He'd give Kevin another few minutes and then he'd have Rev ping the GPS on Kevin's radio. The worst that could have happened is the teen went outside and was hiding in one of the boats. Even so, the GPS would find him.

Chapter 22

Sighing, Adam pinched the bridge of his nose between his two fingers in a vain attempt to push back the headache building between his eyes.

"I don't know," Aiden said.

Chelsea didn't seem dissuaded by the answer. "It's all right. I didn't think you would. You're his friend. I'm sure all you wanted to do was help."

"There wasn't much I could do. He wouldn't go to the hospital."

Adam stopped pacing at the mention of the word "hospital." He sat down on the couch next to Chelsea and tried to watch the screen unnoticed.

"He can be stubborn, can't he?" She gave him a reassuring smile.

After a solemn nod, Aiden glanced down at the hands in his lap. "I didn't know how to help him."

Behind the teen, another figure came into view. Although more clean cut, it was like looking at an older version of Aiden. The man crossed the room and placed a hand on the teen's shoulder. "Help who, son?"

Aiden whirled around. His expression took on a deer-caught-in-the-headlights look. "Dad!"

The man peered into the LinkWay, his eyes narrowed with suspicion. "I'm sorry. I'm afraid we haven't been introduced."

Adam and Chelsea both introduced themselves. Chelsea added, "I apologize for calling like this, but we're trying to find out if Aiden knew how Kevin injured his shoulder the night he was in town."

Mr. Rollings shook his head, then threw Aiden a questioning glance. "I wasn't aware that Kevin hurt himself. But with all the drinking that night, I'm not surprised."

"He wasn't drinking, Dad. I tried to tell you."

"Aiden, I appreciate you trying to take up for your friend, but his dad said—"

"His dad lied."

Adam's radio chose that moment to come alive. He hopped off the couch and tapped it upon hearing his name. "Kevin?"

"No, it's Rev." There was a slight pause. "I take it you're looking for Kevin too."

"Too?"

"I'm not so sure you want to hear this."

He walked into the living room, out of Aiden's view and hearing. "At this point, I've given up on what I want to hear. It can't get much worse than it is now. Spill it."

There was an exaggerated pause. "Yeah, I went out to get something I left in one of the boats and found one of our radios lying on the deck. I checked. It's Kevin's."

Adam stopped and leaned back against the wall. His hand trembled as he ran it through his hair. This couldn't be happening.

A memory of Kevin saying he'd fallen in the water flashed through his mind. What if he'd lost his glasses? What if he fell in trying to get one of the boats started? "Rev, I want the divers out. Everyone else search this place from top to bottom."

"Understood. But I'm wondering if he might have snuck onto Mark's plane? If it's okay, I'd like to start there."

"Call him." Adam shook his head toward Chelsea, whose eyes were already firing off unspoken questions.

His wife quickly spoke into the LinkWay, then set it aside and moved to stand in front of him.

Chapter 22

"Call me back and let me know what Mark says." He closed the connection and then turned to Chelsea. He grabbed her arm and propelled her toward the door. He wanted to get out on the deck and take a look around. "Come on. We've got to find Kevin."

Kevin rested the back of his head against the glass, bulky flight headphones now cupped over his ears reducing the roar of the engine to a low hum, interrupted only by the occasional crackle of the radio as the pilot reported different information. For the most part, Kevin did his best to tune out the short relays of information.

Instead, he focused on the problem of where to go and what to do once they landed back in the States. In the time since they had left the Center, much of the determination and bravado had slowly plummeted into the reality of his situation. His impromptu escape left him empty-handed. No money, no food, and no place to go.

If he'd been smart, he would have figured out how to get his hands on some of Tyke's money for himself—compensation for all the trouble Tyke had caused him and Dad. He grinned at the thought of all that money at his disposal. It would have been the perfect ending. Tyke would lose and Kevin would be free to do whatever he wanted without anyone's threats following him. How easy it would be to disappear on one of these islands. Then he might even send some money back to some of the investors like Aiden's father and Joe from Galactic Jitters. Then he could say he was trying to make things right, ease his conscience.

He sighed. Too bad it was nothing more than wishful thinking.

"Tango alfa three five delta, this is Ocean Base One, over."

Kevin sat up at the sound of Rev's voice over the radio.

"Ocean Base One, this is tango alpha three five delta, go ahead."

"Mark, we need to know if you picked up a stowaway. Can you verify that, over?"

Kevin held his breath, afraid they would hear him.

"Stowaway?" The confusion was evident in the pilot's voice.

"Kevin."

Mark groaned and then sighed. "I'll put the plane on autopilot as soon as I clear this storm."

"Storm?"

"Affirmative. Radar indicated storms building twenty miles east, but all of a sudden they popped up out of nowhere on the radar. Attempting to circumvent storm, over."

"Roger that. Be careful and keep us informed."

"Roger. If I find him on board, I'll make a bat-turn and get him back."

Kevin knit his brows. Bat turn? A weird phrase, but it was the word "storm" that really worried him. He'd always figured planes were meant to fly through rain. With growing nervousness, Kevin glanced out the window. Dark clouds swirled about the plane on the one side while blue skies drifted on the other.

He must have made a noise because Mark spoke into the microphone. "Kevin, is that you?"

Chapter 22

At first he stayed still, hoping Mark would assume it was another one of the many sounds aboard the aircraft.

"Come on, Kevin. Talk to me. I know you're there."

Kevin held his breath.

Mark lowered his voice. "All right. We should be clear of this storm in another ten minutes. Then we can head back to the Center."

"No," Kevin said forcefully, breaking his silence.

"I'm afraid you don't have any choice in the matter." The plane banked hard to the left.

"But you do." He leaned his head back on the seat. "You could take me to the States. What difference does it make how I get there?"

"We're going back."

"I won't go. I'll drown myself first." Nothing more than desperation talking, but he had to try something.

Mark didn't even pause with his answer. "You think Adam and Chelsea would let you drown? They'd be the first in the water to save you."

"Who says I want to be saved?"

"You do." The pilot flipped some switches. "Otherwise you wouldn't be running from whatever it is you're afraid of."

Suddenly one of the windows across from Kevin shattered. A large piece of hail shot past his head like a bullet and landed on the cabin floor. Kevin screamed. This was impossible. It wasn't cold enough to form hail here.

Cyclonic wind rushed into the cabin. He called out to Mark, but the roar created by the wind overpowered the volume of his voice. Lightning flashed outside. Rain blew in, pelting him. Thunder rumbled. Kevin feared the plane might break apart.

Stephanie M. E. Gallentine / refuge

Freedom? It had all been a trick. A way to lure him to his death. Somebody's idea of a cruel joke. He was going to die. It didn't matter about Tyke, Dad, Adam, anything. This plane was about to become his tomb.

As if to confirm his fears, the plane suddenly plummeted. Like a centrifugal force ride at the carnival, the cabin floor dropped away. He flew upward, slamming into the ceiling. His mouth opened to scream, but it was as if his mouth had gone under a molecular malformation from the sudden G-forces.

In the next instant, whatever force held him to the cabin ceiling gave way. Kevin plunged to the floor below. Saliva pooled in the back of his throat. If this kept up, Kevin wouldn't have to worry about holding down the sausage and eggs burrito he'd had for breakfast. It'd be airborne along with everything else that wasn't secured.

Kevin screamed into his headset, not sure if the pilot would hear him. "Mark! I don't want to die!"

The plane continued its free fall.

chapter 23

As suddenly as it began, the free fall came to an abrupt halt and after a few more bumps, leveled out. Kevin moaned. With slow methodical movements, he worked to pull himself up on the seat and reach belatedly for the seatbelt.

"Are you okay?" Mark voice held more than a hint of hysteria.

"Fine." He groaned into the microphone. Another dip like the last one and he would be searching for a parachute. It had to be safer.

"Kevin, I don't want to scare you," Mark began.

Scare him? He passed scared up as soon as he took on the role of Chicken Little and the falling sky.

"We're going to make an emergency landing until the storm blows over. I need to inspect the plane for damage."

Kevin glanced around. Debris lay strewn across the floor, making the back of the plane look more like his bedroom, except he didn't feel at home in this chaos.

Several minutes later, the plane neared the water. Kevin could see the white caps on the waves. He shuddered, cradling his arm close to his chest and dreading the inevitable bumpy landing. At least this time he had his seatbelt secured.

"Almost there, Kevin. Another few minutes and we should be close enough to land and taxi to one of the nearby islands."

Kevin nodded, not trusting himself to answer coherently.

A gust of wind came out of nowhere and caught the right wing of the plane, pushing it like the sail of a boat. The left wing skirted the water, gradually disappearing beneath the ocean depths until the right wing pointed heavenward.

Something snapped. The engine sputtered and died as the plane smacked into the water.

Kevin's white knuckles clenched the armrest. Below him, water gurgled in. "Mark!" His fingers shook as he fumbled with the seatbelt mechanism.

He couldn't get it undone!

Kevin tried again.

The lock wouldn't budge.

Water now formed a pool below him. He was going to drown. "Mark!" he yelled like a madman about to die.

The pilot stumbled into the cabin. He grasped the ceiling to balance himself. Blood trickled from his right temple. Mark swiped his hand over the stream, smearing it across the side of his face. "Kevin! We have to get out of here." He bent over and undid the seatbelt latch.

Chapter 23

Kevin slid down and splashed into the deepening water. Something yellow appeared from the plane's storage. A raft?

Mark handed him a life jacket. "Put this on, but do not, I repeat, do not pull the cord until we're in the open water."

Open water? No, this had to be a joke.

"Give me your glasses. I'm going to tie this rope around you so we don't get separated getting into the raft."

He panicked. "I can't see without my glasses."

"You won't have to." Mark held out his hand. "I can see you. Otherwise, you might lose them in the ocean."

Trembling, Kevin slipped off his glasses and gave up the only thing that left him somewhat grounded. He felt Mark's hand go around him as the pilot secured the rope around his waist. It cinched up when Mark pulled him toward the hatch.

"Hold on! Here we go." Mark tossed out the raft. A faint whoosh sounded over the storm.

Wind howled around them. The plane shifted and groaned beneath them. Water now covered their knees.

"Don't let go of the rope!" Mark shouted over the storm.

Kevin nodded. He clutched the nylon fibers with a death grip.

Not far away the raft bucked on the water like a raging bull. Mark plunged into the water. His life jacket gave a grunt as it inflated.

Taking a deep breath, Kevin stepped off into the murky fog of the stormy ocean. His hand shook as it clawed at his life jacket in search of the pull cord. An unseen wave toppled over onto him, slamming him beneath the turbulent waters.

Like a vortex, the water had a pull to it. Beside him, his legs kicked against metal as the plane sank to the bottom. Kevin struggled for air. His arms and legs flailed. Which way was up? Eyes open, they stung but couldn't make out anything.

His lungs begged for oxygen, screamed for even one breath.

Someone tugged on the rope tied around him. After what seemed like forever, Kevin broke through the surface, coughing, letting the air rush into his oxygen-starved lungs.

"I've got you." Mark's voice rose over the storm.

Kevin fought to stay above water as another wave collapsed on them. Kevin choked on the seawater. "Help!" his plea no more than a strangled cry as more water rushed into his mouth.

Mark jerked Kevin's cord and the life jacket expanded around him. "I've got you."

All around him, the sea churned. Lightning crackled against the ashen sky.

"Jesus! Help us!" Mark cried out.

As if in response, another wind, stronger than before, gusted around them. Thunder rumbled overhead like a bomb exploding in the air. Waves pummeled them.

Kevin disappeared once more beneath the water. He clung to the rope, the nylon fibers digging into his skin.

Mark, don't let me go! His mind screamed the words his mouth couldn't. Breaking the surface, he kicked with his feet. Somehow, he had to stay above water.

Seconds ticked by.

Chapter 23

The wind stilled. Kevin bobbed in the water.

The steady drum of rain seemed to move behind them. The ocean became calm.

Beside them the raft drifted as if now waiting to pick them up.

"I guess you want these back," Mark said as soon as he hauled Kevin into the raft.

Kevin reached out his hand to receive what he hoped were his glasses. After slipping them onto his face, he got his first glimpse of the world around him. The raft was spacious, room for both of them to stretch out and lie down. Above them a heavy vinyl canopy covered the raft, giving it a tent-like feeling. Mark left the flap unzipped so they could see outside.

"The wind must have blown the storm away." Mark pointed to the sheet of rain that still fell from the sky some distance off. From their vantage point, they saw the waves cresting and falling. But where they now drifted, all was calm. Even bits of blue sky peeked out overhead.

"Oh, Lord, thank You for hearing and answering our prayer the same way You did for Joshua when the sun stood still in the valley of Ahijah." Mark kept his gaze heavenward as he prayed aloud. "The Bible says it was the day You listened to the prayer of one man. Thank you for hearing me also and calming the storm."

"You believe that?" Kevin looked at him skeptically.

"Sure. Any reason not to?"

Kevin shrugged. "I can think of several."

"Then what about that?" Mark pointed to the retreating storm. "What else could have happened back there? Random luck?"

Kevin let his head fall back against the tarp and closed his eyes. The storm stopped, and Mark was ready to give God credit. But what if the storm hadn't stopped? "Who knows?"

"I know. I know God cares and wants to answer our prayers."

Cradling his arm, Kevin glared at the pilot. "You think I've never prayed before? I prayed the night my mom died. I prayed for my dad to—" He stopped. "God didn't listen."

Mark eyed him as though seeing all Kevin's thoughts. "He listened, Kevin. His answer was to send you to someone who could help. Now it's up to you to trust them."

"I don't want to talk about it."

"Okay."

Kevin shivered and leaned back in the raft, dreaming of a soft pillow, dry clothes, and something from Chelsea's drug collection—not necessarily in that order.

"You ready to go back yet?" There was a hint of amusement in Mark's voice as he, too, leaned back against the side of the raft.

The eye roll surely must have said it all. "Right now, not even juvie seems all that bad."

"You never know. Adam may be able to get you out of it."

Kevin snorted. "Knowing my luck, I'll get a life sentence."

"A bit extreme, don't you think?"

He sat up in the bobbing raft and gave Mark a look of pure disbelief. "Ya think? I just experienced some heavenly being's target practice with baseball-size hail. Then I took up skydiving without the benefit of a parachute from ten

Chapter 23

thousand feet up. After normal gravitational forces returned, I'm slammed into the cabin floor. You try to land, and we end up sinking the plane. Now we're trapped in an oversized blow-up toy in the middle of the Pacific Ocean in search of land, and hoping when we find it, it won't be overrun with half-starved cannibals. How am I doing so far with extreme reality?"

Mark chuckled. "I doubt we'll have to worry about cannibals."

"Thank you," Kevin said sarcastically. "I feel so much better now."

When the flap of the raft canopy came loose, Mark leaned over and tied it down. It was then that Kevin noticed the scarlet pool that not only came from Mark's still bleeding head wound, but a large gash on the pilot's leg. The blood ran in tiny steams, filling the vinyl crevices. Like in some horror movie, the blood inched closer to him.

"Are you okay?" The pilot had to be. The man had saved Kevin's life, and Mark had the knowledge to keep them alive. His stomach knotted at the thought of being left alone with little hope of survival or rescue.

Mark nodded and then pointed to what appeared to be a small island not too far off.

Kevin sighed in relief. Maybe they would make it through this alive after all.

"He's on the plane, Adam," Rev said through the radio.

"Good, so they should be on their way back soon." He sighed. This day had quickly deteriorated from bad to worse and showed no signs of getting any better. They had to find a way to buy some time to get the answers they needed.

"I hope so." Another pause. "Adam, something happened in the middle of our radio contact. I haven't been able to raise them since."

"What are you saying?"

"I'm saying, they may be in trouble."

"Do we have a way to track them?"

Rev said, "No, the transceiver isn't picking up on any of our instruments. We're working on the problem right now."

Adam slammed his fist on the table. They had to find them. "Just keep trying to raise them on the radio. Kevin's dad is due in another couple hours. We'll find him if we have to do it ourselves."

"Will do."

Chelsea waved him over from behind the LinkWay. "Adam, Aiden's on again. I think you need to hear this."

By the time Aiden finished his story, the teen looked to Adam like a thousand pounds had been lifted from his shoulders. Unfortunately, that same weight had been transferred to his father. A wide range of emotions played out on Mr. Rollings' face.

Adam knew those emotions must mirror his own. He glanced at the bat Chelsea had placed near the couch, longing for the feel of it in his hands, the power of a single swing. No wonder Kevin had reacted as he did. Adam was the adult, and even he relished the thought of beating something up right now. But violence had yet to get anyone anywhere.

Chapter 23

Through the LinkWay, he saw Mr. Rollings loosen the tie at his neck and pull it off. Bunching up his jaw, he leaned in to the LinkWay's screen. "What can I do?"

Adam sighed. "We need proof. Can anyone verify Aiden's whereabouts that night?"

"Just Rom. He's the one that got me the fix for Kevin," Aiden said.

Mr. Rollings crossed his arms. "Rom's in on this too?"

Aiden nodded. "It was Rom's virus that Kevin used to lock up Tyke's laptop. We had to find Rom to get the fix."

Adam met Aiden's gaze through the LinkWay. "Can we get Rom on the LinkWay?"

"Sure." Aiden typed in the information and waited until the screen split in half and Rom's sleepy face appeared on the other half of the screen.

Curls going in all directions, Rom leaned on one elbow. "Hello?" A small dog yapped in the background.

"Rom," Mr. Rollings asked. "What do you know of all this business with Kevin and Mr. Tyke?"

Rom scrubbed a hand over his face, sat up, and balanced the LinkWay on his lap. "Should we be talking about this right now?"

Mr. Rollings understood the hesitation. "Don't worry. We're all working together on this one."

Rom nodded. "I've been tied up in a major security breach with one of our contracts this week, so I didn't get to download the files until yesterday afternoon. It's going to take some time to sift through them and find information that would clear Kevin."

"Can't you hurry? They're gonna send him back to juvie." Aiden pleaded with Rom.

Stephanie M. E. Gallentine / refuge

"I'd love to, but I'm afraid it's a bit more complicated than that. Right now all the evidence is pointing at Kevin and his father. I can't find anything that directly connects Tyke with any of this. He could easily say he was investigating both Kevin and his father's involvement with their firm."

Adam chose to interrupt. "What about the bank account file that the boys found? Deiseldorf Banc?"

"The bank is located in Switzerland, but when I went in and checked it out, it was under S Ramsey. I did, however, use the account numbers and passcodes in the file and put a temporary freeze on the account."

"What about the video everyone keeps talking about?" Mr. Rollings asked.

Rom plugged something in to the LinkWay. "Hold on and I'll load it up so you can see it."

Moments later, the screen darkened and the faces disappeared. In their place, a grainy black and white security video played. In the vacant parking lot, a dark Volvo drove up, its blazing taillights illuminating the license plate number. T35 6ST. After the car shut off, a small figure in a hoodie stepped out of the car.

"As you can see," Rom narrated, "the camera panned at this point, so there's no way to zoom in and see if it really was Kevin."

Aiden answered for him. "That's not Kevin. I told you. He was at home that night. Everything he did, he did from home."

Rom's face reappeared. "Can you prove that? Could Kevin have driven to The World's Gateway that night and not told you?"

Chapter 23

"He doesn't drive," Aiden said. "He doesn't even have a driver's license."

"Has that ever stopped him before?" Rom crossed his arms and confronted Aiden as though he remembered something.

There was a deep sigh from Aiden's side of the LinkWay. "Once, before his dad got this car, he took the other one out while his dad was asleep."

Adam's eyes widened. "Did he crash it?"

"Yeah. He rammed the back of a car a couple of blocks away from his house. Said the car's brake lights weren't working."

"More likely, he couldn't judge how far away the car was." Adam glanced over at Chelsea, who up to this point had been listening to everything.

The doctor in Chelsea took over. "Was he hurt?"

Aiden shrugged, not really meeting anyone's gaze. "He missed a couple of days of school. Said he got bruised up pretty bad."

Chelsea glanced at Adam. He, too, wondered how much of the bruising came from the accident. However, right now they needed to stay focused on the current issue. Knowing what they now knew, they could revisit old topics at a later date. "Rom, since he crashed so close to home, do you think the judge could take that into consideration. He probably would have crashed into the building before parking that nicely?"

Rom shrugged. "Maybe, but I doubt it. The video has Mr. Ramsey's car clearly identified. It's inconceivable that some random teenager stole the car, put on a hoodie, gained access to The World's Gateway, tampered with their interior security cameras, and then returned the car back to their residence." He took a breath. "See my problem?"

Adam understood the dilemma. All the evidence pointed to Kevin and his father. Someone had obviously gone to a lot of trouble to set this up. He wondered how many other people Tyke had framed. Although he spoke to everyone, Adam locked gazes with Aiden. "Tyke made a mistake somewhere. And if we have to delay our flight back and keep everyone on the LinkWay for the next two days, we're going to find it."

chapter 24

Kevin winced as he and Mark worked together to drag the raft onto the sand.

The pilot stumbled. His knees buckled beneath him, crashing into the sand. A low moan escaped his lips.

"Mark?" Kevin bit back his own pain at the sight before him.

"I'm okay." He swiped at the blood with the back of his sleeve and then slowly rose to his feet. "Just a little dizzy spell."

The pilot took a few more steps, wavered, and then stumbled again.

Sand flew from under his feet as Kevin hurried to where Mark laid on the beach. His knees hit the sand beside the fallen pilot. "Mark?" He pushed back the matted hair and examined the two-inch gash in the man's scalp.

Stephanie M. E. Gallentine / refuge

Mark's bloodied hand took hold of Kevin's arm. Blood smeared his hoodie, imprinting it like a tattoo. Kevin froze. The bleeding had slowed to a trickle, but it should have stopped altogether. A cursory glance at the leg showed an even larger gash beneath the torn fabric. Jagged pieces of skin peeked up through the pant leg. Blood dripped into a small indention in the sand.

"Kevin, you have to . . . help me." Mark forced out the words.

"How? What do I do?"

"Have to . . . close the wound. Stop the bleeding." Mark took a deep breath, licked his chapped lips. "Pour water over the wound. Use my shirt. . . . Apply pressure. Then pull. . . . Tie hair together to hold . . . wound closed."

Kevin nodded. He could do that. Maybe.

He leaned down and probed the wound. It would be difficult to use the hand without moving the arm, but he had to help Mark, had to do what he could. Slowly, with awkward and unskilled movements, Kevin pulled the pieces of the skin together and tied the bloody strands of hair to hold it shut.

Mark ran his fingers over the wound once Kevin had finished. "Good . . . work." The pilot clenched his teeth against the pain.

Kevin looked on anxiously, wishing he had some of Chelsea's medicine with him to give to Mark. "Your leg is bleeding too. I don't think you have enough leg hair to tie that one down."

The older man let loose a chuckled and then squeezed his eyes as if in too much pain. "Duck tape . . . my bag."

"Duct tape?" Kevin knit his brows together. He reached for the small black bag Mark had pulled from the

Chapter 24

raft. Inside, Kevin sifted through several articles until he came to the small roll of bright yellow duck tape at the bottom.

Between painful breaths, Mark instructed him. "Pull the skin together . . . tight."

Rip the fabric. Bite off a couple pieces of duct tape. Use bits of ripped fabric to act as padding to absorb the blood. Then use the duct tape to seal the wound.

Once finished, Kevin sat back in the sand and took deep breaths, trying to erase the gray dots that kept appearing in his line of vision. He looked longingly at the bottle of water sticking out of the nylon bag. His mouth was dry, like he'd eaten some of the sand beneath him. No matter how hard he tried, he couldn't seem to get rid of the gritty taste.

"You need to drink." Kevin held what little was left of the bottle over Mark's mouth and dribbled it in as if he were feeding a baby bird with its small beak open to catch whatever droplets of water he could give it.

"Kevin." Mark held up his hand to stop him. "Drink some . . . for yourself. We both have to stay hydrated . . . or we won't make it."

He screwed the cap back on the now empty bottle. "Who says we're going to make it anyway?"

The pilot inhaled a deep breath. His body seemed to relax a bit. "I set the transponder on an emergency frequency. It'll send our coordinates out. But we need to get something on the beach for an SOS. Anything in threes will do . . . large enough to see in the air. Coconuts, palm branches, wood."

Kevin nodded. "I can do that. But what about the radio? Did anyone say they were on their way to help us?"

There was an exaggerated pause. "The radio quit working before I could get a Mayday call out. But the transponder should be able to broadcast the plane's location."

"So nobody knows where we are or that we need help?" Frustrated, he clenched his fist in the sand. Everything kept getting worse. He remembered Murphy's Law stated that anything that could go wrong, would go wrong. He frowned. Why did Murphy have to pick on him?

Why couldn't he just be normal like Aiden? Great family, great job, able to drive a car. Was that so much to ask?

"God knows where we are, Kevin."

Kevin exploded and chucked the fistful of sand toward the water. "Well, forgive me if I don't find that comforting right now."

"I spoke with Rev. He knows about the storm. He'll get worried if he can't reach me."

With an eye roll, he said, "I don't know. Adam may be tired of chasing me down."

Mark tried to sit up, but then moaned and lay back in the sand. "You're coming to the Center has been one of the best things that happened to him."

"Yeah, right."

"Didn't you say you worked with computers back in the States?"

He nodded, grateful for the sudden change in topic. "Yeah, I worked as a penetration tester for Rollings Security."

"And did what?"

"We were hired to hack into computers to find their system's weaknesses so the company hopefully wouldn't be the victim of a malicious hacker."

"Sounds like you love a good challenge."

Kevin grinned. "Of course. Who doesn't?"

Chapter 24

"You're right, who doesn't?" He sucked in another painful breath. "Adam won't walk away from this challenge, and neither will God."

"You know," Rom said, "if Kevin and his father had gone to the police when Kevin first found the file, a lot of this could have been avoided. The judge will see it that way too. Instead, they took the law into their own hands, to the point of using embezzled money to send Kevin away. It's almost a nonverbal admission of guilt."

Adam's gaze flew up to meet Rom's. "The donated grant was made with embezzled funds?" He glanced over to Chelsea's own shocked expression. If information got out that they'd accepted embezzled money, it might not bode well with their newly acquired contract to build the first underwater prison.

"From the looks of it, yes. William Tyke noticed that some of his financial records didn't seem right after Steven Ramsey got through with them. A few days later they found out it was Kevin who set the virus in their system."

"So why didn't Mr. Tyke go to the police at that point?" Mr. Rollings asked.

Rom shrugged. "Prof talked them into letting Kevin's father send him to the Center. I guess they didn't have all the facts then." Rom stopped to let his hyperactive Chihuahua out into the hall. "Anyway, from Mr. Tyke's account, it seems that some time after that, Mr. Tyke discovered the missing money. Then he found that the amount donated to the Center matched the amount stolen.

"Kevin's father admitted to investigators that the money was directly deposited into his account from The

World's Gateway as interest in the purchased investments, but that after viewing the security tape, he feels sure it was Kevin who electronically deposited the money that night."

"I'm telling you, Kevin never left the house that night." Aiden glared. "I thought you were a Guardian Angel, Rom. Isn't it your job to protect us? But all you're doing is putting Kevin behind bars." Disgust flowed through his words.

"I do volunteer for Guardian Angels, but that doesn't make me God. I can't read people's minds and have it admitted into court as evidence." Rom used his hands to explain. "I still have to dig into files and follow the computer trails to find hard evidence. And from everything you've shown me, Kevin, and possibly his father, are guilty. The video feed alone puts both Kevin and the car at the scene the night of the alleged crime. No one's debating that money changed hands. And neither Kevin nor his father have a provable alibi for the night of the thirty-first except to say they were home. In fact, Kevin's father told investigators Kevin took the car that night and set the virus."

Adam cut in. "We have to be missing something. Has his father or Tyke made any big purchases lately?"

Aiden stared down at the hands in his lap.

"Aiden?" Adam asked.

The teen shook his head, hopeless. "The last time Kevin was here, he was late meeting me at Galactic Jitters. He told me some car salesman called and said when his father came in to get a key replacement, he showed an interest in one of the most expensive cars they sell."

Chapter 24

Rom looked up as though something had caught his interest. "Huh?"

Mr. Rollings suddenly ended his silence. "Rom, can you play that video once more. I think we might have missed something."

"Sure." Rom hit the play button and let the security feed play back again.

"That's it." Mr. Rollings leaned back in his chair, a smug smile playing on his lips. "We got him."

"Who?" came the almost unison reply.

"I don't know. Tyke is my guess." Still smiling, Mr. Rollings continued, "Whoever it was might have filmed this video but not on the night said. I remember because I was at a New Year's Eve party with a fellow businessman, Leon Carter. Mr. Carter held the party in his glass-enclosed sunroom so we could watch the snow."

Aiden smiled. "It snowed the whole night."

"And there was no snow in that video." Adam laughed. Finally, they had a break.

Mr. Rollings sat up. "Rom, I need you to check the metadata on that feed."

"I did, but didn't find anything unusual."

"Back it up. Contact Mr. Damon and tell him you need a copy of the security feed for the twenty-four hours prior to and after that night. Examine all the metadata and get back with me. Look for any discrepancies at all."

"Will do, Boss." Rom went to sign off but then stopped. "Mr. Rollings, I'm wondering about that replacement key. A friend of mine lost the key to his car awhile back. The dealer asked him for the last six digits of the VIN number on his car. I remember my friend being amazed at the ease. No one even asked for any identification other than the VIN and payment for the key. What if someone did that—copied down the VIN and got a duplicate key—not for stealing per se, but for framing?"

"Aiden and I will check on that," Mr. Rollings said. "Seems like a lot of trouble to go through to pull off a scam, but I guess in the security business, nothing should surprise me anymore."

A mixture of relief and excitement flooded Adam. They were going to get to keep Kevin and hopefully put a criminal or two behind bars.

"Adam." The voice came from his radio.

"Yeah, Rev, go ahead. Are they are on their way back yet?"

"I don't know. I haven't been able to regain contact. I radioed in and flight control says they haven't received a Mayday call. Still . . ."

Adam started pacing. "We have to find them. Are you picking up their transceiver yet?"

"Yeah. Looks like they're on some small, unnamed island in the middle of nowhere."

"It means they're alive." Thank God. The relief was tangible. "How far out is Kevin's father?"

"About an hour and a half."

"All right. I need David, Anna Lisa, and our head diver, Pete. He's been trained as a rescue diver. You'll stay here and man the radio. I'll send Chelsea down as soon as we're finished. I need all our supplies ready to go within the hour."

"What's the plan?" Rev asked.

Adam grinned. "We're gonna hijack a plane."

chapter 25

The sun blazed down on Kevin from its position in the westward sky. The skin on his arms had gradually taken on a more baked appearance. Kevin dropped to the sand as he placed the final coconut in his SOS that probably resembled crop circles in the sand more than actual letters.

A glance at the pilot's still unmoving figure worried him even more. Sometime between setting up a makeshift tent and using the canopy from the raft draped over palm branches, Mark lost consciousness.

Despite his own pain, Kevin had tried everything to wake the pilot up. Nothing worked. Not even tipping the water bottle and letting the last few drops slide between Mark's sun-cracked lips. Exhausted, Kevin rested against an outcropping of rocks that dotted the shoreline not far from where they came on land. Salty spray from the ocean rained down on him, temporarily relieving the heat radiating off his skin. He longed to open his mouth and let the water moisten what felt like coarse sandpaper.

Kevin picked up the empty water bottle and submerged it in the shallow water. He waited as it bubbled and filled before returning to Mark and dousing the pilot with the water. If nothing else, it might cool the pilot off. He made three more trips before satisfied that Mark's skin and clothing were saturated.

He sighed. The seawater might cool off the skin, but it didn't ward off dehydration. Somehow, he had to find freshwater to drink. Otherwise, neither of them might make it off the island alive. With a determined glance at the pilot, Kevin trekked off into the thick foliage.

Adam prepared to end the three-way conversation when Aiden stopped him.

"What about Patrick Thomas?" Aiden held up the tiny flash drive. "I don't know if Rom found that file or not."

While Adam listened, Aiden explained what they knew of the now deceased Patrick Thomas. It did seem strange that Tyke would keep an encrypted file full of articles detailing a man who supposedly embezzled a large amount of money from his own investment firm.

"I used his wife's name from the obituary to find a number. But I've been grounded from the LinkWay and haven't had a chance to call it," Aiden explained.

Adam nodded. "No time like the present. I'd like to see how all this ties in together myself."

Chapter 25

Mr. Rollings stepped near the screen again. "Rom, can you get her online and reconfigure the LinkWay so she could only see you but everyone could see her on the screen. I hate to scare her away."

Rom nodded and set to work. "Hold on. I'm connecting now."

A few moments later, a woman who appeared to be in her early forties stepped in front of her LinkWay. Her ash blonde hair was swept back away from her face in a short ponytail. "Can I help you?"

"Yes, my name is Reginald Makelhaney. I'm looking for Mrs. Patrick Thomas."

The woman covered her mouth with the tips of her trembling fingers. "I'm Cassie Thomas."

"Forgive me for calling, but I was researching some articles about your husband."

She pulled a chair close and sat down. "My husband has been dead for a year and a half."

Rom nodded. "I know that, ma'am, and I'm sorry for your loss. What I need to know is did they ever find the person who embezzled the money?"

The woman broke down. Tears coursed down her cheeks. Cassie quickly wiped them away. "Forgive me. But you're the first person who didn't just assume my husband was guilty."

"Would it be too much to ask you what happened?"

She appeared relieved. "Not at all. From the article, you know that over a million dollars from my husband's overseas investment firm disappeared. His partner confronted him, and after Patrick denied any wrongdoing, his partner took it to the police. All the evidence seemed to point to my husband taking this money and putting it into some offshore bank account. No one believed my husband after that. He was arrested and then let out on bond to await trial and the ongoing investigation surrounding the company.

The night he died, my husband begged me to believe him. He said he had proof that he had been framed. He planned to meet someone that night who he hoped would help him."

"Who?" Rom asked the question everyone must have been dying to ask.

Cassie shrugged. "I don't know. He wouldn't say. Patrick sent me to the video store to pick up a DVD of some movie he wanted to see. *Dempsey's Defense*. When I came back home, he was dead." She pressed her lips together and covered them with her cupped palm, trying to hold back the emotion. "The doctor said he had a massive heart attack. But I don't believe it. It was too coincidental."

"*Dempsey's Defense*? Hmmm." Rom appeared thoughtful. "Did you find it odd that it was a movie about an investment scam?"

"I never watched it," she said. "I couldn't."

"Just your typical mystery suspense. The hero saves the day, and the bad guy goes down."

"But in this case, the hero didn't win."

Rom gave her an encouraging grin. "Not yet."

David handed Adam a plastic transport container. His face housed an expression that seemed barely controlled. "Do you want me to stay here with him?"

Chapter 25

"Him?"

"Kevin's father." David rubbed one balled fist in the palm of his other hand. "I will take care of him. No one need ever know."

Adam let loose a nervous chuckle. As much as he knew this was David's way of verbally working out his own anger, he had hoped they could have gotten through this day without him knowing about Kevin's father. "I'm going to need you with me."

An evil smile appeared. "Then perhaps we can 'accidently' drop him from the plane."

"How about we try it my way for now?" Adam accepted another container. "How did you find out?"

"I walked in on Chelsea telling Rev." David clenched his fists at his side. "I didn't know. If I had, maybe I wouldn't have always—"

"Wouldn't have always let your temper get the best of you?" David nodded and Adam continued, "It shouldn't have gotten the best of you in the first place. But that's a topic for another day. Right now, I want to find Kevin and Mark, and I need your help."

The amphibian plane landed with a bump before taking several small jumps as it skirted across the watery runway. The plane slowed and then taxied its way next to the docking side of the platform.

Adam waited as Kevin's father disembarked. He resisted the urge to ball his fist up and give Steven Ramsey a taste of his own medicine. Instead, he nodded. "Steven."

"Adam."

He met Steven's gaze in a silent standoff.

Steven shifted his gaze to somewhere behind Adam.

"Where's Kevin? And what's with all this stuff?" he asked gruffly.

No one in the small group spoke. The wind had picked up, and everyone had something in their hands, ready for Adam to give the order.

"We need to use your plane. Our pilot's in trouble. We think his plane crashed," Adam explained.

Kevin's father stepped in front of the hatch and folded his arms across his chest. "Then let Search and Rescue find him. They're better equipped. Besides, I don't have the fuel." He paused. "Now where is Kevin?"

David launched from behind Adam, barking off a string of Spanish. Adam knew he didn't want to know the translation. At the last second, he caught David's arm, yanking him back before he did something he'd regret—at least Adam hoped the engineer would regret it.

"That's enough, David. Rev, take Mr. Ramsey inside and get him settled. We'll continue this conversation after we get back."

Rev nodded and placed a hand on Steven's back to guide him up the steps to the entrance.

Steven shook him off. His eyes ignited with anger. "We'll settle this now. Where's my son?"

Adam motioned for everyone to start loading the supplies. Then he turned to Steven, thankful for the few feet between them. "Kevin's out there." He motioned toward the vast ocean before throwing a barb of his own. "I'd like to find him while he's alive. Unless you'd rather wait on Search and Rescue. But then he might miss his court date."

Like a punctured balloon, Steven crumpled onto the steps. He clutched his chest. When Chelsea advanced on him, he waved her off. "I'm all right. Go find my son."

Chapter 25

Chelsea wrapped her small fingers around his thick wrist and checked his pulse. The hand shook as she held it midair. "Anna, I want you to stay here and monitor Mr. Ramsey. Rev will be on hand if you need him."

Anna grinned, flipping her waist-length braid over her shoulder. "I'll be fine."

With a defeated wave, Steven motioned for them to go. "Don't worry. Just go find my son."

The plane engine sprang to life. Everything appeared to be loaded and ready to go. Adam reached for Chelsea's hand. Kevin and Mark needed them. And this was one accident that wasn't going to take someone's life. He couldn't save Staci, but God was giving him a chance to save her son. And for that, Adam thanked Him.

Kevin pushed the narrow branch back as he made his way through the dense island foliage. It snapped back, striking him in the face. Kevin winced at the sting, but pushed himself forward. If he was going to find water before dark, he had to keep going.

He plunged into the vegetation. Briars scratched the sunburned skin on his arms and hands. Droplets of salty sweat formed and rolled into the wounds, burning. Every breath seemed labored, like sucking in air from an oven. Water. He hated water. But right now, he could drink a gallon of it and appreciate every sip. He didn't care if he ever had another energy drink or coffee, if only he could have that one sip of water.

Gingerly, he held his left arm as close to his body as he could. No longer could he move it without unbearable pain ripping through the swollen shoulder and spidering out from there. A few steps more and he stumbled. Exhaustion pulled at him. Kevin's knees crashed into the packed earth. His fingers splayed out into the leaves, breaking his fall.

Intense emotions bombarded him. Regret, fear, hopelessness, anger, frustration, desperation. A virtual map of emotions, and he bounced from one to the other in quick, uncontrollable succession.

He was lost. In more ways than one. And this was his punishment—this barrage of emotions as he wandered aimlessly, searching for water—something so basic, yet still out of reach. He pushed himself up, but then collapsed back on the ground.

He couldn't go on. Like a garment, too tight and suffocating, fatigue clung to him. His head felt like a bowling ball, too heavy to lift. Eyelids drooped, and Kevin couldn't fight it anymore. Why fight the inevitable?

As he lay there, he wished for the first time that he would have trusted Adam. Wished he could have had one last chance to talk to him. Wished he could make everything right with Aiden. He hated the way he was. He'd hurt so many people, and those he hadn't hurt, he'd pushed away. All the while, he blamed Dad for all the hurts in his life, but Kevin had left a trail of hurts himself.

In his mind he could see the sadness in Chelsea's eyes when he blew up in their apartment, the disappointment in Adam's. If God likes a challenge, Kevin had certainly given Him one. He couldn't see himself believing the way these people did. But a small part of him wished he could. Anything had to be better than running all the time. He was so tired of running.

Chapter 25

Kevin stared at the empty water bottle in his hand. Even if there was no hope for him, he couldn't let Mark down. The man had a family, a family he obviously loved. Kevin couldn't let them lose their dad. He pushed himself up off the ground and used a nearby palm tree to hoist himself up to a standing position.

"Kevin!"

Someone called his name in the distance. Tightening his grip on the tree, he scanned the area. *God, don't let it be a dream. I'll make everything right . . . somehow.*

"Kevin!" A twig snapped from somewhere close.

Adam's voice. Kevin fell back against the tree in relief, his wobbly knees threatened to give way again. "Adam." He tried to call out, but his voice was too weak, his mouth too dry.

Feet pounded. Twigs snapped. The foliage split in half. Adam emerged from the greenery. David appeared a few steps behind, their faces masked in concern.

A water bottle came into view.

Kevin eyed it as if he'd never seen anything so precious in his life. Everything else faded out of focus. He longed to guzzle the entire bottle. But Mark's need was greater.

Adam held the bottle toward Kevin.

He snatched the bottle, held it to his face, and relished the instant relief its coolness brought.

"Do you need me to open it?" Adam spoke soft and low, as though speaking to a frightened animal.

Kevin shook his head. "Mark," he croaked. "I've got to find Mark."

"Chelsea is with him now." Adam approached him slowly. He slipped the water bottle out of Kevin's grasp.

With a twist, the plastic seal on the top snapped. He handed the bottle back.

He stared into the clear depths of the bottle, lifted it, and took a slow sip. His world tilted. Black spots appeared in his line of vision. The bottle slipped from his hand as he stumbled. Strong hands lifted him and carried him back through the foliage, somehow shielding him against the branches.

And strange enough, David never said a word.

"I'm sorry, Adam," he mumbled after they'd been walking for awhile. "For everything." He meant it. Every word. He just didn't know how to make it right.

"Me too."

Adam's answer surprised him. What did Adam have to be sorry for? This was all Kevin's fault. But he didn't have the strength to ask.

They reached the plane in what seemed half the time it took him to wander away.

"Kevin!" Chelsea rushed out to meet them outside the plane. Beads of moisture gathered at the base of her eyes. With a feather-light touch, she brushed the errant lock of hair off his forehead. "You don't know how good it is to see you."

The slightest hint of a grin pulled at his cracked lips. "Yeah, I do." He suddenly felt a chill come over him and shivered.

Something changed in that moment, and Chelsea became the doctor again. Her gaze traveled over him, taking note of what needed to be done. "Get him in the plane and lay him on the mat. David, I need you to get his vitals and cover him with warm blankets. I have to get Mark's IV going, and then I'll be over to get Kevin's started"

Chapter 25

"Si, Señora."

Kevin blinked back his surprise. He'd never seen David this respectful of anyone.

Adam laid him down on a makeshift pallet in the floor near the rear hatch. Kevin couldn't have cared if it was a concrete slab. They were headed home to safety. Chelsea would take care of him. Adam would help him once he understood. They wouldn't let Dad take him. Everything was going to be okay . . . somehow.

"Adam, I need your help," Chelsea called from across the plane's interior.

He didn't care. He'd only have to endure the pain a few moments more.

Someone lowered a soft blanket over him. He relished its warmth. David wrapped a blood pressure cuff around his forearm, pumped it full, and then slipped the stethoscope into place. The metal felt like ice when it came in contact with his skin.

"Hello, Kevin."

Kevin eased his head slowly around at the sound of the vaguely familiar voice. All the air went out of him. He closed his eyes. It couldn't be. "No," he moaned under his breath. Kevin only thought it was over.

The nightmare had begun anew.

The pilot flashed him a slow, evil grin.

Landon.

chapter 26

"How are you feeling?"

Kevin glared up at Landon. "How do you think?" He wasn't in the mood to play games. Especially with someone who didn't play fair.

Something rolled out of Landon's hand and dropped onto the floor inches from Kevin's head. When David left for a second to report to Chelsea, the pilot knelt down and retrieved whatever he had dropped.

"I would not suggest telling anyone anything, or this plane might never make it back to the Center." Landon gave him a pointed look. "You would not want to be the reason the pilot did not make it, would you?

"Why isn't this plane in the air yet?" Adam appeared on his other side and eyed Landon with suspicion.

Stephanie M. E. Gallentine / refuge

The pilot slid his hands into his pockets. "Sorry. I was waiting for a ready call from you. Thought I would take a second and check on the kid Ramsey keeps talking about."

"Just get us back to the Center. My wife will see to Kevin's needs."

Landon dipped his head forward. "I am sure she will. He looks like he is in a lot of pain. But I am sure she will give him something to help him rest more easily."

Kevin froze. Landon would want him drugged. How much easier it would be for Landon to kidnap him. No way.

"Just get this plane in the air." Adam punctuated every word of his response.

Once the pilot headed to the cockpit, Kevin sat up and leaned against the cabin wall.

Chelsea approached him with what looked like an IV kit and a bag of clear solution. Pressed alongside those items, he caught sight of a capped, prefilled syringe. Using the wall for support, Kevin stood.

"Kevin, what are you doing? I need you to lie down so I can get your IV started as soon as the plane is in the air."

Kevin's hand slid sideways until he felt a cold metal. "Can't it wait till we're back at the Center?"

"I'm afraid not. You're dehydrated and I need to get some fluids in you and then see about that shoulder."

Adam advanced on him.

Adrenaline flooded his system. He couldn't let them drug him no matter how much he longed for something out of Chelsea's drug bag. "Take care of Mark first."

"Mark is fine for now," she said. "There's nothing more we can do until we get back to the Center."

Chapter 26

If they got back to the Center. He had to remain lucid and that meant he needed a place where Chelsea couldn't get to him. If he couldn't tell them about Landon, maybe he could stall them. His gaze panned the area. Nothing.

He chanced a sideways glance to what his fingers had found. A fire extinguisher. Perfect. He dropped his hand and slid across the back wall.

"Chelsea," David's voice called from the other side of the cabin. "I need your help."

While she and Adam checked on Mark, Kevin unlatched the extinguisher and sat it on the floor behind him. He pulled the pin and waited.

Moments later, Chelsea was back. "Kevin, I need you to sit down and let me get some fluids in you."

"I'll drink some water."

"You can." Chelsea sighed, her patience waning. "Later. Right now I need to get fluids in you a bit quicker."

Kevin sank down toward the floor. Adrenaline flooded his system as he wrapped his good arm around the fire extinguisher and shifted it into his lap.

"Adam." There was a note of urgency in Chelsea's voice.

Chelsea nodded to Adam.

That was his cue to yank the pin. He pointed the nozzle outward. Satisfied he could now protect himself, Kevin crouched in the corner. "Stay back!"

"Put it down, Kevin," Adam ordered.

"Not until we're back at the Center." He heaved in a deep breath against the pain. "Now, leave me alone."

Chelsea dropped to her knees and opened her bag. "You're shaking."

"It's cold." His voice sounded small and helpless even to his own ears. Where had his bravado gone?

The melodic cadence Chelsea used returned. She smiled, took several calming breaths, and reclined back on her knees.

Kevin felt himself relaxing against his will.

"Why don't we get you another blanket?" She glanced back. Someone passed a blanket through the door. Chelsea inched closer to him.

"I said, stay back." He tilted the nozzle toward her. "Throw me the blanket."

Although Chelsea probably could have easily overtaken him, for some reason she did as he asked. "Better?"

Kevin nodded as he draped the blanket over himself. Only his right arm protruded from the cover, the extinguisher still holding position in case someone should come too close. He didn't know how far away from the Center they were, but he figured he shouldn't have to stall them too much longer.

Adam squatted down beside Chelsea. He lowered his voice as if trying to copy his wife's tone. "You don't have to be afraid. You're father's not going to take you back. We know what he did to you."

This couldn't be happening. Not here. Not now. The way they stared at him, their eyes full of pity. Through clenched teeth, he spoke in a low and menacing tone. "Go. Away."

Adam shook his head. "We can't do that."

"Kevin, I'm going to give you something that will calm you down so I can work on you. Everything else can wait for now." The soft hypnotic lilt to her voice forced him to listen to all the words.

Chapter 26

The temptation to nod was strong. His chin dipped a couple of inches, then stopped midstream when she uncapped the syringe and flicked the end of it with her finger, effectively breaking the spell.

"No!" He tightened his grip on the trigger on the extinguisher. "I won't let you drug me."

"Kevin—" Chelsea tried.

"Don't you get it? I need to talk to my dad." He had to warn him and hoped he wasn't in league with Landon.

Chelsea shook her head. "I can't wait that long. Besides, I think you've had enough drama for one day." She scooted forward and then stopped, digging through her bag. "Your pain level has to be through the roof."

It was, but somehow the surges of adrenaline seemed to take the edge off. "I'm fine."

"Let her help you."

He turned. David's voice pulled his attention to the right.

Adam rose. He rushed Kevin, wrapping his large hand around Kevin's thin wrist and yanking it away from the trigger. With his other hand, he moved the extinguisher. Chelsea scooped it up and dropped it into a chair out of reach.

"Nooooooo!" With one last effort, Kevin jerked his arm free and smacked Adam in the face. An uncontrollable panic rose within him.

Adam grunted and captured his flailing arm. He held it while Kevin yelled in his ear.

In a flash, Kevin felt a needle jab into his arm. It burned. He tried to jerk away but Adam held him firm. "Let me go," Kevin demanded, but Adam didn't move from his position.

"Just give it a minute or two," Chelsea said.

Adam nodded.

A floating feeling came over him. Little by little, the pain receded into nothingness. His head lulled to one side. Beside him, Adam carefully hoisted him up.

"It's going to be okay, Kevin. You won't have to run anymore," Adam said in a determined whispered. "I'll make sure of it."

By the time Adam placed him back on the pallet, Kevin felt himself drifting to a peaceful place. Light. Flying. Was this what heaven would feel like? He found himself wondering if the reason superheroes took to the sky had less to do with escape and more to do with getting closer to heaven. Closer to something that could help them.

"Adam." He forced the word out through what felt like an oversized tongue that struggled to move. "Talk."

The older man gripped his hand. "We will. But not now."

Chelsea inserted a needle in the crook of his arm. This time he didn't fight it. Cool liquid flowed into his vein. Kevin shivered.

"How's it looking?" Adam asked.

"Aside from the obvious dehydration, I think he may have separated his shoulder this time." She adjusted the blankets around him.

Kevin mentally thanked her from his drugged state. Everything was warm now. Too bad the euphoria wouldn't last.

chapter 27

Adam sat stiffly behind his desk. His shoulders tensed. Every nerve in him wanted to pounce on the man who sat before him and Chelsea. "I know what happened the night Kevin hurt his shoulder." He leveled Steven with his hard gaze.

"It was an accident." Steven leaned back in his chair. "I'm surprised you haven't felt that way yourself when Kevin gets in one of his moods."

"No." Adam leaned forward on his desk and pressed all his weight on his flattened palms. "It's not the teenagers who make me that angry."

Standing beside Adam, Chelsea glared down at Steven. "You know I'm obligated to report this to the authorities."

Stephanie M. E. Gallentine / refuge

"I know." Steven let out a long breath and picked up a small picture of Staci on the desk. His index finger caressed the photo. "But I'm asking you not to."

"Give us one good reason," Adam demanded.

Steven's shoulders slumped forward while his large hands rested on his knees. "You know Ramsey isn't our real last name. What you don't know is why."

Adam waited in expectation. Finally, he was going to get some answers to this maddening mystery.

"My father was a" —Steven paused as if searching for the right word— "difficult man. He adhered strictly to the policy of spare the rod and spoil the child. That rod became my father's most effective weapon and my constant nightmare."

Chelsea's expression seemed to soften, but the lines of suspicion remained. "Why didn't you tell someone? The police would've helped you."

Steven snorted. "My father was the police. He was the sheriff in a very small town. Talking only made things worse—much worse." He rubbed the back of his neck. "Anyway, I started drinking in high school. My father sent me away to college hoping I'd straighten up. It was there I met your sister. She worked at the student center. Within the space of a few months, we married and Staci became pregnant with Kevin. However, I still had another two years of college to finish.

"My parents insisted we move into the little apartment over their garage. I told myself everything would be okay since we wouldn't be actually living in their house."

Adam's gut clenched. Suddenly he wasn't sure he wanted to hear all of this after all.

Chapter 27

"During the next few years, my parents tried to control our family. By then I was drinking heavier than I ever had and Staci took a night shift cleaning the county building to help us save up the money to move. One night in my frustration, I did what I swore I would never do: I shoved Kevin in a drunken rage and bruised him. Staci came home, and we took him to the emergency department. My father had me arrested. I was shocked. All those years he beat me, and the first time I hit Kevin, he throws me in jail."

"Before I could bond out of jail, my father convinced child protective services that not only had I abused Kevin, but Staci had failed to protect him as well. My parents had Kevin removed from our home and placed in theirs."

Adam plopped back down in his chair and raked a hand through his hair. "I can't believe you're admitting that even then you didn't take responsibility for your son. What in thunder was my sister thinking to stay with you?"

"Staci loved me. She believed I could change," Steven ground the words out. "I threw away all the alcohol and promised her as soon as we got Kevin back, we would move and never look back. But then my father told me he would fight me until they had permanent custody of Kevin.

"Then one day, I arrived early to visit Kevin. They had him locked in the basement, punishing him—just like they'd done to me." Steven's gaze never left the floor. "After that, Staci and I knew what we had to do. She found help through one of her online hacker boards. They put her in contact with someone who helped her get false identity papers."

"So you really were placed in the Witness Protection Program?" Chelsea asked.

Steven lifted his head partway and grinned. "Nothing so official. On our next visitation with Kevin, we disappeared. Staci called you to make sure we had a safe place for Kevin, but we couldn't risk anyone—not even Kevin—knowing about you or any of her relatives."

Chelsea lifted a finger to interrupt. "But couldn't your father have tracked her by her name?"

Steven shook his head. "I didn't know until much later in our marriage that she had already been living under a false name. I guess she ran away from home. She always claimed if she hadn't called you that day, maybe you wouldn't have lost your leg. She didn't want to cause her family any more pain."

Adam's gut clenched. He struggled to hide the rush of emotions. *Ten minutes. Oh God, that I had ten minutes with my sister to tell her I didn't blame her. To tell her I loved her and would have done anything to help her come home.*

"You could have all come here. This didn't have to be your last resort."

Steven shrugged. "We were fine, and Kevin was protected."

Chelsea's voice was ice cold as she asked, "So when did the protection stop?"

Adam replied for Steven through a clenched jaw. "When Staci wasn't there to referee anymore." His gaze bore holes into Steven.

"That's not—"

"Yes, it is," Adam said. "All those years. You never overcame anything. Your temper and your alcoholism laid dormant, waiting for the right set of circumstances to

Chapter 27

bring them out. When did you take the first drink? The night Staci died?"

"I—"

Adam rose out of his seat like a snake waiting to strike. "One thing led to another and before you knew it, you were your father's child. You hurt him, Steven, and you trained him to act just like you. I see the anger burning in Kevin's eyes. He runs instead of facing things. Is that what you wanted? A third generation abuser?"

Steven's fists balled at his side and jumped to his feet. "You think I want to be this way? My son is here because I couldn't control my anger."

"You son is here because you used him and then couldn't risk everyone finding out who the real Steven Ramsey is."

Steven flew out of his chair and slammed his fist into the wall. Pictures rattled and then stilled. He turned back to Adam, his face twisted in anger. He thrust his finger out at Adam. "You want to have me arrested? Fine. But if my father gets wind of any of this, he may come and find Kevin. And trust me, I know from experience, anything I've done to my son is nothing compared to what that man is capable of."

Slowly, Kevin opened his eyes while he concentrated on the soft whirring sound of the IV regulator as it ticked away the droplets from the two bags connected above it. A glance at his left arm showed it was now tightly bound in a sling. His shoulder felt almost numb. At first he thought it must have been the medicine until he realized Chelsea had packed it down with padded ice packs.

Through a slight break in the hunter green curtain that separated the cubicles, he caught a glimpse of Mark, who seemed to be sleeping soundly, compliments of Chelsea's drug collection, no doubt. A thick bandage now covered the part of the scalp where Kevin had tied the pieces of hair together. If he hadn't been anchored to his own set of tubing, Kevin would have been tempted to grab the Sharpie someone had left on the silver medical tray and draw a comic character on the white of the bandage. The pilot would have had something to show off to his kids. How else did he say thank you to someone for saving his life?

Bored, Kevin lay back down on his pillow and sighed.

The curtain parted and Anna Lisa walked through, chart in hand. She smiled and pressed the button that blew up the blood pressure cuff attached to his arm. As soon as it was done, she scribbled on his chart before dropping it into the basket at the end of the bed. "How're you feeling?"

"How do you think?" He glared at her, hoping she'd leave. "Where's Chelsea?"

"In a meeting with Adam and your father."

Kevin's eyes flew open, but he quickly schooled his features. No way would she let him out to attend that meeting. That meant he would have to pull one final escape on his own. A plan of action began to form in his mind.

Anna held a glass of ice water in front of him. "I'm sure she'll be down as soon they finish their meeting."

He took a long pull from the bent straw. "Thanks."

"Do you need another shot for pain yet?"

Chapter 27

"No, I'm good. I think I'll just go back to sleep for a little longer."

She grinned and set the cup back on the side table. "Good idea. I'll be in the next room if you need me."

Kevin nodded and waited for her to leave. He had to get out of here and tell them about Landon—tell them everything. He was tired of running, tired of having to watch his back, and tired of living in fear. It was time to fight back. Last time he tried going it alone and lost. This time he would make himself trust Adam. No longer would he live a dual life.

As soon as he heard the door slide shut, Kevin threw back the light cotton blanket. His old clothes were nowhere in sight, so the cream-colored surgical scrubs he now wore would have to do. Twisting his body to get into position, Kevin grimaced as he peeled back the tape holding the IV in place. After one final glance to make sure no one was watching, he clenched his teeth and pulled.

Blood flowed from the site. Like a white piece of paper and a set of finger paints, the sheet beneath him took on the look of a horror movie. Kevin grabbed the pillow and held it over the wound in an effort to stem the flow.

Dizziness assailed him when his feet hit the ground. He grasped the bedrail and lowered his head until the feeling passed. Then he rushed out the door and down the hall. Someone passed by and paused to stare, but Kevin hurried to the elevator without answering any questions. Let them call someone. No one was going to stop him from talking to Adam.

Barging into the elevator, Kevin ran smack into the solid statue-like figure of Rev. Thankfully, the door slid shut before Rev could take him back to the infirmary.

"Kevin?"

He followed Rev's gaze as it traveled down the right side of his scrubs. Blood splatters decorated his clothes like he'd been in a paintball match. Dried blood stained the tops of his bare feet. He blushed. "I yanked the IV."

"I can see that." Rev's hand went for his Icom.

Kevin reached up to pull it away. "I need to talk to Adam—in person."

The ride ended and Kevin raced out of the elevator before Rev could stop him. The man caught up with him in seconds.

Kevin stumbled as he came to a stop; a wave of weakness hit him.

"I think we need to get you back to the infirmary."

Kevin shook his head. "I told you. I have to talk to Adam. It's important."

"Then we'll bring him to you." Rev turned him back toward the elevator.

A decisive kick in the shin caused Rev to loosen his grip enough for Kevin to twist out of it. Rev caught him once more.

"Let me go. You don't understand what's going on here."

"Kevin, he knows about your father."

"Does he know about—?" The rest of his sentence was cut off.

Rev suddenly fell back, writhing on the floor, yelling for it to stop. Twin electrodes had attached themselves to his back. Kevin traced the source. Landon stood not four feet behind them, holding a Taser.

"Stop it!" Kevin shouted.

"Only you can stop it. Come with me or make no mis-

Chapter 27

take, I will kill him. It certainly wouldn't be the first time this device has stopped someone's heart." For a moment, Landon eased up on the switch. A slight chuckle escaped his lips. "I will not lose you this time."

"This . . . time?" Rev forced out the words as his body lay curled on the floor. Before he could explain, Landon hit a button that sent Rev writhing once more.

Landon waited with a calm indifference. "Your choice, Kevin."

chapter 28

"Stop! I'll come." Kevin slowly made his way over to Landon, unable to stand the sight of Rev or the sounds of agony the man emitted.

Landon pulled out his knife, wrapped his arm around Kevin's neck, and then retracted the leads in Rev's back.

Down the hall, the door opened. Dad stepped into the hallway. Blood drained from his face. "What are you doing with my son?" Steven rushed toward them, but stopped short when Landon yanked Kevin's head back and tightened the grip on the blade.

Adam and Chelsea hurried down the hallway but stopped short behind Dad.

Kevin felt the sharp edge press against his throat. He gulped, afraid to cry out, afraid to move even a fraction of an inch.

Landon smirked. "You should have finished your counseling session. Kevin and I would have made our way out of here without an audience."

Dad's face raged. He shook his fist at Landon. "I'll kill you if you hurt my son."

Landon chuckled. "From the looks of it, I would only be mimicking what you did yourself. But I would get my way much quicker, I assure you."

"Why do you want him so badly?" Adam took a tentative step forward.

Landon sneered. "It does not concern you. Now leave, and perhaps I will spare his life."

Kevin gulped and felt the blade dig into his throat. For the first time, he doubted he would reach his real sixteenth birthday. Once Landon got what he wanted, there'd be no reason to keep him alive—just like Patrick Thomas.

"Then maybe you would satisfy my curiosity." Adam stopped a comfortable distance in front of them. He crossed his arms casually in front of his chest. "It's not every day someone comes in here and tries to kidnap my resident teenager. Most would be content to leave him here for me to deal with."

"He is a thief."

"A thief? That doesn't surprise me. What did he steal?"

"Almost two million dollars." Landon's voice lowered but didn't lose any of its steel as he spoke into Kevin's ear. "And I will get it back, won't I?"

Across from them, Adam whistled. "That is a lot of money. I'd be upset too and wondering how a teenager could accomplish such a feat."

"The kid put a virus on the laptop. We lost access to our accounts. We thought perhaps it was a mistake, a

Chapter 28

joke. When we asked for the fix, the kid tricked us and damaged it further." Landon refocused his gaze on Dad. "But his father has given us great insight in how to motivate his son. I assure you, we will get the money, and then perhaps you will get this nuisance returned to you."

Adam grinned and captured Kevin's gaze. "I'd like that. I've kind of gotten used to having him around."

Suddenly, Dad moved toward Landon. His fist clenched and unclenched. His eyes blazed with fury. "I'm going to protect my son."

Adam tried to stop him. "This is not the time."

"Get back, Ramsey," Landon commanded. "I will kill him."

Dad continued his approach. "No, you won't. You still need something from him."

The knife moved. Kevin cried out as the blade lightly sliced his neck, its serrated edge bit into his skin. Warm blood trickled down his neck. His bottom lip quivered. "Stop," he begged.

"Back away, Ramsey!" Adam ordered. "You've caused enough trouble for one day."

Dad took a reluctant step backwards. Slowly, he moved against the wall and slid to the floor. On the other side of the hall, Chelsea knelt beside Rev, her mouth moving as though in prayer.

Adam raked a hand through his hair. "Sorry about that. I can understand why you wanted to get out of here without having to bring that one along." He thumbed over his shoulder in Dad's direction and blew out a long breath.

From somewhere outside his fog, Kevin heard Landon say something. He sucked in a deep breath in an effort to clear his head. Somehow, he missed the last exchange but sensed Adam working at trying to calm the situation down.

Adam gave Landon an understanding nod. "You must mean the Deiseldorf account."

Landon stiffened behind him. "How do you know of this?"

"I have a teenager in my keep. I make it a point to know many things." He gave Kevin half a grin.

Kevin hoped Adam could read the gratefulness in his eyes. For once, he was glad Adam hadn't given up on his quest for knowledge.

"That man right there." Adam pointed to Rev who hadn't moved from the floor. "That's my computer guy. I guarantee you he can get the information to you right now if you want to go into my office."

"Bring the computer out here."

Adam seemed to consider it and then nodded. "Rev, bring us the laptop."

Chelsea extended her hand out to Rev as he pushed off the floor.

Landon exhaled on the back of Kevin's neck like a dragon impatiently waiting for his dinner.

Something snapped in the air behind them.

Landon whirled. He jerked Kevin around by the neck.

Kevin yelped.

A paring knife from the kitchen spun through the air and caught Landon's arm. The kidnapper cried out. His arm fell away from Kevin to grasp the wound.

A surge of adrenaline swept through Kevin. He scrambled out of Landon's reach. Chelsea and Dad converged upon him.

Chapter 28

Landon dropped to the floor. A knife protruded from his right arm. Down the hall, Anna Lisa hung back, a satisfied smirk on her face as she swung her braid over her shoulder. "Better be glad I missed on purpose."

Mole Woman!

Kevin grinned. Never mess with a woman with that much hair who competes in knife throwing competitions.

As Adam approached the downed criminal, Landon reached for his Taser that had fallen from his hand. Adam's eyes widened with understanding. Landon's fingers curled around the weapon. Adam rushed forward and kicked the Taser out of Landon's reach.

"It's over, Landon."

Landon chuckled.

Adam bent over to pull Landon to his feet. Landon took his serrated knife and plunged it into Adam's leg.

Chelsea screamed.

"No!" Kevin yelled and tried to run.

Dad held him back while Rev rushed forward to help Adam.

Adam looked around and laughed.

Laughed!

Adam smiled down at Landon. "Next time you might want to make sure you stab the real leg." He jerked the knife out. Then he pulled up his pant leg to show off his prosthetic.

Landon groaned.

Braid swinging, Anna Lisa retrieved her own knife and smirked at Landon. "Looks like you could have used a prosthetic of your own today."

Rev joined the laughter. "I told you that leg would come in handy one day. God truly does work in mysterious ways, His wonders to perform."

303

"Get him out of here," Adam ordered. David appeared, and he and Rev hauled Landon to his feet. "Put him in the hyperbaric chamber. If he gives you any trouble, turn up the pressure and offer him a soda."

Kevin looked at Adam confused.

Rev explained, "It's a machine that divers use to prevent decompression sickness. If you dial up the pressure an atmosphere or two, the soda will produce bubbles in his system that can kill him."

"Sweet."

In front of him, Chelsea eyed Kevin carefully. "First thing after we get you fixed up is a change of clothes. Seeing you with almost as much blood on the outside as the inside practically gave me a heart attack. That idiot," she pointed to the receding figure of Landon, "about finished it."

"Son, I'm so sorry." Dad squeezed his forehead between his thumb and middle finger. "Seems I just keeping making things worse no matter what I do."

Kevin stared up into Dad's face and discovered a broken man, but lacked the words of comfort to offer his dad. He needed time to think.

"Sorry seems to be the only word I say to you anymore." Dad sighed. "Almost got you killed this time."

Adam's figure darkened the other side of Kevin. There stood a man who had seen Kevin at his very worst and had never given up on him, never physically hurt him, never used him as a scapegoat. And yet, Adam wasn't his father and the Center wasn't his home.

"Kevin." Chelsea tried to get his attention while she probed the wound on his neck.

Chapter 28

He hissed and stiffened. As soon as she removed her hand, Kevin reached for the remote at his waist and turned off the chip in his glasses. For once, he longed for a blurred world where he could imagine others couldn't see him either.

Wheels whirred along the floor. The fuzzy picture of a metal gurney came into view, and then his world rose and shifted. A warm blanket enveloped him, and then the gurney sailed down the hall and into the elevator.

Kevin moaned. When the elevator did that familiar take off bump, his head and stomach whirled in unison. "Chel, feeling sick."

"I know." Her hand gripped his good one and squeezed. "Keep your eyes closed. That should help. As soon as I can get another IV started, I promise you'll feel loads better. That is, if you'll leave it in place this time."

Kevin could hear the smile in her voice and grinned. Feel better? He probably wouldn't feel anything at all.

The elevator stopped and the gurney careened down another hall and into the infirmary.

Anna Lisa must have arrived ahead of them because Chelsea immediately began barking orders to her. "Anna, I need his scrubs cut off. I'm going to get a new IV kit and then—"

"Already done. I laid it out as soon as I got here."

After that, Kevin lost track of what happened. Instead, he formed an invisible mental bubble around himself to control the barrage of emotions. Feeling nothing had to be better than feeling everything.

Both Chelsea and Anna Lisa murmured words of comfort as they worked. None of them penetrated his bubble.

Like rain on a windshield, their words slid away, leaving streaks and a residue that clouded his thinking.

He couldn't take being surrounded by these people who gave so much. They didn't deserve this interruption in their lives. No promise was worth the price Adam and Chelsea had paid. Not only had he brought a killer to the Center, but the money Dad had given them had been embezzled. The Center would soon be worse off than when Kevin had arrived.

"Dad?" he called out through a voice he barely recognized as his own.

The abrupt sound of heavy footsteps stopping at the side of his bed told him Dad had not been far away.

"I'm here."

"Take me home."

chapter 29

Kevin peered through half-lidded eyes at Dad, who quietly stared down at the electronic reader in his large hands. He wondered how much longer he could hide the fact he was awake. It had given him time to think and make some decisions. As much as he appreciated all Adam and Chelsea had done to help him, it was time to go home. Back to McKeltic.

All the reasons that had brought him here were gone. According to snippets of conversation he had caught, everyone now knew the truth behind William Tyke's connection with The World's Gateway and AsericA Investments. Dad's name would be cleared as well his own.

Finally, he could return to some semblance of normalcy—normal for him anyway. Being here at the Center had its good points, but for the most part, it felt like living separated from the rest of the world, locked away from everything important to him.

Glancing once more at Dad, Kevin remembered how his mother always told him family was so important to Dad that he quit drinking. Kevin wondered if that was still true. Could Dad quit again now that the stress was gone?

Dad looked up and caught Kevin's gaze. He grinned and moved from the chair to the side of the bed. "Hey. It's good to see you awake."

"Thanks." Kevin didn't know what else to say. "Where's Chelsea?"

"She went to get something to drink. I'm sure she'll be back in a few."

Kevin nodded, relieved to have a few private moments with Dad. "I can't wait to get back home."

"Yeah." Dad leaned forward and planted his elbows on his knees. "We need to talk about that."

The shocked expression on Dad's face made Kevin gulp. But he forced himself to go on. "They all know I'm innocent. There's no need for me to stay here anymore. I'll get my job back, stay out of trouble. You won't have to drink anymore. We can—"

"It's not that easy."

"What do you mean, 'it's not that easy?'"

Steven sighed; his shoulders slumped forward. "Adam knows I . . . I . . . hurt you."

Kevin clenched the blanket with his good hand. His eyes flitted across the room. "Tell him what your own father did to you. Tell him it was because of the alcohol. Tell him you've quit."

"But—"

Chapter 29

"I'll help you . . . just like Mom did. I'll even give up coffee and energy drinks if you'll give up drinking."

Steven shook his head. "I can't. Not yet."

Kevin felt his voice drip with venom. "You can't or you won't even try."

"You know your grandfather may still be looking for you. He could still take you from me. I can't take that chance. I'm signing over complete custody to Chelsea and Adam."

The air rushed out of his lungs as though he'd been punched. Kevin searched Dad's face, hoping for some sign that this wasn't really happening. "You can't leave me here."

"Adam will be good for you." Steven gripped the metal railing of the bed and stared at the curtain that separated the cubicles. "I . . . I'm not . . . you'll be better off here."

"No, I won't. I want to be home. I want to be able to go hang out with my friends at Galactic Jitters. Why won't you even try?"

"Because I . . . I'm not ready . . . I mean . . . I like having a drink after work. I'll eventually quit, but I don't know if I can right now."

Something in Kevin gave way. He sat up in the bed and tried to swallow, but it felt like his Adam's apple had lodged in his throat. Conflicting emotions waged war in him. How many times had he made excuses for Dad in his mind? Dad had been drunk. Dad was under a lot of pressure at work. Tyke had blackmailed him. Dad still felt guilty for the death of his mom.

But this. This had no excuse. Dad would quit drinking for his mother, but not him. Was he not important? Was Adam not so much the safe place but the convenient place to keep Kevin? Anger raged in him. He clenched his teeth together, trying to hold it in. "So that's it. You won't even try?"

Dad balled his hand into a fist and drove it silently into the mattress. "I have a plane to catch." He pushed himself off the mattress and started toward the door.

"Get out," Kevin said, his tone venomous. Rage surged through his good arm. Kevin shoved the small bed table across the room in the direction Dad had taken. The table narrowly missed him. Instead, it clattered against the wall. Heavyweight plastic dishes flew and scattered like shrapnel.

Dad never looked back.

Kevin grabbed an errant pair of surgical scissors and sent them hurdling across the room. Not even that calmed the frustration within him. His pillow was next, and then he searched for something else to throw, something to destroy. The only other thing close enough was a clipboard with his medical chart on it.

He lifted the metal clipboard into the air.

The curtain parted. Chelsea rushed over. Her delicate fingers wrapped around his wrist in her gentle and yet firm grip. "That's enough, Kevin." She reached up and wrestled the clipboard from between his tightly fisted hand.

"Go away, Chelsea."

"No," she said in her softest tone.

His voice cracked against the warring emotions. "I want to be alone."

"That's what your father did, didn't he? Always left you alone, whether you needed to be or not." When Kevin scowled in response, her gaze didn't linger. Instead, she

Chapter 29

picked up the clipboard and flipped up a few pieces of paper, her eyes flickering back and forth as she read. Her hand disappeared into the pocket of her lab coat and reappeared with a click pen. After making a notation, she snapped the metal cover down and placed it out of Kevin's reach. "How's your pain level?"

"Fine."

Chelsea nodded and moved to the other side of the bed. He flinched when she replaced the icepack that had slid to the floor earlier. "I'll get you something for the pain—"

"No," he said. He needed the pain. It kept him grounded, gave him something else to concentrate on. Maybe if the pain on the outside reached a high enough level, the pain on the inside would diminish. In response to her probing gaze, he turned his head and focused on some crevice in the white textured wall.

She sighed. Her cool fingers pushed back the hair from his forehead and then gently turned his chin so he faced her. "Do you know how much I love you?"

Kevin swallowed. Why couldn't she just go away and leave him alone? He didn't need her love.

"I know you don't want to be here." She fixed her gaze with his and held it. "I can't say I blame you. But I'm glad you're staying."

"Did you and Adam force Dad to leave me here?" He narrowed his gaze. The edges of the blanket wrinkled in his tight fist.

"No."

Kevin wanted to nod but he couldn't. Like an unstable building, any movement could cause every emotional barrier to collapse.

"Although we didn't ask him to turn over custody, we did ask that he allow you stay until he got some help with his alcoholism."

"My dad's not an alcoholic. He was just under a lot of stress."

"Then why couldn't he stop?" she asked.

Kevin didn't want to talk about it. "I can't stay here. The money my dad gave you—"

"Has been returned." Chelsea seated herself along the edge of the bed in the place Dad had vacated moments before. She slipped a folded piece of paper out of her pocket. "Kevin, what are you searching for?"

He rolled his eyes and then glared at her. "Who says I'm looking for anything?"

"This."

Kevin unfolded the paper. It was his bus ticket. Adam must have spotted it when he went digging for the bottles of medicine. Although wrinkled and the ink only half-legible, it still represented freedom lost. He blew out a long sigh.

"You know, sometimes what you're searching for doesn't take a bus ticket to find."

"You don't know what I want."

"Maybe not. But I know your running hasn't solved anything yet. So far, it's only created more problems."

He glared up at her. "So is that your little speech for getting me to stay here? No thanks. I'm going home."

Chelsea crossed her arms. "And then what? You stay until things get out of control again and then you run?"

"Isn't staying here running away from my problems? Wouldn't you rather I face them head on?" he challenged her.

Chapter 29

"Last time you faced your problem head on, you came back with your arm practically wrenched off and afraid to tell anyone what really happened. You and your father need some time to work things out at a safe distance." She grinned softly. "Besides, having you here is an answer to a prayer."

He swallowed hard. Over the last year, he had been labeled a burden, a juvenile delinquent, a hacker, a nuisance, but never anyone's answer to prayer. He forced himself not to allow her to get to him. "Maybe I don't want to be anyone's answer to prayer."

"Too late for that."

"So to give you an answer, your God had to take me out of my home."

Chelsea shook her head. "We didn't take you. You were given to us."

Kevin grimaced at the fresh reminder that he wasn't wanted at home. Emotions of sadness and rage came together like fire and ice. He didn't know which one had more power. When her hand touched his arm, Kevin flinched, jarring his shoulder. His teeth clenched at the surge of pain that traveled through his arm.

"Kevin?"

"I'm fine." The pain chose that moment to spider down his arm.

Blowing out a deep breath, he pulled himself up in the bed and looked for something to drink. Chelsea must have misinterpreted his movement because her arms suddenly went around him in a hug. He squirmed, but her hold tightened.

A small sob erupted from her.

Kevin stopped. This was the first time he'd heard Chelsea cry. Suddenly he felt bad for pushing her away. He raised a tentative hand and wrapped it around her.

It proved to be all the incentive she needed. "I know you don't want to be here." Her small hand stroked the back of his head. "It may be your dad will get the help he needs and you can go home soon. But for right now, give us a chance."

"I don't belong here."

Chelsea pulled away from him and swiped a hand across her wet eyes. "Yes, you do. You know your mom ran away from home too. When Staci called Adam twelve years ago, that was the first time he'd heard from her in five years."

Kevin stared back at her, listening.

"Staci wanted to make sure there was a safe place prepared for you so you wouldn't have to feel the need to run."

"But Adam . . . " His words trailed off.

"Adam's been grieving too. He feels guilty for not being able to help her back then. He wonders if he could have found her if he searched harder." She stood and with a broad smile handed him the electronic reader Dad had left behind. "Face it, Kevin. God knew this was the place your bus ticket was meant to bring you."

chapter 30

"So when are you guys leaving?" Kevin asked as he stared into the LinkWay. Aiden lay over the end of his bed and stared back at Kevin through his own LinkWay, which sat on the floor of his bedroom. From the position of the LinkWay, Kevin could see empty Galactic Jitters cups, crumpled food wrappers, and at least one pair of dirty socks stuffed under his friend's bed.

"In about an hour." Aiden rolled over and grabbed what looked like a folded newspaper. "Well, it happened."

"What happened?" Kevin asked warily.

Aiden grinned and unfolded the paper. "It's just like you said. We're heroes."

The headline stretched across the front page in bold letters: "Teens Save Citizens' Investments." The article named both him and Aiden as the main people responsible for exposing a local investment scam and for posthumously exonerating Patrick Thomas of any investment fraud.

"I don't understand, Aiden. It's not over until they catch Tyke."

"But Tyke can't get to the money. And my dad says the FBI sent out an International BOLO, so Interpol will be looking for him if he somehow makes it out of the States." Aiden typed in a link for the online be-on-the-lookout picture and information on William Tyke. "Rom said to tell you he found the spot where the video feed was altered, and after checking the security feed for that auto place, they found Tyke buying a key to your dad's car."

"Too bad they didn't catch Tyke before he left town."

"Rom tried. He put a clip-on GPS under the back bumper of Tyke's car after he got suspicious of Tyke, but Tyke dumped his car as soon as he crossed over into Kansas."

"How's my dad?"

Aiden glanced down and shrugged. "Okay, I guess."

"Is he still drinking?" He tried not to sound too hopeful.

"I don't know," Aiden said carefully. "I heard Prof telling my dad that your dad just wanted to be left alone."

Kevin nodded. "Sounds like Dad." He searched in his mind for something else to talk about. Then he spotted a can of Energy X on the bedside table. "Hey, did you get my order?"

Aiden rolled his eyes. "Do you think I'd forget? Come on. This is your best friend you're talking about. I got a case of Energy X as well as five bags of Mocha Madness I bought at Galactic Jitters."

Kevin grinned from his own position on the bed, pil-

Chapter 30

lows propped behind his back. "You are the man, Aiden. You are the man."

"Like there was ever any doubt." Aiden replied smugly.

Kevin laughed. He cracked open one of the last Energy X cans he had left and took a long swallow. He was so tired of being tired. Since his injury, Chelsea had insisted that he stay inside the Center. Video games were out since it hurt his arm to play for very long. Movies . . . well, he'd seen all the good ones. He was tired of vegging. School work had been impossible to concentrate on. More times than not, the pain medication, which he'd only recently stopped taking, wore him down to the point he had no motivation whatsoever.

"How long do you get to stay?" Kevin asked.

"Dad said Adam invited me to stay for the month. Prof arranged it so I could do all my schoolwork over the LinkWay too.

"Sweet." Kevin drew out the word, excited to see his friend. A loud voice called out Aiden's name on the other end.

Aiden cocked his head to listen. "I gotta go. That's my dad. I guess he's ready to leave. I'll see you tonight."

Kevin nodded and then warned him. "It'll still be daylight when you get here."

"Is that good or bad?"

"Depends on how long a day you want and how much caffeine you bring."

"Let's just say, I'll be well prepared."

Stephanie M. E. Gallentine / refuge

Pencil in hand, Kevin sharpened the newly drawn section of the page where the hero, Saphearon, once again triumphed over his archenemy, Zezima. He held the page out in front of him and examined it once more. The cape needed a bit more shading. Angling the pencil, he applied a light shade that helped the rest of the figure stand out in the frame. He smiled. Perfect.

He sat the clipboard back on his lap and checked the other drawings. In the final frame, Saphearon thanked the new team member for her help. Mole Woman's braid now hung clear to the floor. Her costume, made from invulnerable duck tape, gave her an almost harlequin appearance. But it suited the character in a deceptive way.

A long yawn escaped his lips. Frustrated, he reached for the can of Energy X. A knock sounded at the door. Kevin glanced up and scurried to find a hiding place for his drink.

Adam walked in, spied the can still in Kevin's hand, crossed his arms, and frowned.

A mischievous grin appeared on Kevin's face as he set his drink down on the bedside table as though it were no big deal. "Hey."

"Hey, yourself." Adam pulled up a chair and eased himself down into it. "You trying to get on Chelsea's bad side?"

He rolled his eyes. "I'm sick of being tired. I'm sick of being cooped up. I feel as though I'm losing time. I'm too tired to do anything. And it's like Fort Knox down here. Someone fixed the back door so no one can use it without setting off the emergency alarms in the entire underworld." Kevin plopped back down on the pillow and then grimaced when he landed on his shoulder wrong. He

Chapter 30

glared at Adam. "And don't think I haven't noticed every time we get visitors now, someone magically appears to visit me or keep me company until they leave."

"You're right."

Kevin couldn't believe it. "Just like that? No argument?"

"Why? It's all true." Adam leaned forward and planted his elbows on his knees. "Until the authorities locate William Tyke, there isn't one of us here who is willing to take the chance of a repeat performance by one of Tyke's henchman."

"You could send me somewhere else," Kevin suggested.

"I'll let you run that one by Chelsea." He chuckled. "But no, we have no intention of sending you away."

"What about everyone else?"

"Let me clarify that. No one wants you to leave. Not even David."

Kevin nodded.

"But we're taking precautions just the same, and we're praying." Adam tapped an open page of the Bible Chelsea had left on the desk. "We're asking for God's protection and taking precautions of our own."

"About that . . . " Kevin's voice trailed off. He picked some invisible lint off the comforter and tried to think of how to say what he'd been thinking about. "I've been doing a lot of thinking since the island."

"Oh?" Adam asked.

Kevin focused his gaze on the open Bible Chelsea had brought to him a few days before. A group of highlighted words seemed to jump off the page. *I go to prepare a place for you.* Chelsea said God had always known Kevin would need a place to go. A Refuge, she called it, same as Mom. Kevin remembered the time in Galactic Jitters when he wondered if a place existed where he wouldn't have to fight anymore, a place he could be normal. As much as he hadn't wanted to admit it, this place seemed to qualify.

He took a slow deep breath, suddenly unsure of how to say what he was feeling. "Just . . . keep praying for me."

"I never intended to stop."

Kevin stared at the wall, afraid to meet Adam's gaze. He gulped. "I think it might be working."

There was a slight intake of breath before Adam answered. "Me too."

"Now I didn't say I was ready to do whatever you do"—he quickly clarified, waving his hand in the air—"to become a Christian."

"Okay."

"But I'm willing to listen."

Adam nodded. "That's all I can ask."

"Thanks." Kevin stacked up his drawings and tucked them into his binder. "For everything."

Adam's lips parted and then closed as though he were about to say something but then changed his mind. Instead, he nodded again. "You're welcome."

Kevin took another long sip of Energy X. "But for now, can I get out of here? Maybe go on a boat ride or something?" The mood in the room had become too serious, too emotionally charged, and he needed an escape before Adam talked him into more than just listening.

Adam sat thoughtful for a moment. "All right. But how about we try something different?"

"Different? Like what?"

Chapter 30

"Well, with us beginning construction on the underwater prison, I figured we needed some transportation to watch the progress. Rev did some research and found us a small submarine."

"What?" Kevin laughed. Disbelief colored his tone. "A sub? A real sub?"

Adam nodded.

"No way."

"Now, it'll only hold ten people on top, but it has a mini sub attached to the bottom that can detach for small research missions and can also double for a hyperbaric chamber when needed."

"When did you get it? Why didn't someone tell me?"

"It was delivered the day after the Australian police took Landon away, but Chelsea and I ordered no one to mention it around you until you were feeling better." When Kevin opened his mouth up to argue, Adam went on, "You needed the rest, and if you'd found out, you'd have found a way to get up there. Am I right?"

Kevin grinned sheepishly. "How is it?"

"Don't know. I've been waiting on you to take her out."

Kevin pushed back the blanket and searched for his shoes.

"Not so fast. You haven't asked what the cost is yet."

"Cost?" Kevin narrowed his eyes in suspicion.

Adam nodded. "It'll cost you one can of Energy X. That one." He pointed to the open can.

Kevin's face fell. "Come on, Adam. Let me finish it. It'll keep me awake for the ride."

"Your choice." Adam pushed his hands into his pockets, rocked back on his heels, and waited.

Stephanie M. E. Gallentine / refuge

Growling through clenched teeth, Kevin set the can down. "Fine." Then he muttered under his breath, "You better be glad they don't taste as good as they once did."

Adam smiled. "Maybe I should start charging you cans of Energy X for everything."

"Not gonna happen," Kevin declared.

"We'll see." But a teasing smile accompanied the words. As they stepped out into the hallway, Kevin paused.

"I'll be right back. I forgot something."

"Oh?"

"A pillow." He pointed to his shoulder.

Adam nodded. "Oh, okay."

Kevin hurried back into the room. His laptop came into view about the same time as the pillow. He stopped, remembering all the family pictures stored on it, and how much Adam longed to know about Mom. Keven blew out a long sigh. Adam had done so much to help him. Sharing memories of Mom would be something he could give in return. Kevin reached for the laptop and then headed for the door. "Now I'm ready."